Night Stalker

The Cities Below, Volume 6

Jen Colly

Published by Jen Colly, 2025.

This is a work of fiction. Similarities to real people, places, or events are entirely coincidental.

NIGHT STALKER

First edition. March 4, 2025.

Copyright © 2025 Jen Colly.

ISBN: 979-8230045779

Written by Jen Colly.

Also by Jen Colly

The Cities Below
In the Dark
Bound
Beneath the Night
Sheltered
The Guardian
Night Stalker

Watch for more at https://www.jencolly.com.

To the strong, wild, and uncontrollable women in my life: my mother, Connie, my daughter, Sofia, Lisa, and Kate.

To Ryan. My husband. My everything. None of this would be possible without you. From your encouragement to begin this journey, your dedication to editing, your creation of my brilliant new covers, my website...and my author picture! Thank you for your support, your love, and for being my hero every time 'the tech' tries to take me down. I love you.

Many thanks to my editor, Piper. You are a treasure, and I cannot wait to work with you again.

Thanks to my beautiful work friend, Connie, for the creation and existence of the word 'fuff'. You didn't believe I'd use it, did you?

Chapter 1

MIAMI, FLORIDA

"Hey, Rita!" Jake called out over his shoulder, fumbling with the door as he juggled the grocery bag from one hand to the other, trying to free his finger from the key ring. "I know I'm late. Don't be mad. I had to track down those zebra cakes you keep eyein' but never pick up."

Silence met him. Jake's instincts screamed in warning. A sense of dread crawled through him and landed at the base of his spine. Something was wrong. Rita hadn't scolded him for bringing back sweets, and his big ol' Rottweiler hadn't barreled through the house in his typical overly enthusiastic inspection of any and all food entering his territory.

He pulled his key from the doorknob and called out, "Rita?"

No answer. The kitchen light glowed beyond its threshold and into the living room, but lit nothing more than a door-shaped path. Jake turned, flipping on the hall light, and scanned the entry. Rita was lying at the bottom of the stairs, blood across her chest, beneath her body. The grocery bag slipped from his hands, hit the floor with a heavy thud.

She was alive, and reaching for him. Jake was at her side in a heartbeat, kneeling even as he peeled his jacket off and wadded it up, applying pressure on her chest directly over the wound. She curled her fingers around his wrist, her grip frighteningly loose.

"Hey there, beautiful," Jake said as he brought her hand to his lips for a kiss. It was hard to control his voice, to turn off any emotion as he watched his best friend sprawled out and bleeding, but he shut it all down and let the training take over. Panic, rage, and grief would help nothing, so he pushed them aside.

She'd taken two bullets to the chest. Major vitals were hit, by the look of things, and he had no way of knowing how long she'd been struggling to breathe. She wasn't going to make it, and he knew it deep in his gut. Just like he knew by the still outline of his dog down the hallway that ol' Rumford was dead. Best he could do was keep Rita calm and stay with her.

Jake pulled out of her hold too easily. She was losing strength fast. Fishing his phone from his jacket pocket, he dialed 911 and waited for the gal on the other end to finish her spiel. When she was done, all he could say was, "One-one-two-five-four North West Fourth Street. Officer down."

Nothing more was needed. Even if they made it here while she was still alive, there was no way they could work the kind of magic needed to save her in the back of that ambulance. Didn't stop him from praying those boys could make it happen, but every second ticking by did her in, and he was helpless to do anything but watch.

Rita swallowed hard, tried to speak, but nothing came out, and she was starting to panic. Jake tossed his phone onto the floor and grabbed her hand again, making a soft hushing sound.

"It'll be all right," he said, the words feeling like less of a lie than they should. "Just give it a minute. I got you."

Seconds seemed to last forever, and she was struggling. Her gaze suddenly darted around, like she couldn't see him. Jake moved closer, staying in her line of vision.

"I'm still here. Don't you worry none. I won't leave you." He smiled down at her, but it probably didn't look real. It was all he could manage just to force the corners of his mouth to turn up.

Rita twitched, her muscles clenching. Probably not entirely her doing at this point. Suddenly he realized why his words hadn't felt like a lie. All right didn't always mean healthy and upright. Sometimes it just meant no more pain and suffering. Whether rescue got here, or she passed from this world, the pain and fear would soon be over.

"I know, babe. I gotcha. Give it a second." He knew when he'd said those last few words that she didn't have long. Her lungs were stuttering for each breath in and out, and he couldn't even hear the sirens yet. Once before, he'd held onto someone he loved and prayed for a miracle, even if it meant they'd pass quick if that was the only way to end the pain. Here he was again, holding the hand of his best friend and making the same prayer.

Rita went still, her muscles slack, and the silence of it all rocked him. She'd let go of life while holding on to him. It wasn't fair. Wasn't fair that this prayer had been answered when the last hundred weren't, but he was thankful just the same.

He couldn't readjust her body, and it felt wrong to get up and move away from her, so he stayed, hanging on to her hand.

The phone rang, joined by the buzzing vibration he felt through the floorboards. He looked to the floor beside him. It wasn't coming from his phone. A little numb, his movements slow, he searched for the sound. There on the second step, Rita's phone was lit up. Unknown number. Jake cocked his head to the side in confusion. Didn't make sense for her phone to be on the stairs.

Jake picked it up, forcing his voice to remain level. "Hello."

"I may not have liked my brother, but he was mine." The voice on the other side of the phone made the hairs on the back of Jake's neck stand on end. Tulio Suarez, the man who was supposed to be at the raid coordinated by his SWAT team today. Instead they'd encountered his brother, and Enrique had been intent on going down in a shoot-out. The lazy, harsh edge of Tulio's voice continued on, "You took something from me, Jake Martin. Now I've taken something from you."

"You screwed up." Harsh and low, Jake's voice was downright scary, even to his own ears. "I got nothing left to keep me here. I'm coming for you."

"Come find me. We'll play again," Tulio said, the superior gloat in his voice making Jake's stomach churn. "After I tell Mother what you've done to her favorite son, of course."

The connection went dead and Jake set the phone back on the stairs. Anger settled in, cold and hard. Jake had studied the Suarez brothers' background, and he was well aware both parents lived in France, though not in the same location. Tulio would already be on his way out of the country. He'd gotten away with murder. If Jake was actually able to find and kill Tulio, best case scenario? Extreme jail time. Jake had no false hopes, though. The drug runner's boys would be on high alert, and would likely shoot him on sight. Either way, the end result would be the same. Life over. Going after Tulio was a suicide mission.

"Yeah, you're all right now." Jake kissed Rita's hand one last time and set it down gently beside her still body. Her death would not go unpunished, even if it meant he was walking right into his own. "I'll see you soon, partner."

Jake pulled his badge from his pocket and left it half tucked under Rita's hand. He only paused to stroke Rumford's back one last time, and then he walked out that door. Jake didn't look back, not even when the wail of the sirens finally sounded in the distance.

• • • •

Somewhere over the Atlantic Ocean

"Hey, Rita!" Jake called out over his shoulder, fumbling with the door as he juggled the grocery bag in his hands. He turned, flipping on the hall light. The paper bag hit the floor with a heavy thud...

Jake gasped, jerking awake from the dream like he'd just surfaced from swimming in an ice-cold lake. Thank God he'd left his body belted into his seat even after the buckle up light had blinked out, 'cause his soul had damn near left his body just now.

It took him a hot minute to come back down, to shake the crisp images of the dream. Well, sort of a dream. More like the intense recent past stuck on a loop inside his skull. He rubbed his hand over his face and took a few long, deep breaths to recenter, but it wasn't quite enough.

Jake dipped his hand into his chest pocket in search of a little comfort. He drew out a cherry sucker, peeled the wrapper, and popped it into his mouth. If anyone had been disturbed by his less than manly freak-out, they did nothing more than send him a funny look before going back to minding their own business. This was probably the best place to glitch, he supposed. Most people weren't comfortable on planes for one reason or another, and he didn't expect he was the only one having trouble on an over-the-ocean flight.

Pinned in next to the window, he looked down the row. The mom on the end pretended to ignore him, but kept glancing sideways, keeping a sharp eye out. Jake looked down at the little girl to his left, sandwiched between her mother and him. Poor kid. She clutched that teddy bear way too tight as she looked up at him with wide, watchful eyes. Bad luck to get seated next to a stranger still coming to terms with what had happened only hours ago. He'd probably scared the daylights out of her.

He opened his mouth, meaning to apologize, but noticed she'd switched over from startled fear to curious interest as her cautious gaze kept darting to his mouth. Jake grinned, the sucker stick twitching between his lips. Worked every time. Everyone was a sucker for a sucker.

Jake reached into his pocket and produced another sucker. Lemon Lime. He held it up in silent offering. The girl nodded her head eagerly, but when she went to reach for it, Jake pulled it just out of her grasp.

"Ask your mama," he said, pointing to the pretty brunette on the other side of the girl.

The woman, who had been listening intently, seemed to weigh her answer. She looked him over for a brief moment, then she nodded, making an assumption about his character then and there.

The little girl popped out of her seat and stood anxiously beside his knee, all adorable and bouncy. She took the sucker and eagerly unwrapped it, taking an exploratory lick before stuffing it into her mouth. Climbing back into her seat with all the grace of a blinded bird, she threw herself from the seat back to the armrest, then popped up onto her knees.

Raising her hand to block the glare of sunlight coming through the window, she looked him dead in the eye, and with the unfiltered concern of a six-year-old, asked point blank, "Are you okay?"

"Me? Just fine like sunshine," Jake said, a big ol' grin surrounding that sucker stick. He wasn't surprised by the question. The way his mind and body had woken him up had been more than a little spastic. "Nothing but a bad dream. It can't get me when I'm awake, right? So I woke up. A little too fast?"

She nodded, her poor bear in a tight headlock, and then the sucker clicked against her teeth as she spoke. "It scared me, but not for long. I asked if you were okay because of your sad spot."

"My what now?" Jake asked, keeping his tone light and teasing.

She leaned forward, getting right up in his personal space, and poked him in the middle of the forehead. "Right here. Where your eyebrows are all crunched together."

Jake huffed a little laugh. "Just thinkin' really hard. That's not easy for some people, you know?"

She giggled, seemingly satisfied with the answer, throwing herself against the seat back again. After a couple forward and back bounces, she settled, rolling the sucker on her tongue and chattering to her mother.

Jake rested his head back, looking out the window at the cheery blue sky. Someone shifted behind him, and his left hand went to his hip, a reflexive habit to make sure everything was in place, but nothing was there. He felt naked, exposed. No badge, no gun.

Captain Edwards had texted him shortly before he'd jumped on the plane. Nothing aggressive or threatening. Just an appeal to his good nature with a short and sweet, '*Come on back, Jake. Let's do this the right way.*' Jake should have absolutely followed his captain's suggestion, but instead he'd chucked the phone into the nearest garbage can and boarded.

His SWAT team had known Tulio was vindictive. They'd been prepped for an attack and had responded accordingly, but no one expected him to show up in their homes. To do that, Tulio would have been monitoring them in return. He'd known Rita went to Jake's home and to expect a big dog inside.

Everything after finding Rita had been a nasty blur. Somehow he'd managed to make his way to Miami International and get himself onto a plane to France. Lifting his right hip, he removed his wallet from his pocket and pulled out the picture tucked between his insurance card and a business card for a towing company. He'd done that on purpose to keep the picture from bending. It wasn't much, just a chunk of a picture cut out from a group photo of his unit. He and Rita had been inseparable from the get-go. Best pals, meaning they didn't put up with each other's bullshit.

The other picture tucked in there was of him and his pup on the beach. One of the few selfies he'd taken in his life. His pup hadn't been a pup for a while. Rumford had some serious age on him, but he'd been the best, protecting Rita right up until he couldn't.

A small, not so coordinated hand thumped his elbow, reached over him, and pointed at the picture. "He's pretty. You miss your dog?"

"Yeah," Jake said, his throat tight. "I'm going to try and sleep again. Maybe it'll take this time."

"Okay," the girl whispered loudly.

After returning his wallet to his pocket, he tipped his head back and closed his eyes. A few seconds later, the girl's little hands were stuffing something fuzzy and squishy between his crossed arms and his chest. He cracked an eye open and watched her. The pale pink, flat bear flopped over his arms.

"Whatcha doin'?" he mumbled.

"You keep her for the bad dreams, but just for the airplane ride," the girl said, patting her pink friend on the head. "Her name is Pancake."

"Thanks, little darlin'." Jake smiled, soaking up this moment, reminding himself that there were still good people in this world. These were the people he fought to keep safe. He'd go to the ends of the earth to stop Tulio from murdering another innocent soul.

Chapter 2

PARIS, FRANCE

    Dulcina zipped and buttoned her military cargo pants, the waist riding low on her hips. This style gave her body freedom to move and she would need it tonight. Foot propped on the one rickety chair in the room, she laced her boots to her ankles, leaving the top partially undone. Again, freedom. Somehow, over the years, the act was no longer simply about dressing. This preparation was ritual.

    Snagging her black, sleeveless top off the low footboard of her narrow bed, she slid it over her bare skin. The snug, thin material tugged slightly on the tiny silver ring pierced through her left nipple. That single ring was the sole proof she carried of her identity. Engraved with the name Casteel, the ring was the mark of Balinese royalty. Though Dulcina wasn't royalty by blood, and not a Casteel by birth, circumstances through her adoption had placed her in line to rule the vampire city of Balinese.

    While the mark of royalty was a requirement, remaining inside the city was not. Unless tragedy befell three of her family members, the responsibility would never be placed on her shoulders.

    Tipping her head upside down, she fluffed her thick black curls until the short locks framed her face like a dark halo. Dulcina smiled, a sly twist of her lips. Time to hunt.

    Her sinewy body moved with a lethal grace as she crossed the main room of her small apartment. Deftly, she drew her Bowie knife from beneath her pillow. Tossing the knife up, she snagged it mid-air, effectively flipping her grip on the handle before sheathing the blade at her side. Now she was ready.

    Dulcina stepped out into the muted light of the hallway, leaving her petite apartment behind. The shadows seemed to move with her, but it was a trick of the eye. She kept to them on purpose, minimizing the amount of time she was visible to humans. The darkness was her ally, her camouflage, and occasionally, her savior.

Her gaze darted left then swiftly to the right as she emerged onto the sidewalk above ground. Women who walked alone in the evening were often unwitting targets for demons, vampires, and common street thugs. Not Dulcina. There was nothing in this world left for her to fear.

Suspicious and solitary, she was the perfect fit for life as a Stalker. Her direct and decisive temperament tipped the scales in her favor. Dulcina didn't believe in second chances. Demons got one shot. One. If a demon killed, she put it down. Permanently.

A cluster of giggling women off to her left drew her attention, but not for long. She'd become accustomed to the sounds of night, and to the nature of humans. She moved away from them, the soft soles of her boots lending to her stealth.

Although there had been a spike in demon activity these last few weeks, it had not been followed by an increase in human deaths. This was a good thing, and would in theory prove the Stalkers had the demons scared straight, except for the fact that demon activity ebbed and flowed like the tide. The constant? Very few deaths at the hands of demons.

During the four years she'd been above ground, dedicating her life to the safety of her people as a Stalker, she'd rarely had the chance to actually hunt a demon. What she did was more like...patrolling. When she'd first arrived in the city, it had taken her all of a matter of months to get her bearings and discover demons rarely killed. They were as efficient and elusive as vampires in taking only the modest amount of blood they needed. Most of them left their meal alive and sufficiently disoriented.

It had been a rude awakening to realize everything she'd believed as a child was a lie. Demons were not lurking down every alleyway ripping throats out and targeting the innocent. She'd seen demons kill within her own city. She had witnessed the gruesome aftermath firsthand. Yet she had rarely come across that kind of outright aggression on the streets of Paris.

While this skewed her perception, it also gave her a clearer view of the world she patrolled. Dulcina did what she did best: adapt.

A muffled thud followed by a grunt traveled through the air and bounced off buildings. Dulcina smiled. Demons were rarely involved in a street fight, but they often gravitated toward the sound, lingered, and drank from the last to leave. Pro tip number one: Tail the loser.

Tracking the sound through the maze of buildings and side streets, she prepared for the most likely scenario. Men often brawled outside taverns and it made for a rather enjoyable show. Another grunt and a shallow splash of water drifted to her ears. Someone had disturbed one of the many puddles still dotting the streets from this afternoon's rainfall. What sounded like solid blows, one after another, was enough to make her cringe. By the sound of the quick succession of punches, two men may have ganged up on one.

Dulcina might feel a little sorry for the poor man, but this wasn't her fight. He'd either end up in a hospital or dead. People lived and died by their choices every day, every night.

She slipped into her Spirit form, invisible to the eye, and eased closer. The sounds seemed to come from a beautiful corner building a street ahead. When the building came into full view and nothing moved around the entrances or fence-lined sidewalk, she gravitated toward the darkest back alley.

Murmured voices threaded toward her, making it easy for her to find their source. The short, narrow alley opened to a small cutout in the building's structure, giving wider berth for deliveries.

She'd found them. One man, his dirty blonde hair catching the light as he moved, bent to punch the poor soul on the ground. The felled man curled his body tighter, muscles instinctively trying to block the blows. The second brute, bearded and much stockier, stood on the other side of the victim and kicked him in the stomach. This time, the poor man's reaction was minimal, which generally meant he wasn't long for this world. Unfortunate, and brutal, but none of her business.

A third man watched from the left, his wild gaze gleefully tracking every blow. The excitement in that brutish-looking man's face spread, reached his eyes…turned them red. Demon red.

"Finish him," the demon said, his voice so deep it didn't even echo off the surrounding walls.

Everything inside Dulcina zinged to life. This was no longer a simple exercise in observation, no more lingering to make certain the man wasn't killed after they fed from him. A demon had just given an order to kill.

Rules of engagement? Kill only those who have killed and protect the innocent. Yes, there were only two firm rules, but the interpretations varied. Killed could mean the physical act, or a direct order that had been carried out to its end. Clear and near attempt to murder also fell under that category. Those considered innocent translated to humans, demons, or vampires. A Stalker would protect any of them if necessary, as long as doing so would prevent knowledge of other species.

As one of the men was demon, reason stood the other two might be as well, and yet something about this entire situation was off. Most demons ran in packs, but if all three were demon, why weren't they feeding? They had no reason to draw attention by beating this man. Meaning…the downed man was likely a vampire, or perhaps even another demon.

No, Dulcina was not permitted to kill without sound reason, but a direct order to kill another had been given. If any one of these men attempted the kill, two men would be marked for death. The man who gave the order, and the man who intended to see it through. She grinned. This night just become significantly more interesting.

Being eager didn't mean being stupid. Every detail of the situation flooded into her senses, her brain consistently recalculating. Dulcina had never in her life stopped to plan a strategy. That wasn't how being a Stalker worked, and it was why she was damn good at her job. Charging into chaos half-cocked was a given, and her adaptability ensured her survival.

The stockier man moved to follow the direct order and drew a knife. Raising his arm, he built momentum to strike just as Dulcina took her solid, corporeal form behind him. Sinking her Bowie knife deep into the meaty part of his upper thigh made him howl in pain and he whipped around to glare at her. The man's eyes flashed red. Confirmed. Demon. Two out of three.

The stocky demon took a back-swing at her, and she ducked, twisting the blade as she yanked it free of his leg. In the next breath, she vanished again. Invisible. Untraceable.

Wounding was a gray area she used to get the job done, and until the Stalker Lord told her to cut it out, she would use every tool in her arsenal. She didn't often get the chance to prevent a death by demon and she took full advantage of this gifted opportunity.

Dulcina appeared a dozen feet away from the cluster of men, and the eyes of the third man with dirty blond hair did a double take at her swift travel in Spirit. As he recognized what sort of species stood among them, his eyes shifted to red. Three demons. Fabulous.

None of them moved, but when she made no further motion to attack, the injured demon clamped his thick paw of a hand over his damaged leg and growled, "Not your business, Stalker."

"Everything is my business." She sighed, shaking her head as if the poor demons didn't know any better. She was burning for a fight, craving physical exertion and a keen rush of adrenaline, and she wasn't above provocation.

"Not tonight," the craggy faced leader hanging back said evenly, bearing a confidence he should not possess.

"Want me to leave?" Sheathing her Bowie knife, she spread her arms wide, making her challenge tempting. A tactic she'd learned from her volatile foster mother. "Make me."

The shaggy-haired man stepped toward her, but at the silent signal from their unspoken leader, he stopped.

"Leave her." The leader's gruff voice faded as he turned away from her and looked back to the body on the ground.

Everything about these three demons left a sour burn in her gut. They were not sightseeing above ground, searching for a lost or strayed relation, and they certainly didn't intend to drink from this victim. Yet, to have recognized her as a Stalker, they were familiar with the strict rules applied to demons here in Paris.

"You know you're done, right?" she said, her authoritative tone carrying a weight she was more than capable of backing. "This is over."

The craggy-faced leader changed tactics, producing his own knife and whipping it at her. Dulcina weaved just to the left and then slid back into her previous position. The knife clattered on the ground behind her. This demon had already been marked for death, but now? He'd actively attempted to kill a Stalker, thus ending her patience. Abruptly.

Dulcina took two measured steps back, never taking her eyes off the demons, and plucked the thrown blade from the ground. The demon, who had been so eager to have a go at her, suddenly shuffled backward, closer to the fallen man.

Legs braced, Bowie now securely drawn in her right fist and the demon's blade in her left, she waited for them to make the first move. The demons each pulled a knife, the silvery glint catching what little light shone down on them. She wasn't surprised. The weapon of choice for any vampire or demon was a blade of some form. It drew far less attention from human society than the loud blast of a gunshot.

Dulcina glanced at the victim. Still unconscious, but alive, his chest moving in a shallow rhythm. The demons must have perceived her as weak in that moment, assuming her attention was drawn to the injured man out of feminine care and concern, because the leader charged her.

He'd lunged forward, blade first, exposing his arm. Now here was a moment, an opportunity laid bare. She brought her Bowie knife down hard on his arm. The skin on his wrist was instantly sliced deep by her well-honed blade. Tendons severed. The knife he'd wielded fell from his hand a mere second before he howled in pain.

His garbled cursing would bring unwanted attention. Without a second thought, she cracked him on the head with the butt of her knife, and he jerked once, then lost consciousness. Blessed silence.

The muscle-bound demon with the injured leg lumbered toward her, doing his best to appear menacing and aggressive. The show might have worked on someone less seasoned.

Dulcina never flinched, and had no reason to fight fair. A breath before he struck, she vanished, appearing behind the demon. She drove her Bowie knife up and under his rib cage. It took effort to push through the thick muscles of his back, but she was more than capable.

Lungs punctured, the shock of it split the demon's focus enough for her to make a second strike into the softer flesh of his side. The bleed wasn't enough to weaken a demon of this size, but combined with the fluid now entering his punctured lungs, he struggled to do much more than turn and gape at her. He dropped to his knees, crumpled to the ground. He was down, but not dead.

Two disabled. The shaggy blonde was wiser than the other two, or possibly more afraid. He didn't advance on her and didn't run to help his friends. That wide-eyed glare of his made her think the events had been a bit much for him to take in, but when his leader roused, lifting his upper body from the pavement, the blonde rallied and yelled, "You can't just butcher us on the streets like animals, Stalker!"

"Look around you, demon. Yes, I can," she warned. "I answer to a higher power."

"Leave her!" Struggling to stand, holding his battered skull with his good hand, the leader never stopped giving orders. "We've done our job. Time to go."

"No," Dulcina said, shaking her head slowly and pointing at the other demon. "Just him."

Swaying under the effects of what was likely a concussion, as well as blood loss from his severed inner wrist, the demon leader relented, "She's right. You go on. Leave us."

He hesitated, but after a moment the blonde turned away from them, looking rather shell-shocked, and made his way through the door, bolting it shut behind him.

Dulcina turned her attention fully to the remaining two demons, her grip instinctively tightening around the hilt of her knife. "You know what I am, and you know the rules we all live by."

"I do," the craggy-faced leader said with a nod, dropping his hands to his side.

She approached, watching for telltale signs of an attack. Sure enough, the demon tensed, springing forward. Dulcina functioned purely on reflexive instinct, stepping into him, taking the impact of his good hand on her throat. The instant his fingers curled around her neck, she slid her Bowie right between the demon's ribs. He jerked back, his instant reaction to push away from her out of self-preservation, but it only opened him up for a second strike. Straight to the heart.

The demon sank to the ground, muscle control fading fast. Some genuinely gave up, offering their throat. The rest fought back, expecting a woman to act as a fragile female and not a warrior.

Dulcina tugged her blade from the demon's chest and wiped the black blood onto his shirt. Weapon now sheathed at her side, she turned on her heel, making her way to the poor soul the demons had pummeled into the ground. A street brawl wasn't normal behavior for demons. They fed, killed, and vanished. Whatever happened here was out of the ordinary, and it hadn't escaped her notice that the demons had sported a few cuts and bruises of their own before she'd shown up. Her curiosity was deliciously piqued. An average vampire who could take on three demons long enough to reciprocate some damage? Well, now, that was a man worth meeting.

Caution had never done Dulcina any favors, and so she approached the man as she approached life. Confidently. She made certain to keep the downed demons in her line of sight. Some resurrected swifter than others. As she moved closer, she could see the victim's hair was a tawny brown and not the telltale black marker of her vampire species. Probably demon, then. Disappointing.

Within her home city, everything was constant, rules set in stone. But up here in Paris? Nearly everything she'd known for a fact down to her core was...flexible. Not all demons were bad, drinking from humans was not prohibited, and the once horrifying thought of a demon city named Jericho was now truly of no consequence. Some rules, however, were not fluid. If this damaged man was a demon, she'd have no problem seeing him to his home. That is, if she could get the location from him, and if he lived. Vampire? Well...that got slightly more complicated as he appeared to be a half breed.

Dulcina cringed at the thought of helping a stranger. Dealing with normal folk was a pain in the ass. They didn't understand her, and she sure as hell didn't understand them. She sighed and dropped to a crouch, poised on the balls of her feet.

"Let's see what you are," she said aloud, hoping her voice would trigger a response. Some men swam in the mire of pain, unable to surface back to consciousness, and others woke fighting. Vocalization was just a little preliminary test before she touched him.

Face down on the pockmarked pavement, half lying in a rather large puddle of rainwater, the man gave no reaction to her voice. Two fingers to his neck, she searched for a pulse. It was there and steady. He lived, and would continue to do so, unless he gave her a reason to finish him.

Dulcina clenched his shirt in her fist and rolled him onto his back. Cautiously, she placed her entire palm over his cheek to catch his temperature. He was warm but not demon hot. The cool puddle he'd been sprawled in might have altered his body heat, but there was one sure way to discover the truth. She lifted one of his eyelids. Hazel.

Dulcina drew back, confusion skittering through her thoughts, desperately plucking facts to make his existence logical. A demon's eyes defaulted to their primal red when they were unconscious. He was decidedly *not* demon. It was highly possible she'd come across the lesser-known, but immensely powerful, combination of human and vampire her people called Forbidden. It would explain how he'd been able to hold his own for so long against three rather large demons.

Carefully she lifted his busted, bloodied lip to expose his teeth. Flat, even teeth. A vibrant curse broke past her lips. He was *human*! Knowing his species with absolute certainty left her with even more questions. Dulcina gripped his chin, tipped his head toward her, then away. No bite marks on his neck. The demon trio hadn't been trying to feed from him.

It didn't make sense for demons to pass up a feeding or to simply pound on a human for fun. Were they trying to get something from him? Logical on the surface, but humans rarely knew or possessed anything of value to demons. Period. They were, in fact, rather useless.

Dulcina glanced back at the unconscious demon. They'd been armed, so why hadn't they flat out killed him? No knife wounds or excessive amounts of blood marred his body, but that didn't necessarily mean the human wasn't severely injured. They were fragile creatures.

Carefully, she lifted his arm from where it rested atop his ribs. Her manipulation, though slow and deliberate, wrought a pained groan from the man. His eyes blinked open, those hazel greens flitting around without really focusing on anything in particular. Tension filled his muscles and he gritted his teeth, but when he started to lift his head, it all went wrong. He was able to muffle a cry of pain before collapsing back to the ground.

"You can't move, can you?" Dulcina said, and that's when he saw her for the first time.

Alarm reached his eyes, creased his brow, and he opened his mouth to speak, but ended up gasping in a short breath, which seemed to only cause him more pain. He appeared utterly defeated, and for a flash of a second, Dulcina regretted her words. She'd forgotten how fiercely men loathed losing control of any situation. Typically, she didn't care, reveled in having the upper hand, but she got the sense that something about his predicament, even beyond the physical injuries, truly wounded him. Poor thing.

An unfamiliar pang of sympathy flashed through her, but she quickly dismissed the reaction. Sweeping her hand over his head, checking for further damage as she soothed him, she softly said, "No use denying it."

Dulcina froze with her fingers speared through his short hair, and after a halting moment, swiftly withdrew her hand. Interesting. No, this situation was not normal, but more concerning was her out-of-character behavior. She wasn't the comforting type.

The light in his eyes seemed to fade, then he jerked back to consciousness with a vengeance, eyes frantically searching for an enemy she knew damn well he couldn't see, let alone fight.

"They're gone. It's just me here with you," she said firmly, putting her face directly into his line of sight. "Come now, enough of this in between. Die or fight."

His hand shot out and gripped her arm. Human and weak, he could never harm her, and so Dulcina simply let him hold on, cautiously watching his every move. By some miracle, he pulled himself halfway off the ground before crying out in pain and falling back to the ground, unconscious.

"Rest easy. I'll see you safe," she said, disentangling his hand from her arm. That was when she saw his knuckles. Deep red gashes split his flesh from the backs of his hands to his elbows, his skin spattered with blood that was not entirely his own. Black demon blood made him a colorful mess.

Dulcina lifted an eyebrow in disbelief, and a healthy amount of admiration. He'd fought back and got a piece of at least one demon. She could respect a fighter.

If he were one of her kind, she couldn't very well leave him to the authorities who would whisk him away to the hospital and discover another species. As he was human, she could easily walk away. Except there was a small chance this man retained a memory of the demons he'd fought. On the other hand, if he remained clueless, there was no need to alter his life so drastically. It was a dark night, and no man could expect to fare well in any fight against three men, so perhaps he'd been unaware of their exceedingly powerful nature.

She sighed. Delays.

Yes, she was annoyed, but Dulcina refused to leave this man without knowing for certain how much he knew about vampires and demons. She'd take him home for now, and when he regained consciousness, she could gently ply him with questions. If he knew nothing, he would be free to go, under observation, of course.

However, if he knew anything at all about the demons that had pummeled him into the ground, his life would be irrevocably altered. Many Stalkers would swiftly execute a man with knowledge of the other species, but Dulcina didn't have it in her to snuff out the life of a human with such an abundance of dogged courage.

Chapter 3

PARIS

Jake opened his eyes, more than a little uneasy to face whatever this run of bad luck had left him alive to battle. Everything was dark and quiet, and the warmth around him suggested he was indoors. He couldn't be certain though, since not a sliver of light trickled in through a window, a crack under a door, or gap at the edge of a curtain. Nothing.

No reason to keep looking at stuff he couldn't see. The important thing was he'd lived. He hurt too damn much to be dead. Sweet Jesus, it even hurt to breathe.

Flat on his back, his body felt like a mass of bruises and cuts. His face throbbed, no doubt swollen from all the fists that had made direct contact with his thick skull. Come to think of it, more than a few hits had landed on his cheek. Like a man reading Braille, Jake lifted his hand to search his face for any serious injury, but the jolt of pain that ricocheted through his entire left side gave him all the answers he needed. It wasn't just his handsome mug. Everything was bad. Those big boys who'd swarmed out of the club to protect Tulio had done some serious damage.

Served him right. Dropping his whole life, jumping on a plane, and chasing a murderer across the ocean to a different continent had been a dumb-ass move. If Mama were still alive, she'd skin his hide for this one. Granted, he hadn't done anything yet, but even now, he intended to see this through to the end.

The end. There was always an end. To everything, and everyone. What burned in his gut was the bitter injustice of Rita's young, healthy life being stolen from her. Anger had never gripped him this hard in the past, and vengeance had never rooted so deeply in his heart.

This revenge, chasing after a man to kill him? Yeah, Mama would have dragged him back home by his ear and cuffed him upside the head. This wasn't like him at all, it was just...he had nothing left. Mama was gone, his fiancée had stepped out on him, and Tulio had shot his dog and then his partner. Finding Rita dying on the floor of his home...well, it had flipped a switch he hadn't known was inside him.

Jake had nothing to lose, and while keeping his rage at a low simmer, he did what he'd been trained to do. He tracked Rita's murderer, and because he hadn't followed even one ounce of protocol, he'd damn near caught up to Tulio in Paris.

That's as far as he got. He'd been working his way past the bouncer at a gambling house when Tulio had stepped into his line of sight. Acting every inch the boss he thought himself to be, Tulio had just grinned at him, and then with a short whisper to one of his men, he'd turned his back on Jake.

He'd held his own rather well, until two more men had come out of the dark. Jake's chest throbbed, and he reached with his good arm to gingerly touch the spot. It was sticky with blood, but nothing fresh seemed to spill from him, so it couldn't be too bad. Setting his arm back down caused a whole new sensation of pain to wash over him.

Jake groaned, and instantly winced, holding his breath until his arm was back on the bed. He couldn't be sure, but making that guttural sound might have hurt worse than moving his arm. Not a good sign. Yeah, he was a mess, but for the moment, his attackers were no longer punching him. He didn't much care what had chased them away, or who had picked him up off the pavement. He was only thankful that his bruises weren't still being bruised.

Something shifted nearby, and he strained to focus on the movement through his ringing ears and aching skull. The movements were soft, but they were deliberate. Was this person a friend or enemy? Sure, he had other questions. How bad was the damage?

Why had he been brought here? Where was here? Why the hell wouldn't those men go down when he hit them? He wouldn't ask anything, though. At least, not yet. He'd often found he could get more information from his silence than an all-out interrogation.

There was a subtle change in the atmosphere to his left, but he still saw nothing. No definition, no shadowing. Were his eyes even open? He didn't have it in him to pretend to be unconscious, and he really didn't want to face an unknown person lying on his back. Slowly, he moved his arm away from his body, sliding his hand along the cool sheets to the edge of the bed, which was surprisingly close. He gripped it, tried to pull himself upright, but only managed to bite back a groan as sheer agony shot through his body. He collapsed back onto the mattress, each breath hurting worse than the last.

Pinpoint stars danced across the blackness of his vision, and he barely noticed the presence of a person at his side. A cool cloth touched his forehead and instantly Jake stopped moving. It felt good, that soft cloth wiping away the sweat and heat. The tension in his forehead relaxed, especially when the smooth strokes gave him the distinct impression a woman held the cloth. He also had the sense that he was not in immediate danger, not if she was caring for him. The rhythmic, tender application was comforting, lulling him.

Too soon the cloth warmed, and she pulled away from him. Dripping water echoed in the silent room, and then it was back, coolness returning to soothe the bridge of his nose, his cheeks. Again, the cloth was rinsed and cooled, and this time applied under his chin, gently over his neck, and across his collarbone. Heavenly. For the third time the cloth was taken away, and he waited for who knew how long, anticipating its return.

A piping hot, sloppy wet cloth slapped across his shoulder, making him jerk, and not just from surprise. Sweet baby Jesus, that smarted like a son-of-a-bitch! He flailed, an automatic response he wasn't able to rein in quick enough. With his good arm, Jake tried to fight off whoever was hurting him. He was too weak to accomplish anything more than swatting in that general direction. She was unmovable, holding that hot cloth over his shoulder with a firm pressure that pinned his upper body into a position he really wasn't happy with right now.

"Stop," a female voice commanded, firm and resolute. He did, but only because his failing effort to remove her hand might be causing more pain than her less-than-tender care. "Your shirt is fused with the wound. Hold still and allow me to separate the two of you."

Her imperial tone did as much to stop him from moving as her words. Sounded like maybe this woman was used to getting her way whenever she spoke, and that might be a good thing right now. He certainly couldn't help himself in this state, and she was willing to get her hands dirty.

Getting fabric out of a knife wound was pretty important, but if not done carefully would reopen any scabs already forming and hurt like hell. Jake had no idea how long he'd been out. Too long, was his guess. This wasn't going to be fun.

After an agonizingly long moment she pulled the cloth away, but his relief was short-lived. Another splash and a swish, and that hot cloth came back with a hearty slap onto his shoulder. Gritting his teeth, he pushed past the pain, trying to focus instead on the drips of water sliding over the top of his shoulder.

"Try and hold still." She sounded annoyed. Messing with an open wound didn't seem to bother her, but something—

Jake gritted his teeth as she slowly peeled the cloth away, this time taking his shirt along with it, removing congealed blood as it went. His muscles clenched, trying desperately not to move, not to cause himself more pain, but in seconds he was gasping for air, sending a different kind of pain ricocheting through his chest.

One more tug from her and the tension on his skin released, his shirtsleeve at last separated from his wound. Her nimble fingers rolled his t-shirt sleeve up and over his shoulder. She wedged a towel snugly between him and the bed, then poured water over the exposed, damaged flesh.

Jake buckled down and clenched his fists tight, doing everything he could to stop from twisting away. Sweat beaded on his forehead, his skin flushed once more, and each shortened breath sapped his energy. The pain was becoming familiar, constant, and that was worrisome.

The woman spread a dry towel over his shoulder and swept her hand over it twice to soak up water, and probably a little blood. A bark of pain escaped his lips, and before he could control the reflex, he'd reached up with his good arm, trying to bat her away. Her fingers closed around his wrist in a tight grip, her surprising strength swiftly ending any intentions to stop her.

"Easy. You'll live, pet," her smooth feminine voice cooed, then gently placed his arm back on the bed at his side, careful to do the work for him so he didn't have to use his muscles and cause himself more pain.

Jake opened his mouth to speak, but a wave of exhaustion crashed over him, and then he was fading back into the dream world.

• • • •

Jake's mind reentered the present in a panicked state of confusion. He was moving. No, being moved. Was he being lifted? How? There was only the woman... Jake groaned as he was forcibly shifted yet again. It felt like he was being propped up, but on what? The questions came rapid fire, one after another, clogging his foggy head.

Whatever was behind him moved and settled, then...breathed? A steady, easy rhythm of breathing pressed against his back, and that body definitely belonged to a woman.

How had she... Jake let his good arm slip off his ribs, and he encountered a leg. A woman's bare leg bracketed his body. She'd somehow managed to lift him and slip between his back and the headboard, supporting him without squishing his ribs like an accordion. Maybe she'd realized that's where he hurt the most, because sitting like this really wasn't too bad.

"Here," she said, her voice soft near his ear as her fingertips brushed his lips.

Naturally, Jake did the only thing he could. He turned his head away. She tried again, this time tapping his bottom lip with something solid and small. Maybe round?

"Stop being difficult. I'm not trying to roofie you. Well, maybe I am. A little." She spoke English smoothly, but the cadence and lilt of her words had him wondering if maybe English was her second language. She spoke again, her voice firmer than before, "They're painkillers. Swallow them."

His hesitation came more from processing her words than uncertainty, and it didn't take him long to nod in agreement. No matter what she was giving him, being out of it was starting to sound pretty damn good. Plus, it wasn't likely she meant to kill him if she was putting in this kind of effort to care for him.

Once again, she held the pill up to his lips. He'd intended to pluck it from her fingers, but his lips weren't functioning right either, so he let her feed it to him. She brought a glass to his lips, and he sipped the water. Sort of. Enough made it past his lips to wash the pill down his throat, and that was all that mattered. The rest of the water slid over his chin and neck, but she was ready with a towel, like she'd known this was going to be a problem. His lips felt swollen, his jaw ached, and that made these little steps feel like hurdles.

"One more," she demanded, and they repeated the slow process.

Jake tried to form words, to ask where they were, or why she was helping him, or...well, anything. Of course, the least urgent request was the one that made it past his lips in some mumbled form of vocalization. "Turn... Light on."

"It is on," she said, then petted the top of his head with smooth, gentle strokes, her fingers dancing over his scalp in the most comforting way. "Your eyes are swollen, and right now they won't open. Give it time. You're safe with me."

She seemed to flinch at her own words, and instantly, with a confident grace he wouldn't have thought possible, she lifted him enough to slip from behind him and ease him back onto the mattress. Lifting him in general should have been difficult for any woman, but then, he wasn't sure how much of this he was imagining.

He heard her moving around the room more clearly this time, her steps certain, like maybe this was her home. Was she a nurse then? No, not likely. A nurse wouldn't use her own body as a prop pillow. A good Samaritan seemed the most likely. Whatever she was, squeamish she was not.

This time, when she came to his side, he heard the scrape of wood on wood, like a chair being pulled across the floor and closer to the bed. The cool, wet touch of a thick substance on his face had him instinctively retreating deeper into the pillow, but she reassured him with a quick shush.

"What're you doin' to me?" he mumbled.

"It's just clay," she answered simply, but her words sounded distorted. Distant?

"Like a face mask? Want me pretty?" he asked, his words slurring together. "Mmm already pretty."

Well now, that came out a bit sassy. Pain killers must be kicking in big time to jumble his already hindered speech and draw out his long dormant personality.

This woman at his side never wavered. She just kept on applying the chilled clay in smooth strokes. Damaged, in pain, his senses severely altered, Jake was feeling mighty vulnerable at the moment. He had no idea what would have happened if she hadn't found him, if he'd been on his own... Except he wasn't alone. She was here. He reached out, his fingers gently encircling her wrist as she kept on making those measured strokes across his face. She didn't brush off his hold, didn't put his hand back onto the mattress, and that little bit of contact felt good.

When finished, she lowered her hand and gingerly removed his fingers from her wrist, setting his hand onto the blanket with a slight squeeze. "Once the clay takes the swelling from your face, I imagine you'll be very pretty."

"Damn straight," he mumbled, and slipped directly into a drug-induced sleep.

Chapter 4

PARIS

Dulcina embraced her Spirit form before floating out into the night like a ghost. The act was a habit, and a good one. Invisibility kept demons from following her home.

Up the street and around the corner, she released her Spirit, her stride measured and sure. She savored the rapidly cooling evening air that held a sweet, floral smell. It was one of the many things that represented her freedom. When she'd first come above, in the not-so-distant past, she'd simply sat still and breathed in the night air. The whole-body sensation of the wind washing over her, ruffling her clothes, and moving her hair, had taken some getting used to after a life of living in a stagnant underground city.

Dulcina had spent hours tracking the subtle changes in the air, transfixed by the way the world above had a breath of its own. It had taken her time to adjust, to compensate for how a living, moving environment affected her senses. Sounds came from anywhere and everywhere, and were whisked away just as quickly. It distorted perception, and yet she'd adapted.

When immersed in her Spirit form, she registered little of these nuances, which, to a certain extent, could be beneficial. Spirit was often necessary, but her personal preference? Hide in plain sight and let the environment feed her information.

A tiny twinge of guilt had her glancing back in the direction of her home as she walked away. Dulcina shouldn't be above, not now, not when an extremely vulnerable human lay injured within her home. Though, honestly, he was the reason she'd left. Caring for him had been...too much. Too much contact with a person, too much thought about what she would and wouldn't do with him, too much of a whole other body occupying her small home. Too much unwarranted empathy. She'd needed to breathe again.

All the things she thoroughly was not, as a woman, had just been thrown in her face. Dulcina wasn't nurturing, didn't share her space well, and generally didn't give a damn about anyone.

Taking that man home, tending to his wounds...it wasn't like her. Dulcina had never been kind or giving, certainly not understanding or gentle. She was the woman who sliced open a demon's throat to avoid its pathetic pleading. She took what she wanted, whether it pertained to her next source of sustenance, or the life of a demon. Dulcina had never tried to look at the world through the eyes of another, and she'd certainly never had any inclination to comfort any person in need.

For a woman who had never backed down from anything in her life, the fact that she'd retreated above ground to reconnect with herself was unsettling. Perhaps the change within her was a result of the recent lack of demon activity. Sure, she'd just encountered three demons, but the brief scuffle had been less than satisfying.

It had been weeks since she'd fought a demon, and she was starting to go through withdrawals. She was an addict in search of a fix. Her nerves were frayed, her body twitchy, and her thoughts scattered. She thrived on action, on physical exertion, and if she didn't find some soon, she'd have to settle for her second favorite activity. Sex.

A sly smile curved the left side of her lips at the thought. Not many men could handle her, and she'd made it a point to sample a wide variety. Her favorite bed mate lived in Balinese, and she hadn't been there in well over a month.

If the human had any memory of the demons that had laid him out, then she would be dropping him off in Balinese for safekeeping. She hoped he did remember. It would give her the perfect excuse to knock on Nicolai Moretti's door. The brutish, barbarian-like nobleman was a fascination she'd revisited time and again. A round or two with Nico ought to release some of this aimless tension.

Foreseeable future planned, Dulcina strode down the street, shoulders back and senses on high alert. The night was young and people still walked the streets. This was the safest time of night, for humans and demons. As always, she used this time to observe patterns and find familiar faces.

In the back of her mind, though, she revisited a single worry about returning to Balinese. Seeing Nicolai held a great appeal...returning home did not. Only a few, such as her foster family, truly appreciated what the Stalkers did for the vampire race. Most believed a vampire became a Stalker for the love of the kill, and therefore feared them. Murder was the unforgivable sin. The distinction didn't legally carry through and apply to demons, though Dulcina remained shunned for the most part.

Perhaps shun was too harsh a word. The genteel people of the aristocracy made a grand show of leaping from her path and displaying fear, as if her presence would spread her love of killing. The laugh that bubbled up in her suddenly came out as a breathy, indignant huff.

Their behavior was only an irritant. They could walk into the sun for all she cared. She executed demons on behalf of the innocent children, to preserve their naivety and give them a future without fear. She'd known none of those things as a child, and that was where the difficulty resided. Returning home brought back too many memories of the great demon attack that stole her parents' lives. Subsequent incidents that had nearly taken the lives of her foster parents and siblings shadowed even the most pleasant memories in that city.

She loved her foster parents, Cat and Navarre, but seeing them both nearly killed in the demon attack, and yet again throughout the following years, had made something in her snap. She coped with distance. As an adult, she rarely saw them, but when she did, it was only for short visits. Now, the only two people from Balinese she allowed in her life on a consistent basis were her brother in tragedy, Jovan, and her rough-and-tumble lover, Nico. Even with those two, contact was few and far between.

She and Jovan had gone their separate ways the moment he'd followed her above ground, and she had no arguments. Dulcina deeply understood the drive he felt to hunt demons. She missed him and his similar mindset, but not so much that she would seek him out. She cherished her solitude, as did Jovan.

The underlying reality was they had different goals. When Dulcina first came above ground, she'd been so determined to find the lost demon city of Jericho, to eliminate demons at the source, and she'd worked tirelessly to achieve that goal. The only way to find Jericho had been to track the demons, and for years, she had. She patiently observed them with knife bared, ready to kill should they discover her presence. Some seemed aware of her shadowing them, while others were not. What she'd learned over the years was substantial.

Every demon could take Spirit, very few demons attacked humans, and even fewer ran amok causing true physical harm to either human or vampire. It was all one giant conundrum.

The stories she'd grown up with boasted of the atrocities done by demons on the streets of Paris. The carnage and vitriol a demon was said to leave in its wake was enough to terrify most vampires into remaining underground for a majority of their lives. Simply put, she'd found none of those tales factual.

Perhaps eons ago the city was overrun with the creatures, but from all she had witnessed, never in her lifetime. The blatant falsehoods and inaccuracies had made her question the existence of Jericho.

No demon's words, attire, or direction of travel had ever given her a hint as to where they lived. Paris, Jericho, or perhaps some other demon city. Their accent mimicked Parisian, though a demon dialect sounded more guttural, their word choice lowbrow.

While she'd never been able to pinpoint their origin, the information she'd gleaned from tracking them had been valuable. Simply put, most demons were not a threat, and the ones she had eliminated were loners, deviants, or thugs. This blew up every so-called fact she'd been taught about demons.

What was the point of finding Jericho then, if there was no origin of ultimate evil to snuff out?

Early on she'd been more than prepared to defy her Stalker Lord once she found Jericho, and kill them all, but the more she'd witnessed demon behavior, the less she believed all demons were like the ones who'd attacked her home and killed her family. Most nights she patrolled the streets, calm and vigilant, without incident.

Over the years, her focus had shifted. She'd begun to understand demons weren't driven as creatures, but as men. They had their own individual goals, priorities, core values. Just as she'd known some inherently evil vampires, she'd witnessed several rather angelic demons. The facts seemed to defy logic, until she realized who had taught the logic.

Vampires had a long history of hating demons. Not only were demons held responsible for the entire vampire species seclusion underground, they'd also been blamed for any vampire death above ground. The demon attack on Balinese that had killed her family and targeted all in a position of power didn't help the perception. What many vampires refused to acknowledge was the root of the attack. They'd discovered years later that the leader of that attack had been vampire. Hellbent on ruling the city of Balinese, Vidor had betrayed his friends, city, and species by aligning himself with demons.

Her foster family had nearly paid with their lives for that discovery. That day she'd learned a valuable lesson. Evil came in all shapes, sizes, and species.

While Dulcina tended to shut off her connections with others and shut down her emotions, she'd opened up her senses and observation skills. These days, Dulcina was nothing if not an excellent judge of character, motivation, and intention. It's what kept her alive. She'd also gained a sort of sixth sense. Yes, the night breathed, but it also left signs for her to read. Tension in the air, nervous energy from the humans, and even the phase of the moon gave her clues as to how the night was going to play out.

In this moment? Nothing. She felt no urgency, no itch to turn around and glance behind her. The night was truly peaceful. The people walking together lingered, leaned on one another, smiled. A demon walked into a bistro. Sounded like a bad joke, but he had, and it was none of her concern. She would find no evil tonight.

Dulcina followed the demon inside the corner bistro, keeping her distance. She didn't know him, didn't want to spook him. Demons were jumpy when encountering vampires. Neither were here for a fight, just food. She placed an order, then backed farther out of the way than necessary so as not to draw attention, and waited patiently like any other human. They were a lively bunch tonight, these humans, diving into their revelry with no thoughts of tomorrow. The blessings of a short life, she supposed.

The wait wasn't long, and when a waiter handed her a paper sack heavy with her order, she took it with a smile. Another trick of blending in among humans. They smiled when they spoke to each other, especially in meaningless conversation.

Stepping back out into the street, Dulcina glanced down at the bag in her hand, and rolled her eyes. She'd bought the human food, for no other reason than she didn't want him to die from hunger while in her care. And yet, the simple fact that she'd made the effort to be thoughtful and pick up soup annoyed her to no end.

Never had she thought she'd see to a human's needs, let alone do so within her own home. Stalkers mingled closer to the subpar species more often than vampires or demons, but he was still a foreign creature to her. She'd observed humans, walked among them, but to have one of her own? She wasn't interested, and it wasn't possible.

If by some chance miracle his fragile human mind blocked the fact that three otherworldly creatures had beat the snot out of him, then his thin grasp on reality would leave her with an easy fix. Let him heal, and send him on his way. As of yet, he hadn't remained conscious long enough to have a full conversation.

She didn't like leaving him alone. He was a fighter, and the minute he returned to some semblance of himself, he was bound to start searching for an escape route. She knew it with certainty, because that's what she would do.

Entering her building at the main floor, she descended the stairs that led below ground level. Halfway to her door, a subtle shift in the stagnant air around her set her senses on high alert. Someone was in the corridor with her. No demon had ever followed her home, though she'd long suspected they had the ability, and only two vampires knew she lived here. One, the Stalker Lord, never approached her. In fact, she could positively say she'd never recognize him in a crowd. The other? His watch dog.

"Entertaining?" The single word stretched out, elongated in a deep, thick Spanish accent. Rafe's voice came from no particular direction. Commonly referred to as The Wraith, or the Lord's Hand, he was often the last thing a reckless vampire saw before his or her death. The executioner was rarely seen, and never swayed.

"You know me," she said smoothly, a lazy shrug lifting her right shoulder. "I don't cook."

Scary thing was, Rafe probably did know her. Very well. Her guess? He'd already been inside.

Dulcina turned to face...well, the thin air his Spirit occupied. Still, it felt better than leaving her back exposed. As Rafe hadn't shown himself, and likely would not, she spoke to no spot in particular. "To what do I owe the honor of your presence?"

His deep chuckle floated around her, and even that seemed to curl with an accent. "Ah, there's the aristocrat you keep hidden deep within."

He'd likely come for the human, and playing this game wasn't necessary. "Do I need to call Geoff?"

"The body mover need not be involved... Not as of yet," that thick, deeply accented voice said, suddenly to her left, still disembodied, and creepy as hell.

"He's barely been conscious." She stated only facts, not giving Rafe any reason to go back in and kill the poor, wounded soul. "And he hasn't been lucid long enough for me to question him."

Disconnected, scrutinizing, Rafe's voice floated toward her. "He was attacked by demons. You think he did not notice their red eyes?"

"I'd like to find out for certain before passing judgment." Keeping her best smooth and diplomatic tone in play, Dulcina arched an eyebrow, allowing her surprise to show. "You make it sound as if you watched him lose a battle with demons, and left him there to be beaten to death. Rafe, I never knew you were that cruel."

"Death is death," Rafe said, his indifference clear, so much so that had he been corporeal, she imagined he would have shrugged.

"A death you could have prevented." Dulcina tilted her head in mock pondering. "What would your lord think?"

"Tell him, if you like." Rafe's lazy pattern of speech sifted to her from yet another direction. "Or not. He knows what I am."

"The Stalker Lord's judgment need not have any bearing on this matter," she announced with a confidence she felt to her core. "If he lives, and if he is aware of other species, I'll take him to Balinese and leave him there."

"See that you do," Rafe said, the last word fading off into nothing.

Dulcina waited a moment, until she felt his presence fade. Gaining the attention of the Stalker Lord and his assassin was never a good thing. She needed this human healed and out of her home. Even incapacitated and unconscious, he was nothing but trouble.

Once inside, Dulcina locked the door behind her, though it did no good at all with a vampire like Rafe lurking about in Spirit. She glanced over at the bed, feeling as if she'd walked back into a dream state. The reality was too bizarre to be something made up in her mind. A man was truly lying in her bed. She had placed him there, and yet it was still such an odd and unnatural sight.

She'd had her fair share of men, and she'd never been extremely particular. Tall, short, lean, thickly muscled, in bed, out of bed... Dulcina took pleasure when and where she found it, and walked away without a second thought.

The only true exception had been Nico. She'd returned to him several times. Something about being with her, completely free in the throes of passion, was healing to Nico on some level. She'd sensed it immediately, and in that first encounter, had watched his mind stabilize as it had honed in on her.

Yes, liaisons with Nico had been thrilling and athletic, but other men had similar attributes. She'd asked herself many times, why him? Why did she keep returning for him? Her only rational explanation was that something buried deep inside her trusted Nico more than she'd trusted any other in her life. That alone was special, and that trust had healed her as well. Did it mean she wanted to shift to the permanent status of mating the man? Absolutely not.

Every man she'd had, other than Nico, was nothing more than a good carnal connection, but rarely twice, and never in her bed. Even Nico had never been allowed into her personal space. Maybe that's why the man spread out on her single mattress right now was messing with her head. This was something she'd never seen before.

A moan of pain snapped her back fully to the here and now. His hands were clenched tightly into fists and his face contorted in pain. She set the food down and approached the bed, leaning over to brush her hand across his fevered forehead. Instantly he reached for her. Dulcina allowed him to capture her wrist. The action had become his habit, his ounce of control. His fingers were hot, a sign his body was using a lot of energy to heal.

Gently, she swept his scruffy, dark blond hair off his forehead. He looked weather-worn, the deep creases on his face likely attributed to a hard life, more so than age. Rough around the edges. She liked a man with a little wear and tear on him.

If Rafe had decided to kill him, this defenseless human wouldn't have stood a chance. Plus, the drugs she'd used to sedate and mellow his pain left him vaguely aware of his surroundings until the dose faded from his system. Normally, Dulcina wouldn't give a damn, but not with this one. She admired his spirit and had a driving urge to know what kind of man could take on three demons and live. That is, if he lived.

She'd found no severe external bleeding, but while that would be a blessing for a vampire, the rules were different with humans. They were fragile. Torn vessels healed at a slower rate, bones took an eternity, and if an organ had been damaged? She'd never know until he died.

Even in sleep, he kept his left side guarded. Whatever pained him the most, it was beneath his palm. Slipping her hand under his, she ran two fingers over his protected side, applying a slight pressure as she searched. She found the source of his pain easily, and a strangled sound became trapped in his throat as he gripped her wrist tighter.

His hand locked around her wrist didn't hurt, but something about the intensity of his hold spoke volumes. His touch relayed more than physical pain. She looked up, and Dulcina held his gaze in the dim light. Those rich, hazel eyes, peeking through slightly swollen eyelids, were leery of her every move.

The desire to make him more comfortable with her presence led her to sit on the edge of the bed as she faced him. She allowed him to keep hold of her wrist. He couldn't hurt her, and if he thought that less than formidable grip on her wrist gave him control in his vulnerable position, then he could keep that illusion.

"Ribs are likely fractured," she offered on a whisper, having the need to reassure him. "Not broken."

Scrunching his eyebrows, he looked up at her with an expression that said, 'Well, yeah.' He shifted his shoulders, making an effort to sit up in bed. She let him struggle, watching in silence as he valiantly held back any sign he was in pain. After a brief moment without much progress, he swallowed hard, beat back his pride, and without a hint of question in his voice, said, "Help me up."

"Why?"

He pointed to the bathroom. With a nod, Dulcina gingerly helped him into a sitting position, then steadied him as he eased onto his feet. Nothing appeared severely damaged on the lower half of his body, and when his first two steps seemed sure enough, she released him. His shuffling walk across the floor was slow and deliberate, and after a short time alone in the bathroom, he returned at the same careful pace.

She moved out of the way, allowing him to approach the bed on his own. He eased toward the edge of the bed, and eventually sat. She watched the battle in his mind shine through his eyes as he remained there, sending the mattress a leery glare. It wasn't difficult to sort out his hesitation, and truly, there was only one solution.

Dulcina took over. She walked right up to him, placed her hand on his back, between his shoulder blades, and eased him down to the mattress. Surprisingly, he trusted her, and let his weight fall against her hand.

"Amazon," he mumbled.

"Invalid," she countered, her response too swift to pull the amusement from her voice.

The left corner of his lips twitched in what might have been a smile, until that last moment where his ribs shifting to settle against the mattress had him tensing in pain all over again.

Dulcina hadn't actually enjoyed anyone's company before, but this man? She looked forward to his moments of clarity, and the humor in his words. There was a fire in him she admired.

Between the pain and the drugs she had him on, his eyes were a bit glazed over. He was functioning purely on instinct. Once she weened him off the medication, his personality might be vastly different, though she sincerely hoped not. His little digs were ballsy considering his position in life at the moment, and if what she'd seen of him so far was any indication, she'd enjoy his company very much.

Chapter 5

PARIS

Jake's whole body hurt with an aching stiffness he was afraid to test. A miserable wave of dizziness swept over him, paired with enough nausea to make him wonder why the hell he was fighting so hard to beat back the bliss of unconsciousness.

The short trip to the bathroom had winded him, his body protesting movement after being stagnant for God only knew how long. Jake opened his eyes. He was pretty lucid at the moment, and needed to take advantage of that window. It probably wouldn't last long. He could see much better than the first time he'd tried to get a look at his surroundings. The swelling around his eyes must have gone down, but with sight came a fantastically mild sense of panic. He didn't know where he was, how badly he'd been hurt, or in whose hands his life was being held. Jake recalled very little after his world had been flipped like a flapjack.

His ribs were busted. He didn't know how bad for sure, but he'd nursed a few cracked ribs in his time. There was a slight comfort in the familiarity of that specific pain. Meant his ribs did their job and protected his guts. Now he just had to be careful and keep each breath shallow to help limit the biting pain.

He licked his dry, cracked lips. The scab he encountered on that fat bottom lip stung, as it should. He'd had his face bashed. The swelling was mostly gone, leaving behind the ache of deep bruises.

Suddenly the woman's face hovered over him, her image a little hazy as his eyes struggled to focus, trying to pull out her features in the shadows of the light coming from behind her head. Her short hair framed her face like a dark halo, and that was all it took for pieces of his memory to slowly return. Her care, gruff though it was, had put him on the road to mending. Her voice? He remembered it clearly. Rich and sure, her words had filtered to him as he slipped in and out of consciousness. She'd been trying to help him this whole time, but he'd never seen her face...or her eyes.

"Are you...like them?" Jake asked softly. Damn, it hurt to talk. Just those words sucked all the energy from his body, drained the air from his lungs, and made his ribs twinge. When she didn't answer, he elaborated, "Your eyes red, too?"

Cocking her head slightly, the woman moved closer. She must have understood he wasn't able to see her clearly between the dim room and his recovering vision. Directly above him, she leaned down, now inches from his face, and though he couldn't tell exactly what color her eyes were, he could clearly see they were not an eerie red.

"Satisfied?" she asked. It was like she understood his need to verify.

Jake slowly reached up, stretching out his good arm, only to find that when he touched her cheek, the short distance wasn't an illusion. She was truly right there, about ten inches away from his face. When she didn't flinch at his touch, made no move to draw back or turn away, he used the opportunity.

A gentle brush of his fingers over her cheek got him close enough, and then his thumb caught her upper lip in a quick sweep, revealing a fang.

Sweet baby Jesus! He jerked his hand back, the effort sending another shudder of agony through his body. Damn, but if that little bit of movement about took him out, then he didn't have a shot in hell at escaping.

The woman no longer leaned over him, but sat on the edge of the bed. Calm. He could see her better now, with just the low light blocking the finer details of her face.

She seemed to be waiting patiently for something, so Jake asked point blank, "The men that did this...to me, they had fangs. Red eyes. Your eyes are clear, but your fangs are... What are you?"

One corner of the woman's lips turned up into a sly smile, and in a rather seductive voice, she said, "I am vampire."

Vampire? Okay, wow. Why not? The burly men with red eyes and long, pointy teeth who had attacked him on the streets of Paris had already severely altered his perception of reality.

"Enough...playing. If you're gonna...kill me, do it," Jake snarled through clenched teeth, the pain of speaking altering his speech pattern and draining the impact out of his words.

"You're asking me to kill you?" she asked, her words stiff, unfeeling.

"At this point, yeah. Get it over with. Blacking out...I can handle, but not the guessing game. Don't leave me wondering if I'm going to see you when I wake...or finally get a peek at those pearly gates."

She thrust her shoulders back, notched her chin up. "I have never killed a human. There would be no point in saving your life only to steal it from you."

"You saved me?" Stuck in the awkwardness of the moment, he paused a moment and prepared himself to speak through the pain, to ease the breath from his lungs so it wasn't such a jarring event to his ribs. "I appreciate you doing...whatever it was you did. Don't remember it, but appreciate it. Ah, damn, it was my fault. Sorry. Shouldn't have let them...get the upper hand."

"You're human. You have no upper hand." She shrugged, her tone so certain. "Be content you survived."

"Ouch. Hurts when you...step on my ego, you know?" Jake paused to draw in a slow, shallow breath, his tender, bruised muscles around his ribs screaming at him from all this talking. He wasn't ready to stop, though. Felt good to do those little things that proved he still lived. "I can...hold my own, but glowing red eyes... They make a man stop...and pray to God."

"You get used to their eyes," she said simply, like it was something that would soon become familiar. "And you learn to pray before you leave home."

Damn. Well, that told him a couple things. First, this woman knew exactly what those things were with the red eyes. He hadn't imagined it at all. And second? She considered them dangerous, as well as a part of her everyday life.

She took hold of his left wrist and pulled his arm away from his body, methodically sliding her fingers over his ribs, beginning at his sternum and sweeping down his side. Jake groaned as she prodded a particularly painful area. Once she moved off that spot, it took him a few moments to catch his breath.

Moving his left arm hurt, breathing hurt, and from the way she was inspecting his ribs, she must suspect the same thing. Bone damage. This was not the first time he'd come out of a fight a little battered.

"What's your name?" he asked, trying as best he could to ease away from her searching fingers.

"Why do you want my name?" she asked innocently, her fingers suddenly pushing more firmly along his lower ribs.

"Ah, Christ!" Jake barked out, then gritted his teeth as a second jolt barreled through him from his shout. Damn, that hurt! He glared at her, seething with anger and frustration. He'd never raised his voice to a woman, never let his anger loose on the gentle gender, but this one...

"You didn't answer my question," she said, flashing her fangs as a tiny smile curved her lips. Smiling? What the hell did she find so funny?

Jake opened his mouth, but before he could get a single syllable out, she pushed down on another rib with a single finger. Absolute agony shot through him, seizing his breath, making his muscles spasm. Jake struggled to control his breathing, along with any other physical reactions that might jar his ribs further.

When she'd finally stopped poking at him, Jake glared at her, teeth clenched together. He struggled to regulate his voice, but it still came out as a low growl. "Can't curse your name, without...your *name*!"

"Dulcina." She finally gave it up, and then she laughed. Outright laughed. It was a sweet, feminine sound that severely contradicted the torturous creature he now knew her to be. Even her short, black curls bounced happily around her face.

"Startin' to hate you," he mumbled. He had to pause to slowly draw in another breath, but then added, "Dulcina."

"Hate? Be grateful I got to you in time." Dulcina stood and grabbed the blanket, pulling it up mid-chest, then tucked him in awkwardly. "Nothing's broken. Just a couple fractures to match that knot on your head and your bruised face. You'll be a multitude of colors for a short time, but you'll live."

Dulcina got up and crossed the room. She didn't ask if he needed anything, or if she could help with the pain. No false comfort. The woman defined no-nonsense.

Biting back his frustration, he said to her, "Ribs need wrapped."

"Is that what your people do?" she asked with a strange amount of humor in her voice. "Wrapping is useless. Even for a human."

"Nah...not about medical. I know me. If I don't...wrap them, I'll forget I'm all busted up...and do something stupid," Jake said, squeezing his eyes shut, taking another moment to recover.

She shrugged, bringing over a bottle of water with a straw, and holding out two pills in her hand. "Maybe later. When I'm in the mood to torture you again."

Jake studied the sound of her voice, her facial expression, anything to pan out if she was joking or not. He couldn't tell. Dutifully, he swallowed the pills, eager for anything that would shut down the searing waves of agony. Letting go of consciousness for a while with those pain pills she'd been feeding him on the regular sounded like a real good plan. Holding tension in his muscles was an instinctual response to protect his already damaged body, but it wasn't actually helping anything.

Jake let his eyelids slide shut, listening intently to her shifting around the room, the rustle of clothing, but didn't have the strength to turn his head and find her in the dim light. Exhaustion settled over him like a weighted blanket. He was miserably uncomfortable, but too damn muscle-sore and bone-weary to move. Besides, moving would only jack up the pain. He couldn't lie on either side and put pressure on his ribs, meaning he was relegated to his back. What hadn't hurt before was beginning to ache now, bad. Didn't matter. He was stuck. Flat on his back and staying there.

The mattress dipped at his hip, too deep for her to just be sitting on the edge. He got the distinct impression that Dulcina had put her weight on her knee at his side. Jake cracked his eyes open, to find she'd shut the lights out.

Suddenly, a flurry of motion above him suggested she was climbing onto the bed, and...over him? She settled down at his side, between him and the wall, still and silent. He hadn't thought about it before, and of course, she had to sleep somewhere, but... Jake cleared his throat.

"What?" she asked, her tone sharp and demanding.

"You sure about sleeping here by me?"

"I'm not shy and it's my bed." Dulcina moved, the direction of her voice sounding as if she'd rolled, facing the wall. "Touch me and you'll be sleeping on the floor. Your choice."

"Fair enough," he mumbled, a tiny smile trying to curve his busted lips. Feisty, this one. "I get it, but...cold."

Without another word she lay still as death, but Jake knew people. She was alert, and he was certain that even should she doze off, she'd be awake and ready to fight in the blink of an eye. He sensed a warrior's spirit in her.

Vampires, and red eyed creatures that weren't exactly vampires, walked the earth. He knew better than to think she'd let him go free knowing these different beings existed. This was a secret he could understand her kind being willing to kill to protect, and yet, she'd been offended at the thought of killing him, so...he'd been captured. At least, for now.

Injured and severely weakened, his tools for survival were limited. He had to keep Dulcina convinced he was worth keeping alive, and flat on his back, he wasn't very useful. All he had going for him was his charm, which was sorely lacking at the moment.

Jake had a natural ability to attract and please women. Mama always said she'd been shooing girls away from the house since the day Jake first cracked a smile. He'd learned to tamp it down over the years. Too much natural "smooth" got him into trouble most of the time, so he'd settled into the harsher side of his personality, the cop side.

He'd been playing cop for so long, Jake wasn't exactly sure he could turn that charm back on like a faucet, but it was worth a shot. Chances were, if Dulcina became emotionally connected to him, she'd lose her focus and start to trust him. If he could get her to fall head-over-heels for him, he could gain his freedom in no time.

The soft glow of the nightlight in the bathroom seeped into the room, and it wasn't much, but his eyes were adjusting. Jake let his gaze drift over to the vampire lying beside him in the darkened room. The soft curve of her bare shoulder peeked from the thin blanket she'd tossed over herself. Dulcina might not be human, but she was a woman. Women needed things, and each was different. Some needed protection, others coddling, some needed affirmation. It was possible he could coax her into believing he'd always be here with her, had no intentions of abandoning her, then split.

Ungentlemanly, and something he'd never done in his life, but it would be easy. Jake just had to pinpoint that unfulfilled need and she'd let her guard down.

Dulcina rolled over, her sleep-tousled hair wild with those short locks falling every which way. Her face was pressed into the pillow so hard it pushed her lip back from her teeth, showing a little fang. Jake smiled, couldn't help it. She was something else.

Mama always told him if he was ever serious about a woman to take her camping. That's how you get to see the real woman all cranky and looking like a disaster, the one you'll wake up to every morning for the rest of your life. If you don't like what you see, don't care for how she acts in the little hardships, then don't drag it out. Mama had been one smart lady.

"You're staring," Dulcina said, her words half muffled by the pillow.

Damn. She knew. Time to see how far his charm could get him. "Yeah, well, I like what I see."

Dulcina mumbled something that sounded a hell of a lot like she'd meant 'fuck off' but came out more like 'fuff'. Amusement curled inside him at her little mumbled morphing of the two words, and it was about to break free into a laugh, but then she rolled over, throwing the blanket over her head so hard it bared her thighs. Wow. The woman was all muscle. Toned and strong, those curves seemed to snare all the light in the room. Jake cleared his throat, trying to distract himself from the shot of lust that had just barreled through his battered body. He hadn't expected that, not with his mind and body focused on other problems.

"What?" she huffed from under the blanket.

"Still drinking in my fill," Jake said, and while he'd meant to sound matter-of-fact, his voice had gone a bit husky. He fully expected her to give him another 'fuff' for his words alone.

She groaned her annoyance. Instead of cursing at him, or giving him an earful for looking, she threw her blanket over *his* head!

Jake grinned under the blanket, thoroughly entertained by her reaction. Damn, this woman was likable. He bit down a smile. Playing this game might be more fun than he'd anticipated.

Chapter 6

PARIS

Dulcina woke, instinctively recoiling from the heat tucked snugly against her side. The unfamiliar sensation set her on edge, adrenaline spiking through her, and she reached for her knife hidden beneath her pillow.

Quickly processing her situation, she took note of her surroundings. Her home was still, silent. Nothing moved, nothing... Breathing. Even, sleep-softened breathing. Ugh! Dulcina thumped her face into her pillow. Twice. She'd completely forgotten about the human.

Having someone else in her home was disconcerting. This man's presence made her want to leave, seek solitude, or find something to kill. She popped up on her elbow and glanced across the room at her clock, in an effort to know how much longer she needed to endure his presence. She smiled when she saw the time. Witching hour. Time to hunt. Heedless of her minimal attire consisting of a tank top and underwear, Dulcina climbed over him, her weight causing the mattress to rock with her movement.

She stepped free of the bed, the recoil of the mattress jostling the man. He groaned in protest, but made no other effort to move or speak. Dulcina didn't give a blessed damn if she woke him, kicked him, or if he'd died in the night. The human was an inconvenience.

She was beginning to feel trapped, restrained by barriers of vampire laws, the human in her bed, and her own decisions. Her tiny home offered no escape. She paced, attempting to plan the night ahead of her, but her mind constantly wandered back to the man. Her gaze followed her thoughts.

His deliciously toned forearm rested over his stomach. She had a thing for cut muscles and strength, and she'd have to be blind not to recognize this human was powerful in his own right. She shook her head hard. He was a distraction.

Dulcina dropped down into a plank position, her bare toes supporting the lower half of her body. Physical exertion focused her, and she needed to redirect her thoughts. With precision as smooth as any trained dancer, she lifted her left leg up into the air, held the position for a few seconds, then dropped the leg to tap her ankles together before raising it in the air again. The ebb and flow repeated, until she switched legs and began again. Strength and agility were vital to her survival, and she couldn't let her abilities fade or her routine fall by the wayside.

The man shifted in her bed, and she cranked her head around, watching him intently until he settled back to sleep. Everything about this situation was irritating. No, she would never have left him to the demons, or to die on the street, but this broken man was not a burden she'd envisioned bearing.

He'd been beaten badly enough, she'd assumed he would have zero memory of the event. Nope. Not this human. He'd been hyper-aware of the fight, knew he'd been on the losing end, and as a result, had flat out asked her if she was the same red-eyed species as the demon who had attacked him. Right there he'd lost the right to call his life his own. Dulcina snorted. Human should have kept his mouth shut.

Dulcina changed positions, settling back solidly into her plank, and got back to work, awakening her upper body with a round of push ups. Half a dozen in, she froze in place. Something just changed. She listened intently, searching for the reason her senses had suddenly shifted to high alert. She was being watched. Sheets rustled. Dulcina glanced over at the bed, and found the man's gaze on her. The swelling around his eyes and lips had gone down significantly, his face now only marred by puffiness and bruising.

"You okay?" the man asked, a deliciously sleepy grit to his untested voice.

Ignoring his question, and what the sound of his voice did to her insides, she stood and turned the interrogation around. "How are you feeling, pet?"

"Jake," the man insisted, his name resonating through the silence of the room.

She smiled, refusing to repeat his name. "And?"

"Feel like I've been kicked by a mule," he said, raising his good arm to rub his chest, but it wasn't long before the effort seemed too much.

Those hazel eyes of his fixed on her again, tracking her movement across the small room like he was seeing her for the first time. Maybe he was. Between his swollen eyelids and infrequent consciousness, he hadn't been completely aware of his surroundings. Soon he'd be a real problem.

She made a point of showing him how little she was concerned with his presence. Dulcina pulled her black leather pants from the drawer and slid her legs into them. Then, without any hesitation, turned her back to him and peeled off her thin black tank top.

A strangled groan came from the bed. Not necessarily one of pain. Dulcina cracked a smile. A real smile. She knew she looked good, and if her well-toned body was affecting the human, then it seemed he was recovering quite rapidly. Pulling a fresh, tight T-shirt over her head, she finally turned back to him as she snagged her boots from the floor. Catching a glimpse of him in the corner of her eye, she found he was, in fact, watching her intently. When her boots were laced, she headed for the door.

"Where you going?" he asked, his words a touch sleep-slurred.

"Out. You must be feeling *much* better," she said, plucking her knife from the dresser top. "Took you three nights to notice me leave."

His brows lifted slightly and she could surmise he was mentally taking note of the span of time he'd lost. Poor thing. Must be rough being an inferior species. Dulcina reached for the doorknob, and just as she turned the knob, he spoke. His voice raspy as he pushed for volume, he said, "Don't go. It's not safe."

"No, it's not safe." The anticipation of a chase, a fight, built inside her and a grin broke across her face. "Not for them."

"The red-eyed ones?" Panic surged through his voice and he tried to get up, but his face contorted as he breathed through what appeared to be a great deal of agony caused by the sudden movement. "Don't go. They'll hurt you."

Dulcina stepped over to him, gripped his shoulder and guided him back to the bed. Softly, she spoke the Stalker's creed, "Only demons die on my watch."

He didn't understand the sentiment, the absolute promise behind the words, and so he pleaded again, "Don't go. Not alone."

Concerned for a woman's safety. Ah, men. Dulcina lifted her Bowie knife from its sheath, flashing him the glinting silver edge. "I'm not alone."

Locking the door as she left her home, Dulcina fell into routine. Rapping her knuckles on the Stalker Lord's door as she passed, she kept moving, slipping out into the night in less than a minute. She wasn't about to let one little visit from Rafe scare her into changing her habits.

She hunted her usual route, alert and looking for a fight, but the night moved on at a dragging pace. All was silent, uneventful. No demons in sight, no rumors of strange or violent attacks. It was like the city of Paris had temporarily stopped all demon activity. She could take this time to pause at a nearby location where Stalkers occasionally met to relay vital information, but she couldn't bring herself to interact with another Stalker. Not tonight.

Her mind was elsewhere. She had a man in her home, and he was more aware of his surroundings than he had been in the last several days. The probability that he would attempt to run away increased each night. He would sleep through the night, as he had, but he'd likely wake with the rising of the sun, whether he saw it or not. The man's internal clock was set opposite to hers.

Jake. She wouldn't call him by his name, dared not entertain or nurture familiarity. In fact, she still didn't know what made her offer him her entire first name. No one else above ground knew her as anything other than "D". The honest answer had just slipped out. His vulnerable state caused her to drop her guard.

A couple hurried by her, out on a late evening date, pizza in hand. Vampires needed food like any other living creature, but Dulcina was extremely picky about the places she frequented, food she ingested.

Suddenly she realized the only thing she'd fed the human so far was pain pills. He hadn't been awake long enough to eat the soup she'd brought him the other night, and she had a feeling that once he was good and conscious, he'd be starving. If the man had been clear-minded enough to worry over her safety, to notice how she dressed, then his mind was quickly regaining focus. She'd best return soon, and with food.

Not knowing exactly how much food he would require, Dulcina purchased an entire pizza rather than just a slice or two. Though she was reluctant to let the night go without a fight, returning home to watch over the semi-alert human was the best decision. Within days he would be a flight risk, and she dare not underestimate his abilities just because he was human. A mouse could still outmaneuver a cat.

The moment she stepped inside her home, she glanced to the bed to verify he'd stayed put. Still laid out, he seemed rather weak as he angled his head toward her.

He smiled, a somewhat forced smile, and flashed her a set of even, white teeth. Unsettling.

"Miss me already?" he asked, the deep gritty tone of his voice doing a number on her stomach, but it was that genuine curl of amusement at the left corner of his lips that put the chink in her armor.

Dulcina laughed. Well, almost. It came out as more of an indignant snort. The words that came from this man's mouth kept catching her off guard, and that was something not many were able to accomplish.

Clicking on the little TV, she wheeled the low metal stand away from the wall and over to face the side of the bed. A couple clicks through the channels and she was on the right station, the show already twenty minutes through. Tossing the pizza box on the bed, she sat near the end and removed her boots.

"Can you sit?" she asked.

"I think so," he said, giving his good arm a tender stretch. "I feel better. Not good, but better."

He began to lift his body, but she could see the movement was already taxing him. Dulcina moved to his side. Leaning over her bed, she took hold of his right shoulder and hooked her palm around the back of his neck. Planting her feet, she used the edge of the bed as leverage and pulled him into a sitting position as smoothly as possible.

Dulcina flipped the pillow upright against the headboard and patted it a couple times, then grabbed hers and double stacked them. "Just scoot back."

He did, gingerly. "Thanks. 'Cause that's what...every man wants. A woman to help him...get his ass up."

"I can knock your ass back down if that's what you prefer," she said smoothly, her left eyebrow gaining a little height at his sudden surliness.

A flash of surprise crossed his face, but then he waved her off. "Nope, I'm good. My ego taking another hit is all, but I'll live."

Dulcina stepped over him and sat, back propped against the wall with legs bent over top of his outstretched legs. Yes, the space was cramped, but physical contact never bothered her, in any form.

Her home didn't have room for a comfy chair or a breakfast table, so improvisation was a norm. She took the pizza box and set it down to her left, between them.

"Hungry...pet?" Dulcina asked, just barely avoiding the use of his name.

His eyes narrowed on her, then solidly corrected her. "Jake."

She smiled. So persistent, this man. Dulcina pointed to the box. "It's all I've got."

"Not a fan of cold pizza," he said, more of an easy statement than an objection.

"It isn't exactly cold. Just not hot." Dulcina shrugged. "Eat or starve. Your call."

He grabbed a slice, took note of how she'd folded her slice, and did the same. They sat in silence, which gave her time to watch him from the corner of her eye. When he'd finished his slice, he scanned the room thoughtfully, then seeming resolved, grabbed another slice. What had he been looking for? Perhaps a refrigerator. Interesting. He'd rather eat what he didn't care for than waste food.

He was an observant thing. Practical. Another sliver of begrudging respect surfaced, and Dulcina forced herself to admit this man wasn't nearly as irritating as she'd first assumed. Other than the fact that he needed tending.

Dulcina settled a little deeper into her position against the wall, intending to shut off her brain until this show ended. Futile. Every little movement Jake made drew her attention. He glanced at the last slice in the box. Her eyes narrowed as she studied him, practically able to see the war in his mind. Some imagined obligation not to waste food battled with the reality of him being stuffed full, and she could see the signs. Leaning back, he stifled a belch. Why torture himself with more food? Must be a human thing.

Folding the lid on the box closed, she leaned over his legs and tossed it onto the floor. When his questioning gaze met hers, she simply said, "You keep eating and I won't be able to lift your ass at all."

A grin flashed across his face, and he nodded, unwilling to fight her over something he didn't truly want in the first place. Crossing her arms over her chest, Dulcina stared at the television, avoiding his dashing smile and the things it did to her libido.

For several moments the sound of the TV filled the space between them, and then Jake reached over a rather short distance, and grabbed her foot. Stunned by his impulsive behavior, she met his gaze, subduing the hot flash of wariness at the contact. All he did was grin again.

The heat of his palms wrapping around her chilled foot was a shock to her system, and after the astonishment wore off, she tugged her foot, but the grip of his right hand was far more tenacious than she'd expected. If she'd so desired, she could have easily freed herself from his grip, but she curbed her more violent responses, well aware she could injure him further.

"What are you doing? Let go," she snapped.

"I haven't been *doing* anything for days. I'm finally feeling good enough to move, but I can't without hurting, and it sucks," Jake grumbled, flinching slightly as his facial expressions tugged on the scabbed tissue on his lips, the bruises around his eyes. He calmed quickly, lowered his gaze to her foot, and slowly moved his thumb in a circle. "Doing nothing is making me stir crazy. I'm upright, and feeling mostly okay. Just let me have a focus, will ya?"

Dulcina's jaw nearly dropped at his admission, not to mention the stern scolding. Not because they'd been the most direct words he'd spoken since she'd brought him home, and not at all because he was telling her flat out what he wanted from her, but because she shared those same sentiments. She went positively stir crazy without a focus. Every night. His words resonated with her, and his resolve sparked her interest.

What would he do then, if given free rein to do as he pleased? An experiment seemed in order. Dulcina released the tension in her leg, gave the full weight of it over to his hands.

Jake slowly drew her foot back onto his lap, the positioning more for the benefit of his bruised and cracked ribs than her comfort. Once she adjusted and settled, he pinned her with a 'pay attention' gaze and pointed to the TV. Directing her? Interesting. To what end?

Dulcina did as he asked, keeping a sharp eye on him in her peripheral vision. Once he seemed satisfied that she'd obeyed, he set to work on her foot. Jake didn't watch the TV with her, and he wasn't keen on catching her reaction to his touch. Instead, he truly threw his entire focus into rubbing her foot from ankle to toe.

Sinfully thorough, this man. After he'd taken his time rubbing every inch of her foot with those distracting fingers and drawing bone-melting circles with his thumbs, he cupped his hands around her entire foot with a gentle, firm pressure. The contact was delicious, warming her in a way that had little to do with physical heat.

Jake tapped her shin, and when she looked up, a question on the tip of her tongue, she saw him pointing to the other foot. This was strange. All of it. A man she didn't know was touching her, taking pains to see to her comfort, while he was still recovering from multiple injuries. This tender, selfless care was something done between mates.

Dulcina flinched. That thought was jarring. She didn't want a mate, never had, but then, she'd never had anyone treat her like a mate. Quickly, she shook the thought from her head and matched his behavior to a different scenario. Servants. A personal servant might be required to do this type of thing for their benefactor.

Vampires took on human servants. This was something she'd been familiar with all her life. It had been uncommon in Balinese, but the number of servants in other cities were higher, mainly due to their location in more populated areas. In some cultures, being an indentured or bonded servant of a vampire was a great honor, and in some cases, a debt to be paid. Other instances boiled down to the simple fact that a human had discovered the world of vampire or demon and could no longer be allowed freedom with such precious knowledge, such as Jake's case. Something had to be done with these humans, and most were servants.

Since living above ground, she'd heard stories of vampires purchasing humans for general labor, household duties, sex, and even blood. There were secret, and often illegal, markets for this very purpose. From what she'd understood, many vampires who found themselves saddled with a human would take the pests to a slave market. Just as quickly as the thought of abandoning Jake to such a place crossed her mind, she dismissed it. Not only was she opposed to handing him an uncertain future, but she had a sneaking suspicion that once fully healed, he would be more trouble than most could handle.

Jake belonged to her, by vampire law. Her servant to do with what she chose. She'd never wanted a servant, never considered the benefits, and had no interest in watching over another being.

"Hey, did I lose ya?" Jake asked, tapping her shin again, pointing at her right foot. It was then she realized she hadn't moved, hadn't switched feet as he'd asked. "I'll stop if it's not your thing, but you're gonna feel a little out of balance if I do."

"And that's bad?" she asked, just to poke at him, to expose more of his personality.

Jake shrugged. "Skeeves *me* out, but everybody's different."

Her gaze fixed on his ribs, the rise and fall suddenly heavier than it had been not two minutes ago, as if rubbing her feet hadn't been a hindrance to him, but speaking was exhausting.

Without a word, Dulcina scooted closer, her legs now over his thighs, and she angled her right foot within his grasp. Jake took it with a pleased grin and set to work. No fuss, no smart remark. The man just got down to business. Would she keep him as her own personal servant? No. Absolutely not. Could she enjoy him while he was here? She actually was, but...

Dulcina glanced up, catching his rich hazel eyes watching her. In the nick of time, she halted the scowl she felt coming on from fully creasing her forehead. Jake was studying her, not as a man calculating his options for escape, or even plotting the ways to take a tumble with her in bed, but with a look that hinted at an open and slightly sensual interest. This was not the look she was used to getting from men, and admittedly, it was one she didn't know how to interpret.

It was Dulcina's turn to point at the TV. "Not interested?"

He shrugged a single shoulder. The good one. "Can't understand a word."

In fluid French, she said, "You crossed the ocean to France, and did not learn the language?"

"I caught 'France', I think, but other than that..." He shook his head, an honest admission. "Got nothin'. Sorry, darlin'."

Anger flashed through her. "Don't call me darling."

"Don't call me pet," he countered, but his tone remained non-confrontational, his touch tender.

They held each other's gaze, neither flinching, until a subtle shift in him relaxed his features and he glanced away. His focus settled on her upper arm, and without even second guessing himself, he touched her. His fingers grazed over the raised scars of her upper arm, and his brows creased. Dulcina pulled away.

"What happened? Who did this to you?"

"Demons like to bite thicker tissue if they are not in a direct position to feed," she said quickly, offering nothing more than facts.

"Easier on the teeth if the strike is missed?"

She lifted an eyebrow, slightly impressed with his quick conclusion. "That's the theory."

Poor man. There was no escape for him. He knew far too much, could rationalize their existence too easily. She'd have to keep a sharp eye on him.

"And the folklore?" Curiosity bled into his tone, though she could sense he was holding back. "Any truth to the whole wooden stake thing and dodging sunlight?"

"It's all some version of the truth. Thanks to Stoker we've become a bit more popular. Not nearly as many torches and pitchforks from the villagers. At least, not in this region," she said with a slight shrug.

Jake laughed, but stopped abruptly when he caught sight of her harsh glare. "Sorry. Thought you were making a joke."

"We've been set on fire, hung, pressed, beheaded, drawn and quartered. The list goes on and on." Dulcina doled out the facts with no reservations. This was the reality of what her ancestors had survived. "Do not for one moment fool yourself into thinking your kind have evolved into compassionate beings. It would be a similar outcome today."

"Less pitchforks," Jake said with a nod, then with a sour twist of his mouth, added, "but more secret facilities, experiments, and dissecting."

"Exactly."

"Probably a healthy round of extermination," he said solemnly. When he looked back up, catching her gaze, he made an addendum. "Again, less pitchforks, but that doesn't make it better."

"In reality, it would be easy to eliminate a good chunk of the species," she said, waiting expectantly to see how his brain functioned. He wasn't going anywhere, his fate already sealed, she just had the need to know how he ticked.

"Centralized," he surmised quickly. "You mean there's a nest?"

She wrinkled her nose. "Ugh, that's movie theater terminology."

"Well then, what do you call a grouping of vampires?"

Watching his cleverness in motion as he connected the pieces of this puzzle was actually thrilling. "People, and we live in cities."

He chuckled, then winced, the motion hurting his ribs. Jake glanced up, and as he swept his thumb sinfully down the arch of her foot, he said, "Sounds far-fetched. A city suggests commerce, sophistication, and technology. Meaning, a healthy amount of people to support a functioning society."

"You think vampires can't function as a society?"

"Now, on that I wouldn't know. I'm not one, so..." He trailed off, still pondering that thought, keeping his focus on her foot. Now his fingers moved to just beneath her ankle on the inside of her foot. Dulcina dug her fingernails into the palm of her hand to stop from squirming. Damn, that felt good, and tickled. "So? Do your people function well in a society?"

"*I* don't." Her answer was so final it drew his attention. "But most vampires form a resilient community."

"But not you," he clarified.

"No."

He kept his focus locked on the task beneath his hands, then at long last, his gaze met hers, and he said, "Seems like these are things you'd want kept secret. Stuff you wouldn't just tell anybody. Why you telling me?"

"Because it doesn't matter how much you know, or don't."

The sweeping strokes of his fingers suddenly halted, and his voice dropped low. "You planning to kill me then?"

"No. Not if I can avoid it," she answered honestly, and when suspicion continued to gleam in his eyes, Dulcina felt compelled to explain. "I can't let you free in this world with knowledge of us. Or demons."

"Demons. The red-eyed ones." Jake pursed his lips together, and after a pause that seemed incredibly deep in thought, he just nodded. "I asked you, didn't I? That's why you felt free talking about them. Because I asked. Thought you were one of them. Your eyes are different, but I'd thought..."

And there it was. Clever man, putting the puzzle pieces into place. "You thought I was one of them. As you would, not knowing the difference. Again, I'm not demon. No red eyes, even in my most furious of rages. No second pair of fangs behind the visible set. And as you can attest by having your hands on my skin, I do not radiate heat like a furnace stoking the fires of hell."

Jake pondered her words, then a wicked grin curled his lips. "Makes you sound lacking in the shock and awe department, vampire."

Her lip twitched reflexively, agitated by the insult. "I don't need genetic glitches to make them fear me."

"Fear you?" His brows creased in confusion. "Why—"

Dulcina yanked her foot from his grasp, quick as a lightning strike, and covered Jake's mouth as she simultaneously drew her knife. She released him only to put a finger over his lips demanding silence.

Jake acknowledged her direction with a sharp nod and sat wide-eyed and silent, staring intently at her like he was asking if there was danger.

She deftly tucked her feet beneath her, ready to strike should the situation call for immediate action. Anyone could have made that subtle noise outside her door. Her prying neighbor, a demon, the Stalker Lord himself... Hell, even Rafe could be lurking outside. It was a likely possibility, and one she couldn't forget.

The movement paused outside, and then a letter slid beneath her door with a slight whooshing sound. A simple delivery. Dulcina gritted her teeth. She hated to admit the facts, but Rafe's visit had made her jumpy, at least where the human's safety was concerned.

She rose from the bed, padded across the room, and stabbed the letter with her knife, plucking it from the floor on the point. Nothing but her name was on the outside, which meant it was not a kill order from the Stalker Lord for her to carry out. She held in her hand a simple letter. Cheating, Dulcina pried open the envelope and glanced at the signature across the bottom first. It was signed *Rollin Casteel & Babette Dautry*.

"About damn time," she muttered, scanning the details. It was an invitation to her brother's wedding, most likely dropped off by one of the very few people who knew her location.

Dulcina sat on the edge of her bed, reading the invitation. Rehearsal was tomorrow. Smart. Rollin knew the more time she had to work over options in her mind, the less likely she was to show. Little did Rollin know she'd just acquired a problem.

Though he wasn't fully healed, she would have to bring Jake with her, and in all likelihood, leave him in Balinese. She couldn't keep a human above ground. This was not necessarily a rule, but something that to her knowledge, no Stalker had ever tried. It posed too many risks. They could grab a phone, escape, speak to someone, so many endless possibilities that might expose their species.

She glanced over at Jake. No longer sensing any danger, he had eased himself back against the headboard and closed his eyes. He drew in breaths slowly and evenly, calming himself, resting.

Jake was handsome, in an average sort of way. Scruffy, sandy brown hair fell over his forehead. His short beard was thicker and darker now that a few days had passed. However, that's where the plain and boring ended.

The hard edge of his jaw beneath that scruff was something she could run her fingertips over again and again. Dulcina made sure his eyes were still closed and then let her gaze wander over everything he'd left exposed, which was a lot. That tight, white tank he wore left little to her vivid imagination, and when he moved to rest his hand over his injured ribs, she had to stop herself from sighing. This man's muscles in motion were captivating. It was so rare to see such a beautifully made human. Honestly, few vampires had this kind of tone and definition.

Dulcina turned her gaze back to the invitation. He had to go with her, of that she had no choice, but maybe this was the perfect opportunity to get rid of the tempting man. She wasn't the type to hesitate. If she wanted something, she pounced. This situation limited her options, her very nature, and she needed him out of her life as soon as possible. If he belonged to someone else, she could put him firmly from her mind.

Maybe she would shock her sweet sister with the gift of a male servant. Maeryn needed a distraction. A project. An injured puppy to rescue. Anything to pull her from the deep depression she'd been wallowing in since Jovan left the city.

"Hey," Jake said softly, and when she glanced over at him, his eyes were still closed. "Whatever you're thinking over there, you're thinkin' it pretty hard. Bad news?"

"No, just...family."

"Hmmm," he said, acknowledging her answer, but never pushing for details. Damn it, another thing she liked about him.

Jake would make an excellent servant for Maeryn. He was attentive, charming and fun-loving, and he listened. On paper, he was everything Maeryn needed more of in her life. Maybe Jake could teach her to loosen up a bit, to relax as he rubbed her feet with sure, strong strokes.

The invitation in Dulcina's hand crinkled. She glanced down, a little thrown by the sudden noise. She'd balled her hand into a fist. The thought of Jake touching her sister didn't sit well with her, the image in her head churning jealousy. Admitting she didn't want to share him led to a far more profound realization. If she didn't let Jake go now, she never would.

Chapter 7

PARIS

Awareness slowly returned as he surfaced from another deep sleep, but he didn't open his eyes, and didn't feel like staying awake. He'd been in the middle of a conversation with Dulcina, listening to her smooth voice, and he'd slipped into sleep. Head tipped back, he'd just powered down. He probably didn't feel the need to fight it anymore, knowing full well he was safe here under her watchful eye.

Each time he closed his eyes, he had no idea how long he'd slept, which was becoming a problem. Waking up felt like a refresher nap. Every time. She had a small clock on her dresser top, but it was analog. He could have been out for an hour, or thirteen.

Hell, he'd been in and out of consciousness so often, the only sure way he'd found to at least mark day or night was the presence of his vampire in the apartment. When Dulcina was home, the sun shone. When she vanished for stretches of time, she was out, running free in the night.

Not that he could do anything about her absence right now. If he walked out the door, he wasn't sure he'd make it onto the street. The pain from his injuries definitely hindered his movements, but it was nothing he couldn't fight through. Every time he moved, he was quickly winded, and, well, that made him sleepy. He was doing it on purpose. Sort of. Jake strategically limited his breathing to minimize the pain. It was a trade-off. In the moments she was gone he breathed deeply, doing everything he knew to prevent pneumonia from settling into his stagnant lungs. He didn't want her around to see him struggle.

Something in the room moved, and he instinctively went still. Cracking his eyes open, he saw what had made the soft scuffing sound. Dulcina stood at her dresser, strapping her Bowie knife to her hips. Gorgeous creature. He seemed to push himself a little harder when she was watching. Some ingrained, primitive drive to impress this female. Yeah, he was going to overdo it again, and he wasn't even mad about it.

She turned to face him, and caught him staring. Too late to hide it, he just gave her a sleepy grin. She gave him nothing. Not a word, or even an acknowledgment. The stone-cold woman just walked over to him, and lifted his good arm. He stirred, blinking slowly to chase the drowsiness away. She often checked on him, poked his ribs, moved his arms, and even monitored the changing colors of his bruises. This was different. She'd moved his arm to her headboard. Without a fight, he watched her put a knot in a cord he hadn't seen her produce, and tighten it around his wrist. Then she tied him to her bed. She tied his injured side as well, but gave him more leeway, restricting movement in that arm just enough so he couldn't reach the other and untie himself.

"Kinky," Jake said, his sleepy voice going a little husky. "Never done this sort of thing before, but I ain't about to knock something I haven't tried. Wish you would have kissed me first, though."

Dulcina froze where she hovered over him, glanced down at his lips, then abruptly spun around and headed for the door. "I'll be back in an hour. Maybe two."

"All right," Jake said with a healthy amount of disappointment. "Hey, what if I have to go to the bathroom?"

"You'll live," she said, grabbing her jacket from the chair.

"What if there's a fire?" he asked, testing the ropes, though not with any true effort.

Her back straightened, and she looked at him incredulously, as if the answer was obvious. "Then you won't."

"Your tender words are such a comfort to me," he said, accentuating his accent and adding a sugary smile, but it had zero effect on her. The instant that door shut, he couldn't resist one more tease. "So, I'll just wait here for you then?"

From the other side of the door, she muttered, "Shut up, Jake."

Jake grinned. She might be telling him to shut his mouth, but at least she'd called him by his name. Progress.

With nothing to do but stare at his feet, Jake scoped out his captor's apartment, but there wasn't much to see. There were two rooms. This room and the bathroom. Dulcina was a woman without needs. She didn't need other people, which was clear by her lack of hospitality. She also required very little to function day-to-day, or so it seemed. With no actual closet in sight, he could only assume that her little three-drawer dresser contained everything she owned. All her clothes, shoes, and whatever she kept on hand. He had to be right about that because there was nothing else in the room. No second pair of shoes on the floor, no coat rack. He hadn't even seen a hairbrush, makeup, or girly hair curling things when he'd been in the bathroom. Toothbrush, toothpaste, washcloth, and towel. That was all. Simple. Spartan sparse.

She was a warrior. Had to be. Jake didn't even know men who lived this minimally. He couldn't imagine any woman living like this unless there was a pressing and constant possibility that she would either pick up and move at the drop of a hat, or be killed just as quickly, and wanted nothing left behind.

No pictures on the wall meant no connections. While some pieces of her life painted a clear picture, Dulcina remained a puzzle. She hadn't exactly taken a dislike to him touching her feet last night, but he didn't think she'd liked it either. She'd been studying him the whole time, her sly little sideways glances assessing his purpose.

He'd have to be cautious. Consistent. The woman was smart and suspicious. Jake had a shot at luring her in, finding a weak point, and escaping. If he could keep her charmed. Honestly, charming her was proving difficult. In part because he hadn't been conscious often, but also, she hadn't been receptive. She didn't act, or react, like a typical female.

Maybe because she was vampire. Or—and he was just throwing darts at the wall on this one—but maybe Dulcina had a few trust issues of her own. She fit the profile. Loner. Tight-lipped. Defensive. The woman shot him down before he got started most of the time. Actually, he kind of liked that part. Jake grinned, recalling her need to have that last word from the other side of the door.

A key turned in the lock, and the door knob turned. Dulcina slipped inside. Quiet as a church mouse, she closed the door behind her and flipped the inner deadbolt.

"Didn't expect you back so soon," he said, trying to tease her about how long she'd been gone. It had probably been just shy of an hour, but it felt like a couple. She didn't look at him, let alone turn toward him, so he pushed again. "Miss me?"

"We're leaving," Dulcina announced, grabbing his duffel bag and throwing it on the bed near his feet.

Jake nodded, because, well, it seemed impolite not to at least acknowledge her, even if he didn't have a say in what was happening to him. Grabbing the bottom of his bag, she flipped it and dumped the entire contents onto the bed, and then swiftly replaced the items one by one. She was packing his bag, and at the same time, verifying none of the contents could be used against her. A quick scan of his personal effects revealed she'd already removed his gun. Smart woman.

Jake cleared his throat. "If this is a 'we' event, would you mind untying me?"

Her sharp gaze locked onto his for what felt like the longest suspended moment of his life. She was making a decision about him. He felt it in his bones. No one looked a man in the eye like that without contemplating an end-all judgment.

Without a word, Dulcina lifted her knee, planting it right between his legs, and braced her palm against the headboard beside his ear. She leaned in close enough for him to smell her sweet, natural scent, to feel her breath move the air between them, and stared him straight in the eye.

"You stay by my side," she said, her voice dark and deadly serious. "You do as you're told. Without question."

"Understood, ma'am," he said with a nod.

Her pause was brief, and Jake felt her move a split second before the chunking sound of metal on wood rang in his ear, reverberated through the headboard he'd been tied against. His hand dropped gracelessly to the bed.

"Hey, now!" Jake snapped his gaze over to see the deep gouge in the wood, the cord split by her knife.

She lunged for the other side, severing the cord so cleanly it gave him a newfound respect for how sharp she kept that damn blade.

Gracefully, like nothing about this situation was out of the ordinary, she pushed off the bed and went back to repacking his bag. Jake rubbed his wrists and stretched out the tension in his back, but kept an eye on her.

Dulcina held up a large plastic bag filled with suckers, inspected it briefly, then lifted an eyebrow at him. "You pack one bag for an overseas trip, and *this* makes the cut?"

"Have suckers, will travel." Jake reached over with a pained grunt, and took the bag from her hand, fishing a single sucker through the small hole in the plastic. He peeled the wrapper off and popped it into his mouth.

"You're insane," she said, and he half believed she meant it.

"They're Spangler," Jake said defensively.

"What's a Spangler?"

"Dum-Dums." He held out the bag for her to look over, but she didn't move a muscle, so he changed tactics. "What's your favorite?"

Dulcina eyed him with a skeptical squint. "Never had one."

Jake rummaged around, pulling out several colors and offering them to her like a tiny candy bouquet. "Here, try 'em all. Myself, I'm a cream soda kind of guy. Curious to know your favorite."

She tilted her head to the side, confusion plastered all over her face. "Why? What does it matter?"

"I guess in the grand scheme of things, it don't matter at all. But it's nice to know a gal's favorite. Never know when it'll come in handy," Jake said with a wink.

"Handy?" The look she shot him was priceless, a combination of disgust and curiosity.

"Yeah," Jake said smiling, the sucker stick twitching in his mouth as he spoke. "Never know when I might need to coax you into a good mood. Any little thing is gonna help with you, Sugar."

She narrowed her eyes. Quick as a striking snake, Dulcina slugged him in the shoulder. The hit rocked his body, jarred his ribs, and rattled the hell out of him. Needless to say, it took him a beat to recover.

"Don't call me Sugar," Dulcina snapped.

Damn, the woman was a hard hitter. Those toned muscles weren't just for show. Beautiful form, nailing her target dead on. Sexy as hell. "Worth it."

She glared at him for a brief moment, then turned away as if his presence was insignificant. Maybe he was to her, and that was just fine. He watched her make the little apartment tidy, putting his towel in the hamper, wiping down the sink, and tugging the shower curtain closed. This woman was definitely a different breed.

A normal woman might rush about, collecting clothes, toiletries, and necessary items for a trip of any length. Not this beauty. Those gorgeous high cheekbones didn't have a dab of makeup on them, and that wild, wavy free hair of hers had been hand-fluffed upon waking and never touched since. She wasn't getting ready to leave, but more like making preparations for her return.

"We're leaving in five. Get up," she said, marching through the room. Grabbing his bag on the way by, she slung it over her shoulder and walked right out the door.

What was her game? Jake was certain he didn't understand the rules she played by, and it left him a little thrown. He was alone. Untied. Seemed like an invitation to escape, except he could never cover any ground with these banged up ribs. He was doing significantly better, but it wouldn't take much for her to catch up with him.

Maybe she'd ducked out to preserve his already pummeled ego. Probably not, but he was happy to take advantage of this window of opportunity to grunt, groan, and suffer through the pain of getting up without a witness.

First, a strategy. Sitting upright hurt, twisting to roll from bed might just bring a tear to the eye, and scooting...wasn't fun, but it worked. Maneuvering his body was tricky, and it took him a minute to sort out what felt the best. He was a little wobbly getting onto his feet, but solid enough once he stood. Jake took a moment to just breathe through the new sensations washing through him as his body settled. He'd been laid out flat for too long.

Dulcina walked in and he grinned at her, gingerly spreading his arms wide. Well, as wide as his injured ribs allowed. She looked him up and down, and said, "You're up. What do you want, a medal? Move."

Jake huffed out a short laugh, careful not to jar his ribs. "There's my girl. All roses and sunshine."

"I don't have to let you live," she reminded him, and yeah, that took a little wind out of his sails.

Holding his tongue, he followed her out the door and into the dimly lit hallway at a slightly more measured pace. He didn't hurt terribly at the moment, thanks to all the pills she'd been feeding him, but certain steps or turns still jarred the fractured bones, strained the bruised muscles.

She moved more leisurely than he'd expected, and at first he'd thought it was out of kindness so he could keep up, but she never once glanced back or seemed concerned about the possibility he might fall behind. There was a big ol' red flag if ever he saw one. Dulcina wasn't worried about him getting away in the slightest. If he made a dash, she clearly thought she could catch him. Hell, she didn't even blink about letting him see the entire pathway outside, or which building she called home. Like she knew for certain he wasn't coming back.

Well, then, did it really matter how hard he tried to snag her attention? Her sympathy or affection? His efforts clearly weren't working worth a darn anyway. Still, he would bide his time, wait for an opportunity for escape to present itself, but only because it was truly the only option at the moment.

He followed her through the main entry and out onto the street. Dulcina approached a medium-sized car, parked right on the curb. As she rounded the back end and headed for the driver's side, she tapped the trunk. "Get in."

"Into the trunk?"

She rolled her eyes and pointed to the passenger side. "You keep irritating me, and I'll make that happen."

Jake slowly raised his hands, palms facing out, in the universal gesture of giving up. He made his way to the front of the car and eased into the passenger seat. The little engine sputtered to life just as he closed the door.

Dulcina didn't seem to have an interest in wasting time. She pulled onto the street, and they were on the move, zipping down roads he'd never seen before. Normally, not knowing where he was would be enough to worry him, but at the moment, he was distracted. The smell wafting from the upholstery of this car was...pungent. It was a smell he'd come to instantly recognize from his years as a cop.

"Something wrong?" she asked, probably noting his change in posture without directly looking at him. Damn, she was good.

"That might depend..." He turned, glancing into the back seat, then pinning his full accusing focus on her.

She laughed, throaty and low. "It's not my car."

"A friend?" he asked, sending her a knowing look. Jake nodded. "It's always a friend's car."

"Geoff puts up with a lot from me and the other Stalkers. He is a friend, of sorts, and he's welcome to his habits of coping," she said with a grin. Nice to see she found her friend's drug habits amusing. Made her seem less cold and unfeeling.

"Coping, huh? What the hell do you do to him?"

"*We* don't do anything to him. He disposes of the bodies," she said, all calm and matter of fact.

Jake had a hard time deciding if her implying she might have killed someone bothered him more than the realization that she'd made a certain word plural. "The *bodies*? That happen often?"

"Not as often as I'd expected." She stopped speaking, focusing on the intersection ahead and the converging traffic. In that moment she looked like a teenager, overly cautious, not yet confident in her skills, but willing to push forward with a bracing sense of invincibility.

"Not as often as *you'd* expected?" Jake watched her closely.

She grinned. The moment she'd made it through that mess of an intersection, she went on talking. "What attacked you, the men with the red eyes? They're demons."

"That's what you kill? Overgrown, superhuman, red-eyed men?"

"Every chance I get." Dulcina's smile was wild, eager.

Jake eyed her warily. Hell, he didn't know which way was up with this woman. He couldn't get a gauge on what was a lie and what rang true. She seemed honest. Direct. But, good God, if she was telling the truth... Could she even kill a grown man? She'd easily maneuvered his injured body around with little effort, and Jake was no lightweight. At this point, he was willing to bet it was a possibility.

Jake inwardly cringed, recalling how viciously he'd been jumped. Okay, yes, there had been three, but damn. The hard fact was he'd been beaten into unconsciousness only a few hits into the fight. He hadn't been caught off guard or taken a whooping like that since he'd been a kid. These guys had been...unnaturally strong.

He slipped a glance over to Dulcina, then took a breath to reword the question cycling through his head. "Is it common for vampires to go after demons?"

"Only vampires are Stalkers, and only Stalkers hunt demons. So, technically, yes, but your typical vampire won't confront a demon unless it ventures near or into a vampire city."

"That happen often?"

"Depends on where you live." She paused, glancing into her rear-view mirror, and seeming to settle now that the traffic had lessened on this straightaway. "In Galbraith, a demon wandering anywhere near the city is completely unheard of, to the point I'm not aware of any documented breach of their gates. The fear of demons is constant, passed down through stories across generations, but not necessarily through personal experience. My city was the same as Galbraith, apart from a couple scattered above-ground sightings. Until the night we were attacked. Demons breached the gate, the attack well planned. It shook us to the core."

"They're just men," he reasoned.

"And I'm just a woman," she said, turning to him and smiling brightly, her fangs flashing in the passing streetlights.

"Okay, point taken, but I assume men were guarding your city. Are you saying demons are stronger than vampires?"

She shrugged, a graceful lift of a single shoulder. "Depends on the individual. Some vampires I've encountered are otherworldly, possessing an innate power I can hardly believe exists. Others have adapted to their life of genteel nobility. I image demons are the same."

"They choose weakness when they have super strength?"

"Humans are no different. Many prefer to be comforted by the weight around their middles rather than utilize the greatness their bodies are capable of, minimal though it is for humans." Dulcina seemed bored, like maybe answering this question was beneath her, but she carried on. "I see many human men, but few look like you. You're strong. Capable. Or, at least you were, before you were damaged. I can see it in your posture, how you move and think. React. What is it you do...did?"

"Miami SWAT." Once the words were past his lips, he instantly realized she wouldn't know what that meant. "It's sort of a specialized police unit. We apprehend some of the more dangerous criminals."

"Ah," she said, with a long nod. "That certainly explains you. Well, then. Could *he* join your unit tonight, at this very moment, just as he is?"

Jake followed her pointed finger out the window to a lanky young man about twenty years old getting into his car. All height and no muscle. "Highly doubt it."

"Aw, why not? Too skinny?" she worked to suppress that sly smile of hers.

"Yep. No way he could pull one of the bigger men on the unit out of the line of fire," Jake said, a twinge of sorrow surfacing as his thoughts flashed to Rita. He'd trusted her, more than some of the other men in his unit.

"What about him? I must say, I like that one," she crooned, pointing at a broad shouldered man walking next to a dainty woman.

"Better, but probably not. It's not just physical. Not everyone can handle the job mentally."

"Now you've got it." Dulcina reached over and tapped the side of his skull, just above his ear, with her index finger. "Not all men are equal. Not all vampires are equal. Not all demons are equal."

Jake scrubbed his hand over his head. "Damn, that means when you jump into a scrape, you can't even guess what you're up against."

She drew in a deep breath, and on the exhale, whispered, "Thrilling."

Jake grinned. Dulcina was an adrenaline junkie, plain and simple. No attachments. Life was a joyride. He'd known men like that. Hell, he'd been that way himself for a stint or two. Sometimes that's just how a person needs to function at certain points in their life.

He might understand her to some degree, but that sure didn't mean he had a snowball's chance in hell of making a connection with this woman. His life was at a turning point, and not a damn thing was in his control.

Chapter 8

BALINESE

The chateau ahead looked more like an intimidating fortress jutting up from the ground, black against the bright moonlight. The imposing structure that marked the location of Balinese far below was more than enough to deter most, human or demon, from approaching. Dulcina drove the narrow gravel path to the front gate, and just to the north side of the walkway, threw the car into park and stepped out. This was home.

Jake climbed out slowly, looked way up, and whistled low. "That your house?"

"This is my city," she corrected, but there was no pride in her voice, only simple fact.

Usually she'd slip inside unnoticed, cloaked in her Spirit form, but tonight she would walk the wide, stone paved bridge leading to the gate of Balinese. The human made swift travel and stealth impossible. Even now he was on her heels, half whispering a dozen questions. The man liked answers, and for that she couldn't fault him, but she wasn't about to comply.

Awareness sharpened and she sensed the presence of another in the slight shifting of the night surrounding them. The shadows crossing the arched doorway morphed into a masculine figure, and he headed straight toward them. Imposing. Serious. Even if she hadn't caught sight of his features in the moonlight, she'd know that hitched stride of his anywhere. Steffen.

Jake's hand curled around her elbow, solid and strong, tugging her backward, stalling her approach. What the devil was he doing? She glanced at him, only to find an absolute resolve in his demeanor as he stepped in front of her, fully blocking her from the approaching man.

She lifted an eyebrow, completely amazed by his behavior. Not only had he been aware of Steffen's approach at nearly the same moment she had been, but Jake intended to protect her. His actions were unnecessary and amusing, but on the whole, commendable. His stance remained sure, confident and resolved. Even though he was the weaker species, he truly intended to face off with Steffen. Jake was fearless, a rare quality she was thoroughly attracted to, and wholeheartedly admired.

Dulcina gently squeezed his shoulder, and as she moved to step around him, leaned in and said low against his ear, "Down, boy."

Jake shivered in response to her words, or maybe her nearness. Either way, his reaction was one she might enjoy investigating. Later. Right now they were under heavy scrutiny from the city's keenly observant Gatekeeper.

Steffen cocked his head to the side, curiously regarding the sight before him, but didn't slow his approach. The Gatekeeper only had so much caution in his reserves. His crushing near-death experience years ago had skewed his perspective on life. Mind scrambled and body altered irrevocably, it was only a matter of time before Steffen left his gate and this world, likely on his own terms. Though while he was here and breath still sparked life through his body, she would cherish the presence of this man she called friend.

"Steffen," she said, nodding. With her familiar acknowledgment of the approaching man, she could almost feel Jake relaxing behind her.

"Dulcina," Steffen responded, respect lingering in his voice.

He stopped before her with his hand on the hilt of his sword, not out of vigilance, but habit. Her height nearly matching his, she reached out to him and cupped the back of his neck, pulling him close. He did the same to her, and they leaned toward each other until their foreheads touched. For a long breath they remained connected. This was no greeting of family, friend, or lover, but a reunion of survivors.

She felt Jake watching them intently, never intruding, but somehow his silent respect of their connection threw her off. Stepping back from Steffen, she smiled, swiftly taking note of his kind, tired eyes.

"I'm only here for one day," she said softly.

Steffen nodded. "Thanks for checking in this time."

Steffen turned, walking at her side as they approached the gate. Jake followed, keeping his distance. She sensed a change in Jake's demeanor, like he was freely giving her space, but would be there in a heartbeat if she needed him. On the surface it seemed respectful, and it was, but she knew he was listening in, gleaning information. With Jake, she got the sense that awareness was second nature.

Clearing his throat, Steffen captured her attention. "Everything is...as it should be."

"What a novel concept. For us." Dulcina had felt the same above ground. Perhaps the entire world was changing. "How does peace feel?"

"Stagnant, and I do not trust it," Steffen said in all sincerity.

"Which is why I long for no such thing," she said, a smirk on her lips.

"On that, we are in accord." At the gate, Steffen stepped back into the shadows, allowing her to pass.

Jake followed her through the arched doorway, close on her heels. She led him through the great room and then left into the kitchen. They crossed the room to the narrow door in the back, both ducking through and into the dimly lit landing. Stairs hugged the left corner of the wall, leading down to a cellar stocked full of wine barrels.

"You know that man pretty darn well, I take it?" Jake asked, a few steps behind.

"Yes." She paused on the stairs to glance back at Jake. Odd, but this was the first time she could recall explaining herself to anyone. She didn't have to, but Jake didn't demand, either. He was simply curious. Was he locking her every response away in his memory? Of course he was, and that made her calculated answers vital to his survival in their world. And the fact remained, she did want him to survive, so she answered honestly, "I know both of them very well."

"Both? What both?" Jake sent her a hard stare. "There was one man."

She smiled, a controlled curve of her lips. "Osric is rarely seen."

"Right. Ninja vampire?"

"Spirit."

"A ghost?" he asked, eyes wide, but mirthful. He thought she was lying, or joking. "Sugar, I'm a believer, but a man wanderin' about in the afterlife hardly counts as someone you personally know. Unless...you and this ghost can carry on a conversation."

"No, not a ghost. At least, not exactly," she said, then pivoted where she stood, exposing her back to the open stairwell. Dulcina drew in a deep breath, tipped her face to the ceiling, and let herself fall.

"Hey!" Jake shouted, scrambling down the few stairs that separated them, and just as he reached out to take hold of her, she vanished. Completely gone to his eyes as she fully embraced her Spirit form.

Dulcina took sinful pleasure in watching his features shift from concern, to fear, and then finally, of all things, he seemed to land on outright agitation. Her disappearance was like a puzzle thrown before him, and he was working on getting himself under control enough to sort it out. She liked that about him, this clever human.

"Darlin' I know damn well you're still here...somewhere. I don't know how you did it, or what kind of trick you pulled, but woman, I know that teasing look. Knew you were up to something," Jake said, possibly louder than necessary.

With what amounted to an inner shake, she appeared nearly six feet below him on the cellar floor, and he gasped, the sound echoing off the stone walls.

"Sweet baby Jesus. How'd you do that?"

"That, Jake, was me moving in Spirit. It's why you couldn't see the second man at the gate." She could tell by the look on his face that he was processing her words, sorting out the details.

"Yeah, but I didn't see anything. No mist, no fog."

"This isn't a movie," she said, rolling her eyes. "We travel in Spirit. As ghosts. We exist in Spirit form and yet we are nothing at all."

He came down the stairs, closing the vast gap between them, and when he faced her, he shook his head. Eyes wide, awe plastered across his face. "Did I just walk into Oz?"

She faked a pout, opened the door near a wine barrel, and patted her thigh. "Come on, Toto."

Jake scowled at her pet reference, but obeyed. It took a smart man to know when fighting back wasn't possible, or necessary. He stepped through the door with nothing more than an indignant grunt.

Biting down on a smile, Dulcina shut the door and led him down the corridor to the left, choosing the long way on purpose. The gray stone walls appeared never-ending, tended to disorient a person, and after only a short time, she noticed Jake had stopped trying to sneak a peek down every corridor they passed. He'd at last caught on that it was pointless to mentally map this labyrinth.

Observing him from the corner of her eye, she made several assessments. First, Jake seemed to realize he was out of his depth here, and still he showed no fear. His eyes flitted here and there, soaking it all in, but his gaze always returned to her, gauging her mood and reaction. She knew with certainty that's what he was doing because, well, that's what she would do if the tables were turned.

He could study her all he wanted. Within hours they would part ways forever, and any tricks and tidbits he'd thought he'd gained would be useless. Even now, she approached her destination from the main corridor, instead of those used privately by the royal family and those few traveling through the chateau. Dulcina's long legs took her quickly around the small lake. At the sound of Jake's hushed whistle of wonder at the marvelous underground spring, she suppressed a smile. He'd been captured by the beauty of falling water and green, dangling plants clinging to a jutting damp wall. She'd lost her child-like wonder so long ago, but she still appreciated that the novelty of an underground water source inspired awe in others.

Jake hurried to catch up as she entered the Casteel wing, and by the time they were once again side-by-side, she'd already knocked on the door to her family's home. The door flew open, and there stood the prettiest, wide-eyed young woman. At sixteen years of age, the youngest of her original family in tragedy looked every bit like a grown woman. Deceptive. Her mind and heart remained that of a cosseted, free-spirited child.

"Hey, kid," Dulcina said. They weren't really sisters, and not even that close, but Oriana had always liked the label of sibling.

In the blink of an eye, the girl threw her arms around Dulcina, hugging her tight. "You came to save her, right? Please tell me you'll save her."

"No, I came home for..." She pushed Oriana off her so she could look her in the eyes. "Save who? What the hell is going on now?"

"Maeryn." Realizing a half second later her one-word answer wasn't enough as Dulcina didn't live here anymore, Oriana sucked in a breath and tacked on, "She said she was going to leave the city. She can't leave! Maeryn is too fragile. She'll get lost. Or worse!"

"Did you tell Navarre and Cat? Surely they'll put a stop to this," Dulcina said, fishing for answers in her sister's disconnected stream of information.

Oriana bit her lip, those wide eyes searching around nervously, but she never responded.

"You didn't tell them, did you?" Dulcina only had to wait a moment before her sister shook her head. "Why not?"

"She swore me to secrecy!" the teen gasped out, then dropped her voice back to a hushed tone. "What was I supposed to do? Betray her like everyone else? She'd hate me!"

Dulcina sighed. Not everyone had betrayed poor Maeryn. Only the most important person in her life.

"All right, calm yourself. Did you at least tell Savard?"

"I did, but..." Oriana chewed her lip once more. "I don't think he believed me."

"The captain can sniff out the difference between truth and lie better than any man I've ever met. If you spoke the truth, he believed you." Dulcina glanced past her and into the home. "Where is she?"

"I don't..." Oriana's voice broke in a forlorn sob. "She hasn't lived here for years, and won't tell us where she hides away. Oh, she's so alone!"

"Stop being dramatic, Ori. We'll have to deal with Maeryn later. Just focus on calming down, dressing up, and getting yourself to the church before they start rehearsals. Maeryn will show up, or she won't, but you need to hurry," she said, pushing Oriana back inside and shutting the door between them.

"Come on," she directed Jake, turning back down the corridor, this time at a quicker pace.

"We heading to church? Why?" Jake said, hurrying after her, his hand clutching his ribs. She slowed for him, though not drastically.

"None of your business, pet," she said, taking an odd joy from his narrowed gaze. She'd tell him, in a little bit, but not now. She had to think.

Dulcina walked on ahead, leaving him to trail behind a couple steps. Neither spoke. Leading him through this maze of a city, she wove through corridors, ducked down passageways. He was hurting, his stamina waning, but he would have time to recover later. She'd make sure of it.

She now had three things to tackle on her short visit. Wedding rehearsal. Unloading the human. Stop Maeryn from endangering her life. The rehearsal would begin in about fifteen minutes, and Maeryn being family, she should be there. Dulcina might not be close with her foster sisters, but she knew them well.

To reach the church, they'd have to go through the heart of the city. With Jake in tow, Dulcina was left without the option of disappearing from the gawking noble class, and steeled herself for the encounters.

As they turned down the corridor leading to the dining hall, her steps became markedly sharper, more hurried. Each carved wooden bench she passed was a countdown. Four more benches and she'd be in the center of the main gathering point of the aristocrats. Those who should be her peers.

A couple rounded the far corner, coming at them, doing nothing more than heading to the dining hall to take their last meal of the day. Aristocrats. Jake tensed when he saw them, tracking their approach.

The woman's periwinkle gown moved like a large, stiff bell as she walked. The black velvet vines over the fabric were a stark contrast in color, but a perfect match to the gentleman on her arm. Other than the black suit and white shirt, the only touch of color he wore was a matching periwinkle cravat.

When the wealthy pair gaped at her and swiftly ducked their heads together to whisper, Dulcina wasn't at all surprised to find their disgusted sneers landed on her rather than the human at her side.

The next few individuals they passed conspicuously dodged them and skirted to the far edge of the corridor. Another gasped, then slipped into an adjoining hallway, completely avoiding her.

Jake stepped up to her side, angling his head to observe her reaction, and whispered, "It's like I ain't even here."

"Is that so?"

He laughed, sort of an indignant snort. "Sugar, they may have looked at me, but they gave *you* the evil eye."

She shrugged, ignoring his astute and accurate observation.

Up ahead, Bayard Hallock walked straight for them. Damn. The aristocrat, deeply entrenched in the old ways, was adamantly opposed to the existence of Stalkers. Though if he knew his damn history, he'd know Stalkers were the reason he could indulge in the wealthy lifestyle he flaunted so shamelessly.

When Hallock caught sight of her, he gaped and sputtered like a bloated fish, no doubt primed to spout his outrage at her presence in the city. She wasn't interested in hearing it tonight. Dulcina deftly dropped her hand to her Bowie knife, tapping her forefinger lightly on the hilt, and lifted an eyebrow at him. Hallock snapped his jaw shut, his uneasy gaze flitting everywhere but on her as he hurriedly ducked into the dining hall.

She turned down the corridor opposite the dining hall door, and Jake leaned near again. "Why are they like this?"

"In this land of tradition, I do not conform."

A teasing light in his eyes, Jake asked, "Conform to what? You not supposed to wear pants? 'Cause then I truly object to you conforming."

When he glanced down, clearly appreciating her exposed midriff from her low-rise pants, she rolled her eyes. She felt the need to correct his ridiculous assumption. "It's against our laws, our beliefs, to kill. To them, I am evil. A murderer. The lowest form of life."

"Would be in my world too." Jake paused for a solid couple seconds, then asked, "You police things topside, right? I mean, that's your job."

"Without us, demons would run rampant, drawing enough attention from humans that vampires would once again become their target. If humans discover demons, they won't realize the difference between them and vampires. That puts us all in danger."

"You keep things in check to protect the people down here. They step out of line, you set them straight."

"Yes. By way of a blade through the heart," she said, not missing for a second that Jake snapped to attention. Like he hadn't exactly realized how much blood was on her hands. "Remember, I have a body mover. If a demon kills, or even attacks with the intent to kill, I put it down. No questions. No second chances. I've long since lost count of the lives I've taken, and whatever number it may be, is not limited to demon."

"And they know it," he surmised, his tone more reserved.

She nodded. "As fact."

Dulcina sensed his astonishment, the thickness of it hanging between them, and that was just fine. Now, he knew exactly what she was capable of. He could hate her like everyone else, and that would make the separation easier. She would retain no lingering desires to keep his company if he loathed her for the blood on her hands.

Chapter 9

BALINESE

Dulcina swept past the mosaic walls and through the open Gothic double doors of the church, Jake following. Immediately, she sidestepped out of the way and under the balcony. Leaning against the wooden support pillar, she watched the commotion up front near the altar.

On the other side of the pillar, Jake leaned too, except where she was trying to blend into the background and observe, he was struggling to catch his breath. He'd kept up with her admirably, and now he was paying for it, his body suddenly needing time to recover from overexertion. Honestly, that was part of why she'd stepped beneath the balcony. He needed a moment before coming face-to-face with people. Though honestly, so did she.

"You're hiding," Jake said, sending her a deflated version of a grin. His exhaustion had most certainly caught up to him.

With a short, soft laugh, she said, "Seems like all I do is hide."

"Can't hide forever," Jake said, trying to measure his breathing.

Poor thing. She'd run him pretty hard these last twenty minutes, and after being bedridden from his injuries for several days, this must be a lot for him physically.

"You just take a seat in the back row. I'll go up when I'm damn good and ready," she ordered, her tone a little grouchier than she'd intended, but it didn't hurt a thing. He didn't need to know she was softening toward him.

"Yes ma'am," he said, and she noted the relief on his face when he passed her. He'd needed the break.

Once he sat, she scanned the church. Watching her family from a distance was nothing less than entertaining. Lord Navarre had his head together with the priest. There were two priests in this particular church, but she was not familiar with this man, and had no name to match his pudgy face. To her, he was simply not a threat, and could therefore be ignored.

Cat stood out the most with her red hair, arms crossed and doing her absolute best to listen to the wedding vision Bette was excitedly describing to her while at her core not caring. Cat tried, and that was sweet. To be fair, she was slightly sidetracked with keeping a sharp eye on her three-year-old daughter. Cat wasn't the most personable creature in the world, but she had been exactly what Dulcina and her foster siblings had needed after the demon attack: A fierce protector.

A sharp whistle suddenly rose above the low din of conversation, and all eyes turned to Cat. Little Josette was the only one who didn't look at her mother. She knew she'd been busted. Up on the top step to the altar, she'd been reaching for a candle when her mother's blaring correction stopped her short. Every bit as obstinate as her mother, Josette slowly lowered her hand, clasped her fingers together behind her back, and continued to investigate the previously inaccessible zone as if nothing had just happened.

Rollin and Soren spoke off to the side, their conversation likely having absolutely nothing to do with Rollin's impending marriage, and everything to do with Guardian business. They'd always got on well, their personalities similar. Both were steadfast, with a sense of duty to rival Captain Savard's.

Scanning the room again, she noted Savard was suspiciously missing. That could only mean something in the city was happening, and he felt his presence was needed elsewhere. He'd come through in the end, when it counted most. He always did.

Maeryn sat on the far side of the church, silent and looking forlorn. Slightly relieved though she was, Dulcina could only wonder at what was going through her foster sister's mind. What had spurred this sudden need to pick up and leave when the shifting of the very air surrounding her often left her frightened and distraught? It was difficult to spot any real differences in Maeryn, as her normal state of being only shifted between the two extremes of mopey and skittish.

Footsteps behind Dulcina alerted her to a newcomer, though with most everyone present, and the steps light and airy, she knew without looking that it was Oriana. However, Maeryn spun around with sheer hope spread across her face. The instant she recognized her sister, the hope dissipated.

Oriana breezed up the aisle, a bright smile on her face, and her round expressive eyes so happy. With a little hop in her step, and a swish of her dress, she slipped into the pews and sat right beside Faith.

Faith, Soren's mate, was everything their foster mother was not, and then some. Where Cat's harsh introduction to reality had prepared them all to fight and survive, Faith was more of a nurturing, patient soul. Soren and Faith were, in a sense, like their second set of parents. Or maybe an aunt and uncle who were always there for you.

Individually, these people were all a mess. But together? This was a family who would go to war for you. No one cared that Faith had once been human, or that Cat's red hair was a blaring sign to the world that she was the dangerously powerful mixed species called Forbidden. They were family. Even when Dulcina had announced to Navarre and Cat that she would be going above as a Stalker, they only nodded their quiet support.

Here they all were—well, most of them—taking part in Rollin's wedding preparations. Dulcina never understood her brother's delay in exchanging vows and marks with Bette, but the family never mentioned the drawn-out engagement. The couple adored each other, lived together, and had been fully committed to each other since the buxom aristocrat had crashed into Rollin at the gate.

They'd gone through a lot together. Rollin had confided in Dulcina that Bette had lied to him, thinking it was the only way he'd be willing to help a stranger. Little did Bette know Rollin had the ability to see the best in everyone. Once proved right by any margin, he would put his entire faith in a person with such tenacity, his mind would never be swayed otherwise. He had listened to Bette's explanation, empathized with her encompassing need to seek out safety, and chose to look at the world from her perspective. Rollin had discovered not only did the world look quite different from her eyes, but that he would forgive Bette anything, because he loved her.

Bette was quite lovely. She had her quirky oddities, such as jumping at loud noises and clinging to Rollin's arm like he was the biggest, baddest protector in the world. Dulcina smiled as she watched Bette slip her arm around Rollin's and gaze up at him. What made them work was their unfailing devotion to each other.

Neither were marked, which was not specifically abnormal, just something she'd noticed. Any other woman might demand that mark to lock in her security, but not Bette. She knew her security came from the man, not the mark.

Dulcina hadn't been around when Bette had arrived, and she hadn't witnessed the hurdles for herself, and that was just fine. It made Rollin happy to tell her their story, which had made her a little biased to his side of things. Rollin was totally besotted with his future bride.

An elbow nudged her hip where she leaned against the church pew, gentle but insistent, its owner seeking her attention. She glanced down to see Jake leaning close to whisper, "Easy now, you look happy. Don't want to give someone the wrong idea."

"I'm happy for *them*. There's a difference," Dulcina said, smothering her smile.

"Looks like any other wedding, and since you came all this way, I assume this is the family."

"Wouldn't be here if it wasn't," she acknowledged, then pointed to Rollin. "That's my brother up there. Soon to be mated."

"Mated? As in married?" She sent him a narrow eyed sideways glance, and he laughed, drawing the attention of those in the church. He quickly turned it down a notch, and whispered again, "Okay, fine. Obviously it is, because this looks like a ceremony rehearsal, but you said it different. Like this means something else."

"This one means a lot," she said softly. "Rollin deserves this. Deserves her."

"All sorts of people deserve happiness. Marriage isn't always the answer to that," he said, his tone hinting at something deeper. A personal experience or aggravation.

"A marriage is…" Dulcina paused to process how to explain their culture in comparison to the norm for humans. "Well, it's what they're already doing now. Living together, sharing a life and a future. A mating is permanent."

"No such thing, Sugar."

"For us vampires, this is a commitment so permanent that if it is violated, execution is acceptable."

Jake's eyebrows shot up. "Execution? For who?"

"The person who strayed, male or female, and depending on the circumstance, it could include the person they cheated with," she said, enjoying the shock crossing his face as he processed her words.

"That's insane," Jake said firmly, then whispered to her, "Don't get me wrong, I do not approve of cheating in any fashion, but execution? Why so harsh?"

Dulcina scanned the church, not willing to approach the commotion near the altar, but her stolen moment of observation from the shadows with Jake was about to end. Soren had caught sight of her and would likely have a few words to say.

She leaned down and whispered the answer into Jake's ear. "Female vampires cannot reproduce until marked, and even then, we are only able to have two children. To take a lover before two offspring have been produced is punishable by execution. After? Depends on the situation."

"So cheating isn't a thing in the vampire city? Er...world?"

"It happens, but it is extremely rare," she said, unable to resist remaining near him. "A mating is for life. What of your culture? They seem...less invested."

"Some are in it body, heart, and soul. Doesn't mean the other half respects the commitment," he said, his voice a little darker.

Now she saw it, that chink in his armor that kept him on guard. He'd been hurt. Probably by a woman he thought would be his forever.

"Listen, Jake," Dulcina said, but then stopped the second she caught sight of Soren approaching swiftly. The trainer of the Guardians, with his height and harshly angled features, intimidated most people.

"Dulcina," Soren said before he got too close, giving her a moment to shift her focus from Jake to him. "How long has it been since you've come home?"

"Too long, I've been told."

Soren agreed with a grunt. "Knife holding out?"

"It's seen inside enough demon chests to put on some wear and tear, but she's just as sturdy as ever."

"Good," Soren said, then glanced over to where Jake sat pretending to ignore them with his gaze fixed on some point at the front of the church. "Steffen said you acquired a human. To house one above ground is not...practical. They are wily and complicated creatures, completely ignorant of our rules and way of life."

"I know."

"Do you? You live by the rules of a Stalker," Soren kept his voice low, cautious of the echo of the church. "Perhaps it's best if you leave him when you return above."

"I'm right here," Jake said, visibly annoyed they were talking around him.

"Of that, I am well aware." Soren looked down at him, a slight curl of annoyance to his lip. "Dulcina, you're needed up front."

And without another word, Soren turned, clearly expecting her to follow. Quick lecture, then move on. Soren didn't like to linger.

"He's a ray of sunshine," Jake grumbled.

"Don't take it personally. He's just overly cautious. Doesn't want to see you lead your kind down here to butcher his wife, friends, and godchildren." Dulcina clapped Jake on the shoulder, then left him there to absorb the weight of his situation.

A step down from the altar, the priest lined them up neatly. Bette had no family here, and so Rollin's large family filled in all the gaps. First Dulcina, then Maeryn, and Oriana. On Rollin's side, Navarre and Soren stood proud. Captain Savard would round out the line, making them even. Friends and family didn't normally stand up with the couple, but this was the royal family, and a show of unanimous support for the heir marrying a woman from outside Balinese was needed.

Dulcina half listened to the priest's rundown of the chain of events. She knew her part. She came in, stood during the long-winded speech about the future of Balinese, the line of succession, and on and on. Then she would sit through the marriage, eat in the grand dining hall for the feast. When night fell she'd be gone, disappearing into the night, as always.

Glancing to her right, she took the opportunity to study Maeryn up close. Nothing about her seemed much different. The young woman was still withdrawn, quiet, eyes downcast. Typical Maeryn. If not for the tip from Oriana about her thoughts of leaving, she'd never suspect something was wrong. Not one thing about Maeryn had changed. Same black melancholy clothes, same sharp bangs cut just below her eyebrows, and same long black hair surrounding her like a cloak. No spark of life lit her eyes, and it hadn't since the night Jovan left, but then, she'd always been hollow without him.

A few obvious directions were given, the exchange of vows rehearsed, a couple tears shed from the bride, and then the procession from the church practiced. Easy. Simple. Dulcina hadn't been invited to many weddings, but she'd crashed a few, hiding up in the balcony. The basics never changed, only the people standing here.

After a few lingering questions were answered, the family started mingling together once again. Maeryn slipped from the church, likely nursing her wounded soul. Again. She'd no doubt hoped Jovan would come home for the wedding, but he never came home. If Jovan wouldn't return for Maeryn, he certainly wouldn't make the trip home for his brother's mating ceremony. Maeryn had held onto hope longer than anyone she'd ever known.

From the corner of her eye, Dulcina noted the exact moment Jake stood and slowly made his way toward her. Brave human. Soren instantly tensed, while Rollin pretended to ignore his approach. She knew her brother was assessing how much of a danger Jake was in every move he made.

Standing near her side, but at a respectful step back, Jake reached a hand out to Rollin and said, "I gather congratulations are in order."

Rollin eyed him warily for all the time it took to draw in a breath, and then shook Jake's hand. "Thank you. And you are?"

"Jake Martin."

"Rollin Casteel," he said, never releasing Jake's hand. "You taking care of her?"

"Dulcie? Nah, can't keep up with the woman. More like she's taking care of me. At least for now." Jake sent her a lopsided grin, his eyebrow twitching slightly as if daring her to contradict him.

Rollin let go of his hand, changing his stance to place a protective hand at Bette's back. "Have a bit of caution, Jake. My sister knows how to use that blade on her hip."

"Thought maybe she did," Jake said, still grinning like an idiot. "Haven't seen her in action yet."

"Give it time," Rollin said, his tone slightly bored, then he pointedly looked down to the knife strapped to her hip. "Are you planning on wearing that knife in church and over your dress on my mating day?"

"I'm not wearing a dress," Dulcina said, eyeing her brother as if he'd lost his damn mind.

"But I..." Bette's voice trailed off, and though she looked crushed, at Rollin's insistent nudge gave it another go. "I've picked out something special for each of you."

Ah, damn. Her reflexively sharp words had been driven towards her brother, not Bette, and she regretted them. It wasn't like Rollin to pick a fight, or her to take the bait, but here she was, awkwardly frozen with all attention on her.

Jake was suddenly so close to her side that his arm made nearly full contact with hers, and even so, he leaned closer and softly said, "Won't hurt a thing to see it before you shoot it down."

He wasn't wrong. Her impulsively defiant behavior often hurt people, and she was rarely around to see the aftereffects. Jake was only asking her to be patient.

"Fine," Dulcina said, recognizing that giving in to Jake's insisting plea was far easier than backpedaling with family. "I'll look at it first."

"Thank you," Bette said, her smile beaming.

"Can't be that bad," Jake said, once again interjecting himself into the conversation. "She looks like a classy lady. I don't think she'd make you put a big ol' bow on your head. It'll be fine."

Oriana giggled, and when Dulcina shot her a hard look intending to shush, her sister covered her mouth. Too late. Once Oriana started laughing, it was nearly impossible to stop her. She was joy incarnate. With her other arm looped affectionately through

Navarre's, Oriana glanced up at him. Normally reserved and steadfast, Navarre seemed genuinely amused by the entire situation.

"See?" Jake said, clearly holding back a laugh that would hurt his ribs. "They're picturing it now. Might be funny to think about, but they'd never do that to you."

Dulcina smiled, just a little. In two minutes Jake had her family wrapped around his finger. Impressive. When slipping in and out of consciousness, he'd been amusing, but now? Jake was engaging and charming. Even so, she'd noticed how easily he'd manipulated the situation, molded the conversation so it came out favorably for both him and her. This was an unexpected skill she'd need to keep a sharp eye on, at least while she still had him.

Chapter 10

BALINESE

Jake did his best to keep up with Dulcina as she led him from the church, down the mosaic tiled corridor, and a sharp left at the end. When the next corridor banked to the right, Jake whistled at the fancy setup.

The logic suggested apartments. Rich apartments. Spaced out double doors along both sides of the corridor were separated by supporting arches. They were underground, so those arches must be functional, but they didn't have to be this pretty. Diamond crosshatch marble ran down the center of the corridor floor in cream and rich chocolate brown. The panels along the bottom of the walls were a decorative wood that matched the ceiling, and that inviting chocolate color filled in the gap between them.

"This is not our stop. Keep moving," Dulcina said, picking up her already swift pace. "I need to talk to Maeryn alone. If she's not ferreted away in Jovan's old home, then I have no idea where to find her."

Jake raised an eyebrow at her unfiltered comments. She was getting comfortable around him, speaking her mind rather than giving him strict direction. For a woman so guarded, it was progress.

Dulcina went straight for a wall panel at the dead end of the hallway, the raised trim thicker than on the longer walls. Reaching for a little handle blended with the chair rail, she opened a door. Of course her city had hidden doors. Behind the surprisingly thick panel, a set of stone stairs twisted out of sight. It wasn't dank or musty, like some old basement, but gave off a cozy sense of warmth.

They followed the stairs down what felt like a full level and Dulcie paused on a landing to open a door. Jake peeked out from behind her, and found himself gaping at a shockingly busy city street. The old-world corridors and fancy décor from the floor above were a stunner, but this was a different kind of surprising. People buzzed by them, paying no attention as they went about their normal life. A few women carried shopping bags, and kids tugged on their parents' hands. It was all so...normal. Other than the fact that every one of them had jet black hair.

"Keep up," Dulcina said, ducking back into the secluded spiral stairs and moving on down the next flight. Whatever she was looking for, it wasn't on that floor level.

"Right behind you," he said, resting his hand on his ribs, and he was hurting, but needed the mental reminder to take measured breaths.

The second he caught up with her, Dulcina spun around and said, "So we're clear, you're not coming back with me. You're getting a new home, pet. You're a gift for my sister."

"A gift?" Jake asked, hating that she'd relayed this information like a simple fact. Not a 'hey, we've gotta talk', or even a 'just so you know'. Just hard, life altering facts. Made him want to put up a fight. "Honey, I'm not a toy to be passed around."

"But you are," Dulcina said, giving him a slow cat-in-the-cream smile. "She needs a distraction. A lost and injured pet to care for should do the trick."

"A gift," he said again, trying to wrap his head around what was happening here. No more chance of escape or of going above ground again.

"Since Jovan left the city, she's been a walking ghost." Dulcina smacked him on the arm, heedless of jarring his ribs, and said, "Cheer her up."

"So she's lost her man and I'm supposed to replace him. Is that it?" Jake asked in a deadpan voice, completely unimpressed with this change of events. "You want me to sleep with her, too?"

Dulcina spun around and glared at him, and her upper lip twitched, just barely a snarl before she brought the reaction under control. Good. He'd hit a nerve. He didn't know where the hell that glimmer of emotion had come from with this ice queen, but he'd take it, especially if he could use it to stay with her above ground.

Dulcina turned away sharply. "That's up to her."

When Jake spoke next, his voice was low and soft. "You don't want her to have me, do you, Dulcie?"

"Don't call me that," she snapped, suddenly face-to-face with him once again. He was stirring up one hell of a hornet's nest, but it might just pay off.

Jake shook his head with a grin. She was the most fascinating creature he'd ever encountered, and he couldn't resist poking at her, just one more time. "If you want to keep me for yourself, just go on and keep me. I'm all yours. Promise you can handle me, Dulcie."

Dulcina hooked her leg around his, and shoved his shoulders back. Jake hit the wall behind him with a thud and a grunt that morphed into a strangled moan of pain. Damn, that had rattled his injured ribs. A glimmer of guilt flickered across her face, but the second he gained control of his breath, her expression was swiftly overshadowed by fury.

Slowly and deliberately, Dulcina said, "What I do with you is none of your damn business. In my world, you are property. Nothing more. Count your blessings I see you as such, and not as a threat."

Jake quickly masked his shock, and as if nothing had just happened, he reverted back to that easy-going smile, pretending for all the world like her manhandling him hadn't been an affront to his ego, her words a blow to his perceived reality.

He leaned closer, his nose nearly touching hers, and dropping his voice to a husky whisper, said, "See now? Can't keep your hands off me."

It was both an observation and a challenge. She wouldn't retreat now, and he damn well knew it, which meant she'd have to acknowledge that she was in fact touching him. Heat rolled between them where she'd planted her hand high on his chest, and he couldn't resist flexing. She'd noticed, and ah, but it was a beautiful sight. Her breathing changed to something a little more shallow and uneven.

If he were being completely honest with himself, she affected him, too. Actually, he'd been enamored with her since he woke to find her taking care of him. Sure, he was playing on her emotions to gain his freedom, but he got the sense that while she pretended she couldn't stand him, she was fighting some deep attraction.

"You don't have to let me go. I kinda like being all yours," he crooned, taking clear advantage of her lack of initiative.

Dulcina stepped closer, pressing her body against his, drawing in a breath that made her move against him in a way that almost had him begging for mercy. Jake kept his mouth shut, but couldn't stop a groan from breaking free as he tipped his head back and savored her touch. He hadn't expected her to feel that damn good all cozied up against him.

"What I want..." Dulcie's sultry soft voice drew his attention and he rallied from her full frontal contact in time to see her rapt gaze settle on his lips.

Jake edged closer, getting lost in his own game, and suddenly needing to kiss her. "What do you want, Sugar?"

"What I truly want..." Her lips nearly connected with his, but she pulled away before they could touch, took a smooth step back from him, and removed her hands from his shoulders. She instantly reverted to the cold, hard woman she presented to most of the world, the aggressive disinterest making its way into her voice. "Is to leave your broken ass here."

Jake blinked a couple of times, his lust-fogged brain trying to process her words, her hurtful tone. Like a champ, he pulled it together. "Aw, come on."

"You slow me down," she said flatly. "Now move."

She took off again, leaving him to catch up. He did, but stayed back several steps this time. The hit he'd taken against the wall still smarted, and now he was babying his bruised ribs a little more–and maybe a bruised ego. He'd been certain he'd read her right. In fact, even now he'd swear on a stack of Bibles that woman wanted him.

Deeper and deeper they traveled, his only marker as to how far down they'd gone into the earth was how many flat landings with a door they'd passed that broke up the endless stairs. They were about five levels down by his guess, and that was a hell of a lot of stairs. Down was easier than up, but he was starting to get winded.

At last, she opened a door and stepped out fully into a dark corridor. Dulcina turned to him and gave him the universal signal to keep his mouth shut. His brows furrowed in question, but he nodded, a short jerking motion of affirmation. He didn't understand why, but that wasn't always important.

The corridor ahead narrowed. The ceiling sloped down and the sides pinched narrow, almost like a funnel. Nothing was down here, save for a single door at the end.

Dulcina cautiously approached, opened the door several inches, and peered inside. Even from a couple steps back, Jake could see the sad dark-haired woman from the rehearsal sitting and staring off into the room at nothing.

Dulcina knocked softly. Emerging from her daze, Maeryn bolted to her feet. Her long skirts rustled as she hurried to the door and jerked it fully open. Her elation faded the instant she saw Dulcina, and became swiftly guarded when her eyes landed on him.

"I thought..." Maeryn lifted her chin, putting on a brave face. She'd clearly been hoping for someone else. "Who is this?"

"A gift," Dulcina said. She barely got the words out before Maeryn let out an enraged wail and threw the door shut in her face.

Dulcina stuck her foot out just in time, catching the door with her boot before it slammed closed. Without asking, she pushed her way into the home. Maeryn wasn't there to stop her. The young woman had already hurried to the bed, where she threw herself across the mattress, and cried. An open, half packed suitcase at the foot of the bed did not escape Jake's attention.

"He's injured, needs a home, and I thought you might enjoy a pet. Someone to occupy your time and attention." Dulcina sat on the edge and stroked her hair. "I'm sorry, Maeryn. I was only trying to help."

"I don't want your help," Maeryn mumbled, her face buried in her arm.

"Maybe not, but take him anyway. Think of him as a companion. A friend." The more Dulcina spoke the harder Maeryn cried, and still she pushed on, "Jovan once spoiled you, catered to your every need, was always by your side. Let this man do those things for you."

"How can you not understand this? Men are not interchangeable like pieces in a board game." Maeryn wailed into her pillow. "Go away!"

"He's not here, Maeryn. Stop sleeping in his home and spending every moment of your life in his memory. You've got to move on," Dulcina urged, though not gently.

Maeryn abruptly sat, tall and proper, her wide eyes shimmering with tears beneath her bangs, and she glared at Dulcina. "You're the only one who ever sees Jovan, and I hate you for it."

Dulcina squared her shoulders slightly. "I rarely see him. He cut ties with everyone. Even to the Stalkers, Jovan is only a rumor."

Maeryn melted into herself at those words, her entire being infused with sorrow as she asked, "Is he safe?"

"Last I knew, but I don't think he's in Paris anymore." Her voice became hushed as she delivered the news.

Maeryn stood, an angelic grace to her movements, even in the depths of her despair. She continued packing her suitcase, methodically organizing the small space, and through her tears, she whispered, "I need to leave. I'm going to another city."

Dulcina reached out, touched her arm to pause her. "What about Navarre and Cat?"

"I'm not ungrateful. I love them very much. But... I don't know what else to do!" Maeryn placed her hand over her chest, splayed her fingers wide. "It's like my heart has been torn from my chest, my soul ripped from my body. I live and I breathe, but I am *empty*."

"Jovan wouldn't want you to leave the city," Dulcina said gently.

Maeryn stared at the wall, numbing out once again, until softly, she murmured, "I don't even know who I am without him."

"You can learn, Maeryn, but what lies beyond Balinese is not for you," she urged, and Jake felt the sincerity of her words.

"But it suits others quite well," she said, finally turning to face Dulcina in a flash of courage that quickly faded.

"It does," Dulcina said cautiously, and her sister's chin quivered at her words. The other side of life suited Dulcina. And Jovan. Just them. The exclusion was tearing this fragile young girl apart. "Maeryn, you have to believe I did not take him from you. I didn't talk him into leaving."

"I know," Maeryn's voice broke, and she drew in a ragged breath to regroup. Somewhat. "He wanted to go. He loved nothing in Balinese enough to stay."

Dulcina seemed like she was struggling to find the right words, and after a couple false starts, finally said, "Can you at least be here for Rollin's mating ceremony? If you're not a part of it...if he's worried about you...he'll be a mess."

Maeryn's chin quivered. "I won't ruin Rollin's happiness, but that doesn't mean I'm giving up. I still plan to leave. When I'm ready."

"There are dangers other than demons out there. If you leave this city, you won't be safe," Dulcina warned.

"Yes, I will," she jerked her chin up, defiant once more. "Captain Savard has made certain I will be protected."

"Has he really?" Dulcina asked, and young Maeryn only nodded, not sensing the lethal change in her sister. Jake caught the flip, felt it like electricity snapping in the air.

Dulcina turned on her heel and marched straight for the spot Jake occupied in the doorway, and when she got there, she pushed him out, soundly shutting the door behind them.

"Problem?" Jake asked, portraying as much innocence as he could muster.

She turned to Jake, those green eyes filled with fire and fury, and snarled, "Keep up."

Chapter 11

BALINESE

Jake had felt incredibly out of place listening in on that personal conversation between sisters. More than that, he'd been totally rejected. Neither wanted him. He didn't care. Not really. Hell, he didn't even truly know them. Still, it was a kick in the shorts. A man wants to be wanted.

While escaping from that young, internally focused female might have been a piece of cake, making it through this maze of a vampire city, complete with invisible guards, would be nearly impossible. Looked like he was stuck with Dulcie.

Though, right now, it was a heck of a struggle to keep up with her. She strode down the hall like the devil himself was after her, never slowing even as she led him into a more populated area of the city. She was a woman on a mission. Anyone in her path leapt away, and then heaved a sigh of relief when she passed by, leaving them untouched.

She ducked into an archway and Jake watched her climb the stairs two at a time. Good Lord above, this woman had a narrow focus. He followed as best he could, the stairs setting him back. His legs pumped just fine, but by the time he'd reached the top, his ribs were burning with each breath, the zinging pain ricocheting around to his back.

This area was bustling. People made for unpredictable obstacles, and Jake was thankful they slowed her down just enough for him to catch up. Like a dog on a scent, she was after something. Normally, he would jump at the chance to hang back and get separated, but not here. Not now.

Her keen gaze scanned the shifting people until suddenly her shoulders snapped back and her eyes narrowed on someone ahead. She'd found her target. Dulcina moved like water, fluid and flexible, as she wove through the people to reach...a man with an honest to God sword strapped to his hip. Damn. Nothing like stepping back in time a few centuries to jar a man's perspective.

Dulcina strode directly up to this man and blocked his path. The bold move gained his full attention, though he didn't seem to see her as a threat.

"Where's Savard?" Dulcina demanded, loud enough he'd caught the name from a good distance back.

Ah, she was looking for the captain who planned on helping her sister leave the city. Apparently she thought this bushy eyebrowed, spiked-hair punk with a stud earring and a sparse goatee had his location. The young man glanced around him, either searching for a way out or maybe backup. The odd reaction set Jake on edge, and he hustled to get to Dulcie. Youth and inexperience had a way of merging with recklessness.

By the time Jake reached the pair the man still hadn't answered, which sparked Dulcina's ire, and then some. Though uncertainty flickered across sword-man's face, he remained fully planted where he stood, not budging an inch.

"I have need of your captain," Dulcina said, just as firm. "Now."

A cocky grin turned this man's pursed lips upward. "You'll have to go through the proper channels for that, miss."

Just as the man got that last word out, Dulcina clocked him hard in the jaw. The force spun him to the side, and she was on him before he could rebound. Her big Bowie knife unsheathed, she'd secured it beneath his chin to hold him in place even as she lifted the radio from his belt with her other hand.

Jake hadn't had any time to react. No, he wasn't at peak performance level right now, but clearly she hadn't needed him. Dulcie had zero hesitation. She didn't wait for permission, didn't want to talk things through, and hadn't even bothered to disarm the man. She just controlled the situation.

Dulcina brought the radio device to her lips like she'd used the thing a hundred times before, and barked out, "Briona! Where's the captain?"

"Identify yerself," the sharp feminine voice with an Irish lilt retorted through the radio.

"I'm pierced, Irish. Give it a guess," Dulcina growled, her hard tone making it clear she was in the right and not to be messed with.

"Jaysus! I didn't know ye were back. What the devil are you doing? There are other ways to go about finding a man," the girl rambled, the tapping of buttons clear in the background. Jake didn't know what she meant by pierced, but it seemed to strike a chord with the woman on the other end of the radio. "He's on level three. And since ye snagged Garroway's radio, I'd say you're no' far from him. Is my Guardian unharmed?"

"I haven't decided yet," Dulcina said, then replaced the radio before releasing Garroway.

The young Guardian's lip curled in a snarl. Jake had seen enough detainees fight back to know the thought of retribution was stirring in this man. Jake cleared his throat, catching just a sliver of the man's attention. "Whatever thought just crossed your mind, I wouldn't try it."

"Even the human can see you should take caution," Dulcina said with a sweet smile as she patted Garroway on the cheek. "You hit a Casteel and it won't just be me coming after your head, but Navarre himself."

His eyes shot wide, that silvery gray gaze slipping to Jake then back to her, and his jaw dropped in sudden realization. "Ah, I see. Pierced."

"Where's the captain?" Dulcie snapped again.

Subdued and compliant now that he seemed to know exactly who she was, Garroway pointed behind him. "Briona knows you, and that's good enough for me. Around the corner."

Dulcina headed for the opening in the corridor, and Jake stuck close to her heels, strategically putting himself between her and Garroway. Just in case. He didn't care to leave her back exposed.

She didn't seem to see anything down here as a threat, and rounded the corner without caution, stepping into a narrow corridor and honing in on a young man reading through a clipboard full of paperwork. An older man stood opposite him, near what looked like the back door to a small shop.

"Something you need, Dulcina?" the young man asked in a cool, superior tone, never looking up to confirm he was speaking with the correct person. He just seemed to know. This must be the captain.

Through a hushed voice, Dulcina asked, "Where are you sending her?"

Her words brought his head up, and with the smooth smile of a diplomat, he finished the last page, the shop owner glancing nervously between them. Then the captain caught Dulcina in a stern gaze. "As we move, if you please."

He shot a glance over at Jake, but made no move to engage him. As the three of them returned the way they'd come, they passed Garroway, still standing in the middle of the corridor. The young captain handed Garroway the clipboard and continued to move.

"Captain," Dulcina called after him, and when he didn't answer, she reached out and placed her hand on his shoulder in a way that seemed more personal than professional. "Please."

He turned, stiff and severe, his gaze flicking to the people moving around them, and sternly said, "This is not a public matter."

At his words, and the hard edge to his voice, Dulcie nodded sharply. When the captain moved again, she followed silently. Jake trailed behind, staying out of this matter as best he could.

The captain led them up the corridor and through a pale, minty green door. He flicked on a single light switch, but it was enough to reveal what kind of people used this room. It was a cafeteria, had to be, and by the size of the little bitty chairs, it was for kids under five.

"Where?" she demanded.

"I'm not *sending* your sister anywhere," the captain said calmly, like he'd rehearsed the words. Or simply knew the question was coming. "She wants to leave. I've merely secured her safety should she decide to follow through...as I have done for all those in the royal family."

And that's where Jake sputtered. "Wait, a royal?"

"Not now, Jake," Dulcie snapped at him, though her angry gaze never left the captain. "She'll be taken advantage of the instant someone looks at that doe-eyed face of hers. You can't do this, Savard."

The captain lifted an eyebrow, either at her directive tone, or at the familiar use of what must be his name, but he ignored the slight. Evenly and gently, he said, "Maeryn is a full-grown adult, capable of making her own decisions, even if her sister believes they are foolhardy."

"You save people. Save her," she pleaded, and Jake's heart about broke for Dulcie.

"I *am* saving her," the captain said, and when Dulcie shook her head, ready to fight him again, he raised his hand to stop her from speaking. "You haven't been here, Dulcina. I'm saving her in the only way she will allow. Trust me."

Dulcie straightened her back, defiant thing until the end, but Jake could see her mind working overtime to process the logic of what the captain had laid out before her, and probably about a dozen other solutions. "Navarre and Cat need to know."

"She tried to tell them months ago, and they never believed she would truly leave." Captain Savard studied her for a brief second or two, then surmised, "But you do."

She shook her head, not in denial, but more...at a loss. "I've never seen her like this before. It's like all her nerves are exposed. That makes her unpredictable, even for you."

"Not at all." The gallant captain flashed her a quick smile, and said, "Have no worries. She will have a guardian angel over her shoulder with every step she takes. My promise to you."

"Who? Where?" she demanded.

Captain Savard shook his head. "Her safety depends on secrecy. If she does eventually choose to leave, no one will know."

Dulcie pulled back, as if she couldn't quite believe how the dust had settled. "You intend to keep this a secret, even from Navarre?"

"You forget, Dulcina, that Navarre is not the only Casteel I serve." The captain offered her a clipped bow and walked directly from the room without looking back. Conversation over. No negotiating. No compromise.

Dulcina followed him just through the door of the cafeteria and watched him walk away, a sudden stillness to her. It wasn't until the captain was completely out of sight that she jerked out of her stunned daze.

"We're staying here through the daylight hours," she announced absently, and this time, when she led him from the cafeteria, she moved slower.

Jake was able to match her pace, but held back a little, making sure she was a full stride ahead of him. A woman who didn't get her way was a dangerous thing. By the way her eyes darted as she moved, her lips pursed together tightly, he could tell she was once again sorting through alternative possibilities. Not much had gone how she'd expected in the last hour, and she was searching for answers. A direction.

He kept his mouth shut, and stayed close. Dulcie must have a thousand thoughts swirling around in her head, and sometimes silence was best for everyone.

She hit the brakes at one of several plain and ordinary doors in the hallway and held the door open, waiting expectantly for him to walk through first. He did, automatically reaching out for a light switch that happened to be right where it should, and entered a space with a familiar setup. Owned or borrowed, he didn't know, but this was Dulcina's room. She didn't seem entirely comfortable here, not like above, but she was more at ease behind this particular door than in any other space in this city.

Dulcina pulled her shirt over her head, tossed it over the back of a chair, and turned to him. Standing there in only her tight tank top, she pointed to the bed. "Sleep. We leave at first dark."

"We? I see. So, 'cause little sister doesn't want me, I guess that means I'm your 'pet' now." Jake bit his cheek to stop from grinning. "I could use a bath. A little scrub behind the ears."

A flicker of interest lit her eyes as she gave him a quick head-to-toe perusal, but then her eyes suddenly narrowed and her cold stare shifted away from him. "I have no need of a pet. I haven't the time or desire to take care of you."

He grinned easily, brushing off the flurry of insults. "I could help you topside."

She snorted at that.

"Suit yourself." He stood, motioning to his upper body. "Just let all this go to waste."

"You're damaged," Dulcina countered, her cool logic coming to the forefront, and she wasn't wrong. Right now, he was damaged. He hurt bad enough the pain was constant, making his brain a little numb to it until something jarred him. His breathing hadn't leveled out from simply walking, and he'd be willing to bet if he lay down right now, he could sleep for twelve hours.

"True." He shrugged, moving only his good side. "But I'll heal."

"You don't have the skill."

"Maybe not." Jake tested the waters, wanting to hide his greater talents in case he needed that ace up his sleeve, but also needing to be found useful so he could stay with her. "I'd be willing to bet I'm better than you think."

She walked right up to him, that 'I'm done' look all over her face, and he ate it up. This woman, all fire and fury, was a beautiful thing. Provoking her was quickly becoming his favorite sport.

Toe-to-toe with him, her voice bled pure authority as she said, "Get in bed."

"Yes, ma'am," he said with unabashed enthusiasm and a wink.

She rolled her eyes as she walked away, stepping into the bathroom and closing the door behind her. Not for one second did he think she trusted him enough to leave him completely unattended. She was listening, taking every precaution. Honestly, in the mood she was in, no way was he pushing any hard boundaries.

Kicking off his shoes, he gingerly slid into bed and lay down, taking care not to over stress his ribs. Jake settled in, watching the bathroom door, waiting for her. His loosely formed plan to lure her into letting her guard down and giving him the opportunity to escape wasn't panning out, and not because Dulcina was all kinds of bristly. He was failing.

The problem? Jake was guarded. Shut down. Had been for years. He worked his ass off at his job, busted bad guys, and was happy to do both. Yet a chunk of him was missing. Like someone had unplugged him. He functioned basically on muscle memory.

The bathroom door jerked open and Dulcina emerged...without pants. A small smile curled the left side of his lips automatically, and he smothered it before she could take note. Dulcie was a tank top and undies kind of girl, and to tell the truth, attraction wasn't the issue. This woman was gorgeous. A head-to-toe knockout, not limited to the normal earmarks of a beautiful woman, though they were present. What had him in knots every time he watched her was the way she moved, agile and strong, her confidence and capability unmistakable.

Dulcie walked up to the bed, but didn't make him scoot over. The woman simply climbed over him and settled in to sleep, seeming unconcerned about Jake being between her and the door, and didn't that just say it all?

This woman had zero doubts she could keep him from escaping. No backup of a rope to keep him locked down while she slept, no hesitation about giving him a head start toward the door.

She was strong. He had no escape, and no way of winning her over. Dulcina knew what she wanted, what she didn't, and how to achieve her end game. No man needed.

Bottom line? Jake was screwed...and not in the fun way.

Chapter 12

BALINESE

Jake's busted ribs prevented him from laying on his side, but he turned his head, watching her next to him. There was a dim light coming from the little kitchen and it highlighted the planes of her cheekbone.

It hadn't been a surprise when she'd climbed into bed with him, but he sure hadn't expected her to face him. That just summed her up, though. She didn't care what he thought, or even if he was there. They lay facing each other in silence and it would probably stay that way. She wasn't a big talker.

She was cute with her hand tucked under her pillow. Not a sweet and innocent type of cute, but like a tiger, all deceptively fluffy and ready to turn on you at any second. Her fingers were probably curled around that big Bowie knife he'd seen her take to bed.

Dulcie was one tough cookie. Even his teasing hadn't made her crack a smile. He wouldn't stop trying. Maybe humor wasn't the way to win her. Maybe she needed a little tenderness. She shifted on her pillow and her short curls flopped onto her face.

Jake reached out, gently sweeping them back. Her eyes flashed open with a start, her hand halfway emerging from beneath the pillow, the gleam off the metal handle of her Bowie knife winking at him. Sleep must have pulled her in faster than he'd thought, to startle her. She stared at him for a hot second, then stuffed the knife back under the pillow and rolled onto her back.

"What?" she mumbled, eyes closed. Clearly she hadn't interpreted his touch as a threat or she'd have put a knife-shaped hole through him.

Jake bucked up his courage, tracing the curve of her high cheekbone with his fingers. "You're delicate."

Her eyes popped back open and she glared at him, angry, possibly offended.

"Not like that," he corrected, doing a little backpedaling once he realized why she didn't care for the word. Delicate, to her, might translate to having a weakness. "I meant your cheekbones."

"They've been bruised and healed. Repeatedly," she said, settling deep into her pillow. "Not delicate."

"The curve of your lips." Softly, he brushed the underside of her lower lip. "Captivating."

She tipped her chin up, pulling away from his touch, though not completely. "Split and bleeding, more often than I can count."

"Damn it, woman, take a compliment," he whispered, harsh and angry. She was absolutely infuriating and if Jake couldn't crack through that hard exterior soon, she'd have him sent off to some deep underground world where he'd likely be killed for his sassmouth and back talk. He needed this to work, but her edginess hit him on some personal level he hadn't quite figured out yet. "I get it. You're strong, capable. I'm not arguing that fact. I'm telling you you're damn lovely. One does not cancel out the other."

Jake cranked around and vaulted off the bed, wincing in pain and biting out a few choice curse words. His physical limitations were starting to piss him off. He needed to move, to get away, except there was nowhere to go. He walked into the little kitchen, paced a few times to distract himself from the pain wrenching through his side, then parked it at the table. Jake plucked an apple from the bowl in the center and spun it around in his hand.

He sucked at effort. When he didn't want women, they seemed to follow him like lost, hungry kittens. Now that he *needed* a specific female to fall for him? Nothing, not even a flicker of interest. It bothered him, really it did. He hadn't even possessed the sense to check his frustration. He'd just let it loose on her, and he'd never done that to a woman. Ever.

She got under his skin. Plain and simple. He might be initiating conversation, physical contact, and laying down signals he was attracted to her pretty thick, but the worst of it was...underneath it all, he wasn't faking a damn thing. The urge to whip the apple across the room suddenly struck him, but at least in that, he restrained himself. Mostly because the motion would hurt the ribs.

He felt Dulcina's presence in the kitchen a tick before she moved around his side and sat on the table in front of him. Jake leaned back, not exactly sure what was happening, and when he did, she propped the foot closest to him up on the table and wrapped her arms around her leg. For a long moment, she rested her chin on her knee, and when she finally looked him in the eye, he had the oddest sense that he was finally seeing the real woman.

"You're irritating," Dulcina said, confident in her assessment. He didn't know what kind of reaction she was looking for out of him with that opener, so he didn't give one. Instead, he crossed his arms over his chest, and gave her room to speak. Her hard gaze never left his, and when she opened her mouth, he knew more of that honesty was about to spill from those pretty lips. "Being around you is unsettling. The more you talk...the more I like you. You're just as blunt as I am and I suppose I don't know how to deal with that."

Jake reached for her leg, the one dangling from the edge of the table, and cupped her calf, just below the back of her knee. He leaned forward, invading her space ever so slightly. "I'm not asking for anything from you, and I'm not fishing for compliments in return. I just wanted you to know what I see."

"I don't—" Dulcina drew in a sharp breath, cutting off her angry words. Then she regrouped, looked him straight in the eye and simply said, "Other than those I consider my family, I don't have conversations."

He sort of enjoyed that little catch thing she'd just done. Like her reflexive response was to tell him to piss off, but she kind of wanted to see where this was going. Yeah, he liked that. "All right, so let's try a regular everyday conversation, like normal people. Ease into it. No pressure."

She might be eyeing him warily, but she nodded.

"So," Jake began gently. "Been curious about something. Why do you live above ground in Paris when you have a whole city right here?"

Dulcina's leg tensed under his hand, and as she spoke, her voice tightened, "That topic does not make for simple conversation."

Okay, that surprised him, and at the same time, maybe it didn't. She was complex, this woman.

"Well then, let's try something different. How about friends from school? Did you have a best friend you want to talk to before we leave?" Jake held up his hand as if asking her to wait, and scratched his head. He might have just botched this twice. "Do vampires even have schools?"

Dulcina straightened and looked past him, her cold stare distant, and thankfully not directed at him. After that, he hadn't expected her to answer, but she did. Steady and low, she answered, "I went to school."

"Yeah? Can't hardly imagine you walking down the hall with a little lunch box, falling into line with other kids." Okay, he could imagine it a little. She was probably just as feisty at half the size.

"School was irrelevant," she said, still a bit distant.

"Why's that?"

"I was nine when demons stole me, and several other children, from my city. The demons, they killed our parents." Cold and harsh, she simply spoke facts. "I knew nothing outside my need for retribution."

Jake nodded because, well, it felt right. Like being on her side without fully understanding, but letting her know he was there for her. "That explains your dislike of demons and why you're not a fan of this city."

"It was an experience that would make anyone dislike demons," she said with a lazy shrug of her left shoulder. "Therefore, I kill them."

"Yeah, but you don't like vampires either." He'd seen the guarded look in her eyes, how she edged away from them, or dropped her hand to her blade. "Do you?"

"I don't trust them."

"Yeah? Why not?"

She threw her shoulders back, instantly on the defensive. "You know nothing of what I've been through, of what I am."

"No, I don't. Not a damn clue," he confirmed. Jake reached up, took her chin between his thumb and forefinger and tipped her face down. When he caught her gaze, he said, "That's why I'm askin.'"

That space of time where she did nothing but stare into his eyes was like nothing he'd ever experienced, and he couldn't explain the relief that washed over him when she finally opened her mouth. "Is this how normal conversations flow?"

"Nope. But this whole situation isn't normal, is it?" He waited and she shook her head. "Okay. So, this is how a conversation flows with me and you."

She looked away for a moment, silent, maybe not wanting to face him, or look her past in the eye. It took her a moment, but eventually she faced him again, though she refused to meet his gaze.

"A vampire brought those demons inside the city, directed them to kill, to take certain children and use us as bait. They didn't know who that vampire was until he held a knife to my throat, used me to lure Cat into the arena. I was sixteen. Cat switched places with me, put her own throat beneath his blade to save me. I nearly lost her." After a long blink, she seemed to settle back into herself, rejoining the here and now. "So, no. I will never like or trust vampires outside of my family."

"That vampire still breathin'?" Jake asked, all but demanding an answer.

"No. I sent a bullet sailing through his skull that night." Her jawline twitched as she clenched her teeth.

Jake had seen the harsher side of life and what it did to people, more so than most in this world. Was nine too young to experience terror and loss? Sixteen too young to take a life? Maybe. Maybe not.

"I am glad you put a bullet in him, but Sugar, I hate to break it to you... Sounds like your problem is with that particular man, and he's gone. That one, you gotta learn to let go."

"You may not believe me, but I have. His death held a satisfying finality. Still...when I come home to visit those I love, I also have to spend time with those I lost," she said, clamping her jaw shut the moment the words slipped out. For a moment, Jake thought she was shutting down, that she wouldn't keep going, but then she softly added, "I see my father's lifeless eyes looking up at me every time I walk the outer corridors. I see Yvette on the lawn..."

"Dulcie, I'm sorry." Jake reached up and stroked her cheek, his heart going out to her. He hadn't heard her mention that particular name before, but whoever the girl was, she was dear to her.

"Don't apologize. You asked, so there it is." She leaned back, pulling out of his reach. "If I were to stay here, I'd go mad."

"From what?" He coaxed. "The memory of loved ones?"

"No, it's not that, not anymore. The sorrow I feel over their loss just makes me wary now." Then with a dead calm that unnerved him, she said, "I'm paranoid, Jake. My mind believes things that are completely irrational."

"Don't we all?"

"Not like this." Her eyes snapped up, met his. "Before the attack, demons hid inside our city, and they looked exactly like us. We didn't know they could change, leave behind their sallow skin, red eyes, and mindless aggression. They were a part of us, functioning members of our society for years, until it was time to attack."

Sleepers. Warfare on the most vicious, personal level. "I can see how that would mess with your mind."

"I don't make friends. I don't trust anyone except my family. I see treachery in every man's face, every woman's eyes. The urge to stay and protect my family is strong, but I know that my suspicions are there without cause most of the time." Dulcina straightened her shoulders. "My unease would only cause panic. So instead I choose to protect them from outside the city. I kill an enemy I know without a doubt is the enemy, one I can recognize with certainty."

"You walked away from your city, your family, to protect them and keep your sanity at the same time. That takes...commitment." Jake saw what many of her people could not. The Stalkers had an important role to play in the balance of their world. So many slipped through the justice system he was a part of and he could only imagine how complicated a vampire's laws would be while contending with the world above ground.

"Everyone I've loved has been killed, or nearly killed by demons." Her eyebrows twitched as she spoke, but her eyes were still unfocused.

"That why you're so determined to keep your sister here?" Jake guessed.

"Maeryn is everything good and perfect and gentle in this world. She's everything I am not," Dulcina said adamantly. "I don't know what will happen to her if she leaves the city. She's not a strong woman. Whatever relationship she had with Jovan, none of us saw, or understood. He walked out, severed that bond, and it left her heart battered and bruised. I don't know how much more she can take."

"Storms make trees take deeper roots," Jake said, his voice suddenly thicker.

Dulcina stared at him, and for a moment, just blinked. "That was profound."

"It wasn't me," he said, straightening in his chair. "That's pure Dolly."

"Who?"

"Dolly Parton. Country music icon," Jake clarified. She shook her head, not understanding his reference. A flash of shock crossed his face before he recalled she lived in a completely different world, twice over. Jake quickly flipped his surprise into an easy shrug. "Doesn't matter. The point remains the same."

"I hope you're right." Dulcina rubbed her palms down her thighs like she was about to be done with him and this conversation. "She's been through so much and it feels like every step she's taken has tumbled her into disaster, set her back."

"And here I thought you didn't have a heart," Jake said, his tone light and teasing, but the words still brought a scowl to her face. "I like that you prove me wrong."

They were both silent for a time. Pondering. Processing. She'd clearly shared more than she'd intended and was beginning to bottle up.

"Listen... Dulcie, I—"

She stood abruptly, walked past him without a word, and climbed back into bed. Message received. Too much, too soon. She was done. Jake stayed at the table for a long while, wondering if he'd made the right decision to try and get close to her, to manipulate her feelings for him just enough to drop her guard. Now that he'd seen a glimpse of the woman beneath the facade, his plan seemed cruel.

Jake returned to bed, and by the way she held herself, stiff and guarded, he could tell she was very awake.

"My family wanted me to stay in the city. Become a Guardian," she said softly, almost as if musing to herself.

"Hey, I understand. Probably more than you'd think," he spoke to her back, but he kept going. Just felt right. "You can't work with these Guardians because you don't trust them. Got it. You can't just throw a bunch of people together and say, hey, be a team. To be a true team, you have to go through a crisis, a tragedy, a war, and come out on the other end different. Changed to your core. Your siblings...those are your team. I see that. And after knowing that kind of trust, that they've got your back no matter what, and you'll do the same for them...you can't fake it with someone else."

Again, silence. He didn't know if she was processing or pissed. Either way, it was best he let it be, so he closed his eyes. The silence was awfully loud as the minutes ticked by and he tried to shut off his mind to sleep.

"If you don't wake up when I'm ready to go, I'm leaving your ass behind," she said out of the blue, her terse words bouncing off the wall she faced and back to him.

Jake smiled. That right there he'd take as a sign of growing affection. This was her way of telling him she was taking him with her. "Wait. You're not staying for the wedding? Isn't that tomorrow?"

"Rehearsals are not normal. My family is the exception as we are royalty." She drew in a weary breath. "I'm certain they want me to stay, but a week is too long. We'll make the trip back."

"Hey," Jake said, feeling confident enough to voice the question that had been rolling around his head. "What did that Garroway guy mean by pierced? What did you pierce?"

"You'll never know." Lightning fast, she reached back and cracked her hand over his thigh. Jake yelped at the contact, more to rile her than anything, but it stung. Woman had some power.

Jake liked this woman, had enjoyed staying with her, and wouldn't mind coming back after he took care of some business, but time was always moving. Rita's killer wouldn't stay in one place for long.

Chapter 13

BALINESE

Dulcina had no inclination to surface completely from sleep. Her dreams had been nothing shy of delicious. She burrowed into the warmth of her bed and sighed, giving herself permission to slip back into that dream state and continue exploring Jake where it was safe in the dream world. Her hand skated over the hard planes of his muscled chest, down his toned stomach. She savored every dip of defined muscle, each inch of this man's taut skin as her hand slid lower. This man had been under her skin for far too long, and she needed this like she needed air, even if she could only go there in her mind. A hint of a smile curled her lips as her fingers brushed past his outie belly button, venturing lower.

The moment he groaned, that rumbling sound reverberating through her chest, Dulcina stilled. Her eyes snapped opened and a bolt of pure shock had her wide awake. She was every bit as randy as any hot-blooded man, always had been, but she had not intended to cross this line with Jake.

Nothing separated them, not even the blanket. She'd pressed her body tight against his side, her arm wrapped snugly around him, fingertips just above his waistline. Her body knew what it wanted, and that she wouldn't refute, but this human did not fit into her plans. Besides, she had a feeling that if she gave him an inch, he'd use it to his advantage. She needed to get out of this precarious position before he woke, or worse yet, returned her touch.

"Darlin', you don't have to stop." Jake practically purred the words, his accent thick and voice rough from sleep.

She rolled away, her first instinct to shove him, but his battered ribs gave her pause. No need to be cruel. Frustrated with herself, and her sudden state of unfulfilled desire, Dulcina left the bed and pulled on her clothes. Jake didn't even move. His gaze followed her, that crooked grin plastered across his face. Smug man.

"What's the matter?" he said, that sleep-raspy voice doing funny things to her insides. "Find out you want something from me after all?"

"Shut up," she snapped, smacking his leg.

"There you go touchin' me again." He stretched gingerly, adjusting his weight to relieve pressure on his ribs. "Just can't resist, can you?"

Could she resist him? She'd always been the aggressor. If she decided she wanted a man, she had him...and she did desire Jake.

Dulcina stole a quick glance, enjoying how he was sprawled across her bed. Yes, physically he was perfection. That honed, compact muscled body type was something she'd always been hungry for, but there was something else about Jake she was drawn to, even craved. She'd never encountered playfulness in a man. Most men she'd crossed were either totally focused on warfare or sex. This had never bothered her because she functioned in rather the same fashion.

Jake was different. The light in his eyes, his teasing words. The way he'd listened to her in the kitchen, focused only on her. She liked him. Damn it. She hated forming connections. "Get up. We're leaving."

With nowhere to send him, no home to leave him in, she didn't have much choice but to take him with her. For the time being.

It didn't take her long to gather what little she'd brought to Balinese. Her main luggage was Jake. Once he'd dressed, his bag slung over his shoulder, she led him out of the city. Like always, she just left. Commitments satisfied, she had no reason to linger. No drawn-out goodbyes, hugs, or false promises of her return.

In silence, she drove home with Jake planted firmly in the passenger seat. To her great annoyance, he seemed happy, like being back on the road was some grand adventure. He hummed along to the radio, paying no heed to the fact that he wasn't familiar with any of the songs. The man didn't know the language, and certainly couldn't carry a tune. Eventually, he dozed off, his hand curled protectively over his bruised ribs.

They entered Paris late in the night and the stillness, coupled with the clear open sky, was a slight balm to the tension that had been coiling inside her. She pulled the car into an alley near her apartment, shut it off, and left the keys in the glove box. Geoff would pick it up next time he came this way.

Reaching over, she thumped Jake on the leg with the back of her hand. He roused quickly, sharp and alert, already assessing his surroundings. When his eyes settled on her, he let out a lengthy yawn.

She didn't say a word, wasn't ready to speak to him. Dulcina stepped out of the car and started walking toward her building. He followed a good distance back, thankfully remaining silent.

Bringing him back to her home hadn't felt odd in the slightest. She'd gotten used to seeing him in her space and on her bed. Already, she'd acclimated to his presence. Because she was lonely? Dulcina took a moment to mull over that last thought. No, that wasn't it at all. For her, there was no sorrow in being solitary. The sense of rightness came down to one single point. She enjoyed Jake's company. All of it. Nothing about his existence was truly irritating. Unlike other men, she hadn't felt the need to disconnect completely, or even take a break from him. That alone gave her pause.

She unlocked her door and let Jake go in first. Like he owned the place, he made himself at home. Duffel bag set on the floor, he kicked his shoes off and immediately made his way to the bed, stretching out on top of the blankets. For the last few days he'd covered his injured side with his hand when he slept or recovered from exertion, and now was no different. She'd pushed him hard on their trip. True, he'd kept up, but he was paying for it now.

Body frozen in thought, she noted something she'd overlooked in her eagerness to drop him on Maeryn's doorstep. Jake was adaptable, easily jumping from one unexpected situation to the next. He never complained.

And when she'd been tucked up against him in her bed, stroking his stomach, he was a perfect gentleman. Irritatingly so. The more she was around him, the more rapidly her libido ratcheted up. If Jake would have taken her hand and moved it a bit lower, shown her how aroused he was by her touch, her resistance would have buckled then and there.

It was wavering now. Her fingers curled at her sides, itching to touch him again. Sprawled out with his eyes closed, chin tilted up, and his neck exposed, Jake was deliciously attractive. She longed to nibble his stubble-covered jaw, kiss her way down his corded neck, taste his skin.

Dulcina turned on her heel sharply and ruffled her fingers through her hair. Pure, exhilarating lust pinged around inside her body, craving an outlet in the form of one self-assured, scruffy man. She wanted him, but what she *needed* was space to think straight with that man out of reach. She headed for the bathroom, dropping her clothes as she went.

"I'm showering," she said, now down to just her tight tank top and hiphuggers, and closed the door behind her.

She half expected Jake to make a comment about joining her, or asking if she needed his assistance. He hadn't said a word. Disappointing, but it was for the best.

Her imagination ran wild. She could just imagine him smiling as he kissed her. Feel the warmth of his breath, the vibration of his laugh as his lips grazed her neck, made his way over her shoulder.

Several different scenarios played through her mind's eye, each more tantalizing than the last.

Dulcina stepped under the spray of water, the heat slowly building. She turned it back down. A cold shower might be exactly what she needed to jolt her from this fantasy. Tipping her head back, she drenched her hair, slipping easily into her normal shower routine despite the abnormal temperature.

The white noise of falling water, however, let her mind wander right back to Jake. He might be playful and teasing toward her, but he couldn't fool her. Underneath it, she was well aware Jake was a survivor.

The baseline of her desires always came down to a warrior. Didn't matter if the veneer was pretty, scruffy, or crass. Jake fit that category. It was the joyful easiness about him that made her comfortable, and that was unfamiliar territory for her. He'd asked her questions because he was interested, and listened for the same reason. Also, he seemed to have a healthy amount of respect for her, which always made a man more tolerable.

Stepping from the shower, Dulcina wrapped the towel around her, wiped down the mirror and stared at the woman looking back. Life was dragging her in an unpredictable direction, and every decision felt like it was vital, changing to the core, and this time it wasn't just her it would affect. Pressing her forehead against the mirror, she lightly thumped it twice. Dragging in a deep breath, she released it slowly, repeating the act three times. She could feel her libido burning, a constant buzz that needed sated, and it was influencing her behavior. Dulcina was restless, lustful, and when her needs were not tended, aggression and poor judgment were just around the corner.

Okay, so she wanted Jake. If she were being completely honest, she hoped he would just walk in right now and peel down. She gasped as that image of him standing in here naked before her flashed through her mind.

An irritated halfhearted growl made it past her lips, and immediately she tipped her head upside down to towel dry her hair. She rubbed the towel a little harder than necessary, trying to force her mind on the task at hand.

This was not something she could allow to happen. Jake would always be here, permanently in her care. Dulcie didn't like to feel trapped, especially not by men, and starting something with Jake would leave her with no escape.

When she righted herself, she noticed the silence, the emptiness now that the running water had stopped. That was life before Jake.

Dulcina bit her bottom lip. Before Jake. Was that how her life was being defined now? Had he made that much of an impact on her? She doubted it, and yet...

Towel wrapped around her body, she peeked out into her home, needing to see him peacefully sleeping on her bed. Jake's duffel bag was missing. And Jake? She threw the door wide. He was gone.

"That shifty son-of-a-bi—" Her snarling words were cut off as she pulled her shirt over her face. Still damp, Dulcina stepped into a pair of sweats that hung low on her hips, and strapped her Bowie knife to her waist. The second she tugged her boots on, she vanished.

Spirit was the only way to catch him, and she floated swiftly from her home, following the path he would have had to take, being human. He wasn't in the building, which meant he was moving as fast as his body would let him, and probably already on the streets.

She emerged at the main door to the complex and tried to see things from his perspective. If he were anything like her, and he certainly seemed to be, then he would head left toward the lights. More lights, more densely populated. Easier to hide.

The first street she investigated produced nothing, and she tried another, not expecting him to opt for the quieter and less traveled option. Two streets over, Dulcina caught up to him. He'd made it a good distance from her home, but his gait was stinted and slow. Perhaps this was why he didn't want to be seen. Injury drew attention, and while avoiding human concern was what he'd intended, Jake was a shining beacon to any demon looking for an easy food source.

Jake had likely run until his ribs hurt too badly. The added weight of his duffel bag over his shoulder throwing his center of gravity didn't do him any favors either.

For a short time, she observed him, studying his movements, calculating his intentions. Jake had a map in his hand, glancing repeatedly from the map to the street signs, and occasionally turning in a full circle. The man had no blessed idea where he was, how to get where he wanted to go. There was no one around to poorly attempt asking, and still it didn't deter him. This was a problem she had to correct, and fast.

Dropping out of her Spirit in front of Jake, her hair still dripping a little from the shower, she blocked his path. He drew up short and immediately winced from the abrupt motion, then leaned forward to ease the muscle tension on his ribs.

"Woman, you scared the living daylights out of me," he hissed through clenched teeth.

She ignored him. In this, his emotions were irrelevant. "You're coming back with me."

"Not happening," he said firmly, bringing his map back up to eye level like she wasn't an obstacle he had to reckon with. "You don't need me, and I don't need you. I got something that needs doing."

"You've got this all wrong. You don't have a choice."

"Sure do. And so do you." He dropped the map to glare at her, a hard unmovable look that most likely worked on others. "Leave me to what I gotta finish."

Dulcina narrowed her eyes on him. Jake's American southern twang was coming out thick, his composure slipping because this was serious to him. Something so important his emotions altered his controlled speech.

Clamping a hand on his shoulder, she said, "Talk to me, Jake."

"None doin'," he said, jerking his shoulder from her grip. The motion had hurt him and he gritted his teeth.

"Not how this works," she said, keeping her tone calm, patient, like she was negotiating. "I talked to you when I didn't want to and didn't know how. Now it's your turn."

"My business is personal."

She nodded in understanding. "There's a Stalker's soul somewhere deep inside you. I respect that, Jake. I do. Doesn't mean you get to run free."

Without warning she threw a punch that landed square on his jaw. His head whipped around, his body following, and when he hit the ground, he didn't get up. She flexed her fingers, and though she hadn't hesitated to unleash her full strength to knock him out, guilt sidled through her heart. Just an ounce. She was hurting him thrice over. One for the crack to the jaw, one as he'd landed on his side jarring his ribs, and again for denying him whatever mission he seemed stubbornly set on.

Dulcina flipped him over and checked his vitals. He breathed, his pulse thumping strong. She hated doing this to him, but if she couldn't get him under control, the Stalker Lord would be forced to execute him. Or worse, order her to do it. She couldn't.

With a heavy, highly irritated sigh, she pulled him into a sitting position. Crouching down, she worked her arms under his shoulders, getting a good hold on him. The only way to move him would be to take him with her in Spirit form. While her innate strength was great, she was not capable of carrying an unconscious man all the way back home. Dulcina took a calming, focused breath, and sucked them both into Spirit and out of sight. Moving in Spirit with another person in tow was not a possibility for every vampire, and even for those capable, it required a diligent maintenance of the body's blood requirements. For a short while, she would have no issues towing Jake with her in Spirit.

Traveling in Spirit with an extra body burned through energy, and she would be forced to take in blood sooner than expected, but that wasn't her main concern right now.

His escape had been entirely her fault. She shouldn't have taken her eyes off him. The thing was, having her eyes constantly *on* him was becoming a problem all its own. The man was desirable in that mouthwatering type of way.

Once inside her building, she descended a level and then moved down the hall. With one last burst of effort, she slipped them both through the closed door and released her Spirit so close to the bed that her knee touched the mattress. The sudden jerk of Jake's full corporeal weight in her arms nearly pulled her down with him. She managed to heft him onto the bed, though not as gently as she'd hoped.

Dulcina rubbed her hand over her brow. She should have made more of an effort to unload him in Balinese, but properly placing him in someone's home took time. He would have been cared for with Maeryn, but anyone else? She had to admit, her screening of other candidates would have been rather aggressive.

Talvane, the highly secure vampire city here beneath Paris, was a possibility. Though it wasn't her first choice, the city was not opposed to the presence of Stalkers occasionally seeking shelter from the daylight, and due to the city's high traffic location they already had a fair amount of human servants. She could visit...

Dulcina shook her head. Hard. There would be no need to see him again. He would be routinely checked for abuse and neglect by the proper authorities. Jake would be fine. Except for this stubborn streak she'd just witnessed.

What was so important he took the open opportunity while still recovering, rather than waiting until he'd healed? It didn't make any sense. What was he trying to accomplish by pushing his damaged body beyond what it could handle?

"Stubborn jackass," Dulcina muttered, even as she tied his wrists to her bed.

Chapter 14

PARIS

The unbalanced clunk of something solid being dropped onto a table roused Jake. He woke like he was pulling himself up from underwater, a slow trudge to consciousness. His jaw hurt like hell, and when he tried to roll and look for what had made the sound, something tugged at his wrist. She'd tied him again.

He instantly went wild, flailing and cursing. He didn't even know if Dulcina was in the room. Jake yelped the second his thrashing became too much for his ribs, and changed his tactic, but didn't stop fighting. He was just plain pissed off, and taking it out on...well, apparently himself. Drawing in a deep breath, he braced for the pain that would follow, and put some serious muscle behind a hard, measured pull on those cords.

"Stop," Dulcina ordered from his left. "You'll destroy any progress you've made in healing those busted ribs."

"What the hell do you care?" he gritted through clenched teeth. He had no plans to stop. This devil woman would have to punch his damn lights out again to take the fight out of him.

Dulcina huffed out a breath in frustration, then climbed onto the bed and straddled his hips, settling her full weight on him to pin him down. Nope. Not in the mood. Jake bucked and jerked beneath her. She must have recognized he wasn't anywhere near done fighting, because that snake of a woman found his damaged ribs and pressed her thumb firmly against a single point. Jake barked out a cry of pain and immediately stopped struggling, then gritted his teeth as he worked through the pain. When he finally opened his eyes, he didn't say a word, letting every ounce of his frustration pour out into his angry glare.

"Was I not paying enough attention to you, pet? Is that why you left?" Dulcina leaned forward over his chest, her face hovering above his. "This better?"

"Dulcina," he growled low, and to be honest, he let that anger slip into his tone as well as dictate his choice on what to call her. No Dulcie or Sugar. Just her given name that somehow held none of her personality. The name she demanded he use but he never had before. Using it now disconnected them, let him be who he'd been before he'd met her. The gut-hurt, vengeance-driven man he hid from her was peeking through, barely leashed. "Untie me."

"No," she said with absolute conviction, daring him to challenge her with just a single upward twitch of her eyebrows.

Jake thrashed again for a moment, but everything was different. With her hips settled snug on top of his, leaning forward like she was, the friction was delicious agony. This time he stopped fighting for an entirely different reason. Jake was completely annoyed, his body strung tight, and...yep, aroused.

The long growling groan he let out served two purposes. First, it bought him time to regroup and get a little blood back to his brain. Second, it gave him something to focus on other than visions of them together in this same position with a lot less clothes.

When he'd recovered enough to look at her, he nodded toward the cords and snapped, "I don't like this."

"That's the point, Jake. You need to get it through your thick skull that you're not in charge here. You're human and vulnerable," Dulcina said evenly, somehow managing to keep her cool even though she was clearly done with his shit. She reached back and pulled a small five-inch blade from her boot. He hadn't known about that one. Jake watched the glinting metal in the dim light of her home, wary of her intentions. At first, he'd thought she meant to cut the ties, but she lowered the blade and deftly sliced off three buttons from his crew neck shirt, starting at the top.

"Hey!" he cautioned, tracking every twitch of her blade until he was left with no buttons at all. Cool and calm, Dulcina peeled that split open, leaving the center portion of his chest bare. On any other day, with any other woman, this might be the start of something fun and a little naughty, but that hard edge in her assessing gaze made him a touch nervous. She was up to something and he had a deep suspicion he wasn't going to like it much.

Flipping the blade's position in her palm, Dulcina pointed it downward, the tip hovering over the inner half of his left pectoral, just over his heart. The metal tip scraped his skin a moment before she broke the surface.

"Hey! Knock it off!" he hollered. She ignored him. Slowly, she pushed the blade into his flesh, splitting skin and muscle.

Jake let a few colorful curses fly, but they slurred together, hindered by his clenched teeth and thick accent. He could do nothing but let his voice take on his pain rather than moving his body and causing further damage.

"Do I have your attention now?" she whispered, her resolve steady as a rock.

His lip twitching slightly, he gritted out a solid, "Yes."

"Good." She leaned closer until all he saw was her face framed by wild curls. Just as hushed, and far more ominous, she said, "The number of nights you have left in this world are precariously hanging by a thread. You leave me and you *will* die. That's a fact. The Stalker Lord knows you are here, as does his assassin. No one escapes them. For the safety of my kind, and yours, you cannot be allowed to live with knowledge of vampires and demons. You run again and I will be ordered to hunt you down and kill you. Should I fail, which is *highly* unlikely, then every Stalker from here to Portugal will be on your tail. If you're very lucky, you'll last a few days."

Jake steeled his facial expression, giving no hint to the shock her statement sent through him. "Then I'll go east."

"Then you'll die faster," she said with a sincerity that hit him hard. No elaboration, no hints as to what would kill him in the east, just a simple fact that if he went that way, he was toast.

Dulcina sighed, looking down at the wound she'd made in his skin. Jake grunted as she slipped the blade from his chest, setting it on the nightstand not far from his head. Blood welled at the punctured split of his skin in his lower peripheral vision, but Dulcina's fixated gaze on that same spot was a sharp reminder of her species.

She dipped her head and flat out licked his chest, blood and all. Jake drew in a full breath, its release shuddering as she drew her tongue over the cut several more times.

"What are you..." he mumbled incoherently, his thoughts scattered as she lapped at that single spot again, this time slower and more deliberate. Her name came out as less of a warning, and more of a tortured groan. "Dulcie. What are you doing?"

"Sealing the wound for proper healing," she said, her tongue dancing over the deep puncture that no longer stung, but tingled and itched. With a final kiss to his chest, she pulled back. "And savoring the taste of your skin."

"Christ, woman. You can't just say stuff like that. Half of it didn't make a lick of sense, and the other half..." Jake shuddered. He didn't know where the hell he stood with her at the moment. He was riding the line between furious and incredibly turned on.

Her hand still lingering over his sternum, she sat tall and softly said, "Jake, the last thing I want is to see you hurt."

"Clearly," he grumbled.

She scowled at him, her head tilting slightly. Now she was getting pissed. Well, good. Because he was testy as hell and it didn't look to let loose anytime soon.

She kept her voice hushed. "You're a real pain in the ass, you know that?"

"Yeah, like being tied to you is a treat." He tugged on the rope cords again.

"Watch it. The chance of me helping you is slowly slipping away every time you open your mouth." Dulcina leaned forward again, arms braced near his shoulders. "You get why this is important to me, don't you? How this is bigger than the two of us? You leave and it's a chain of events I can't stop. First, they hunt you down, but then they turn on me. I'm the one who let you go. I jeopardized an entire race. To save the vampire race—tens of thousands of men, woman, and children—you and I...our lives mean nothing."

Jake gritted his teeth, refused to look up at her. The muscles along his jaw line twitched. He was angry, but not at her. Not this time. She was right.

Somehow it hadn't dawned on him that one man could inadvertently kill an entire race, especially since Jake had no intention of telling anyone what he knew. It wasn't until she'd said the Stalkers would come after her as well that all the pieces fit together. It didn't matter that she was damn good at her job, that she was a royal from a well-known city. They could potentially kill her for endangering a race.

He couldn't look her in the eye, didn't think he could stomach it at the moment. Quietly, he said, "I didn't think it would come back on you."

"My pet. My responsibility."

His lip twitched, almost forming into a snarl. He controlled the reaction, but barely. "Stop callin' me that."

"In my world, a human is one of two things. A pet or a servant. While you were quite serving when you rubbed my feet, I don't see you as a servant. Directing you to accomplish tasks I'm more than capable of doing myself is...tedious and unnecessary. As it seems I am to keep you, I'd rather care for you when needed. It's a compliment, Jake. Accept it as such," she said, though he didn't exactly understand the details. She was keeping him and he was going to be bored out of his mind for the rest of his life.

His gaze flicked to her, then swiftly away. Nothing needed said. His defeat in this matter was evident.

"Back in Balinese, in my home, you pushed me to have a real conversation when I did not want one, so now it's your turn," she coaxed gently. "Talk to me."

The truth wouldn't change anything. She wouldn't release him, and the problems of a human wouldn't matter to her. There was no solution, and drudging up crap he didn't want to revisit would only be heartbreaking. Jake shook his head.

"Jake, I need to understand." That smooth tone of hers seeped into his brain, made him feel like they were the only two people in the world. She laid her palm against his cheek and turned his face toward hers, her thumb brushing in a slow rhythm over his whiskered cheek. "What is it you need to finish? What are you searching for so far away from your home?"

She'd just looked into his soul and guessed half of it, so what did it matter if he told her? It wasn't like she was going to run and tell the police when she was hiding her species from the world. Dulcie was the only person he knew in Paris, and probably one of the few people he would ever know since it sounded like he'd be locked to her side for the rest of his life. If she wouldn't let him track this man, then it was all over anyway.

"In my wallet," he relented.

Dulcina lifted an eyebrow, then rose onto her knees. Though she looked skeptical, when he lifted his hip, she removed his wallet from his back pocket. She flipped it open and spun it around so he could see inside.

"The picture, tucked between the two cards behind the cash," he directed.

She tugged the picture free, the small image cut from a larger group picture. He'd stared at Rita's face on the plane the whole way here and knew the details by heart. He was in the picture too, throwing a peace sign and smirking with a beautiful, strong woman at his side. That was Rita. There was a clear connection between them that could be seen in the photo, and not just because they wore the same uniform. He hadn't realized just how close they'd become until the flight here, but if they always looked like this together, then it must have been obvious to everyone else.

"She's...lovely," Dulcina acknowledged.

"She's my Rita." Jake nodded toward the picture.

Dulcina lifted her gaze to meet his, looking for all the world like she'd just had some deep realization strike her. In a whisper, she said, "She is your fated one."

"Fated what?"

"Fated mate," she altered her wording and the sincerity in her tone got to him. "The one who makes you whole, brings you back from the edge."

Jake nodded. He caught her drift. Some people just seemed destined to find each other and sort stuff out. "I loved her, you know. I wasn't *in* love with her, but... She was a good woman, a great friend, and the best damn partner I'd ever had at my back. Rita saved me, kept me going more times than I can count. Never knew a woman could be that way."

"Why not?" she asked, and Jake could see it in her eyes, the pure, unadulterated curiosity. She truly didn't understand.

"Because I've never had a good woman stay at my side. Had a fiancee once, but she two timed me and left without saying a word. Don't know if she'd had enough of me, or maybe it was the job that got in the way of us. Doesn't matter. No one stays. Never had a partner I could trust at home. Only at work."

"Rita?"

"Yeah. Didn't matter how thick things got, she never left my side. Never flinched. That was more commitment than I'd ever known in my life." Jake shifted beneath her, slightly uncomfortable with sharing these extra pieces of his life he'd never voiced aloud. "Rita changed me. Stomped out the bitterness I'd been clinging onto and gave me hope. Gave me hope, and then..."

Dulcina cleared her throat, her approach more hesitant as she softly asked, "Did she leave you?"

"You could say that. She was killed. In my home. Waiting for me to get back from the carry-out," he said, his words deliberate, his tone low. "I'm not here chasing after a woman who doesn't want me anymore. I'm hunting her murderer."

"I'm sorry, Jake. Truly, I am," she said, placing her arm on his shoulder, her attempt at comfort awkward.

"Yeah, that and two bucks'll get me a coffee." He cleared his throat. His off-kilter statement had him slipping from sadness back into that dark anger that had brought him here in the first place. "The man who killed her...well, he's here. Wanderin' Paris like he owns the damn place. I *need* to put him in the ground."

"Do you know where he is?"

Jake shook his head. "No. I caught a glimpse of him right about where you found me knocked out, but I doubt he's there anymore. I know his habits, and the man likes to gamble. He tends to set up his own hot spot clubs and he likes a particular setting. Classy. Guarded. I almost had him, but those red-eyed devils set me back."

"A lot of time has passed, and you know as well as I that he may no longer be in Paris. What was your plan when you walked out of my home? Your next step?" Dulcina asked, seeming genuinely interested. Take that back. She *was* interested. He'd seen her interact with other people, handle an array of situations, but this right here? The woman was invested in him on some level he didn't understand.

Jake paused for tick and bucked up his courage for a little honesty. "No plan. Can't be more than one bastard named Tulio Suarez. Especially here. His mother is French, but I doubt he'd show up on her doorstep. If he's got connections here it'll be with the underground circuits. Bars, clubs, anything tied to drugs. Was just going to ask around."

"In English?" she teased, but he wasn't in a joking mood.

"Every time I get something good it gets taken away. Rita's the one person I let get close to me, and since her killer fled the country and can't be brought to justice, I'm bringing justice to him," he said, his anger cranking up his volume.

She placed her palm to the center of his chest, the pressure more of a comfort than he'd expected. Like she wanted to be on his side.

"I can't allow you to kill a human," she said, her tone somewhat regretful. "Jake, I understand your need for vengeance more than anyone, but, I tell you truly, it is out of your reach."

"I figured as much." He wasn't at all surprised by her quick shutdown of his plan. He'd left the States with every intention of putting a bullet in Tulio's head and he hadn't really cared what happened after. Anything had been on the table. He could have walked away, been arrested, or shot by one of Tulio's men. Not since he'd put his badge down beside Rita had he questioned his path. Truth was, he didn't expect to live past this mission, and that hadn't mattered in the least, since Rita had been the only thing to keep him going. Jake stared off into the distance, a shade more numb than he'd been a moment ago. "She was my kindred spirit, the one person who knew just how to pull me out of the darkness."

Dulcina sat upright, her hand sliding down his chest until she pulled back and let it rest on her own leg. She was thinking things through. He'd thrown a lot at her, and he could see she'd taken it all in, was trying to figure him out.

"What if..." She paused for a moment, her gaze shifting to the door, and then she lowered her voice. "If you could confirm he's here, is there a way to make your countrymen aware of when he returns to the States? Then they can arrest him upon arrival?"

Hope surged though him. "Maybe. It might be a while before he feels safe enough to return. I'd have to keep tabs on him until he got on a plane, and when he does, you'd have to let me make a phone call."

"I think we could make that happen. I'll help, Jake, but you have to do two things for me," she said, imperious as she sat atop him. "Number one. If we hit a dead end, you let this go."

"And the second?" Jake already knew what the last thing was, he just needed confirmation.

"No more trying to escape."

"Yeah," Jake said, and even as he said it, he knew he'd be true to his word. He valued preserving her life over taking one of a criminal.

"Trust me," she coaxed, tilting her head slightly as she looked down into his eyes, a slight crook of a smile on the left side of her lips.

"I'm trying to. How do you think you're going to find him?"

"I speak French. You don't. Also, I happen to have a friend well connected to...everything. Airlines, car services, drugs, bars, criminals, humans, vampires, rumors, facts. He would know when your man came in and where he was headed. From there, any movement within the city will be easy for him to track," she said, her confidence in this man boundless. "We'll find him."

"When can I talk to your guy?"

Dulcina threw her head back and laughed, a wild laugh that made his insides jump to life, all giddy and drawn to her infectious smile. This time, when meeting his gaze, she sent him one of those looks that said he'd lost all sense of reality. A 'good for you for believing you can fly to the moon on a kite' kind of a look.

This moment between them was special and he could damn well recognize the rarity. There was intimacy in this sharing of secrets, of planning the future. She was with him on this, one hundred percent at his side.

Thank goodness she'd tied him down, because if he'd been free, he would have flipped her onto her back and kissed her until she sighed. Jake cleared his throat, more so to redirect his thoughts than to gain her attention, but it accomplished both.

She slowly shook her head. "He won't talk to *you*."

"So you'll talk to him?" Jake tried sitting upright, his excitement getting the best of him, but he wasn't going anywhere all trussed up with her still parked on top of him. "He's your kind, right?"

"It's not that easy, Jake."

"I'll do whatever it takes to get this guy. Tell me what to do," he demanded. She took a long, drawn-out breath, and for a moment Jake thought he'd lost her. With only a few tools left in his belt, Jake raised his voice to draw her focus. "Hey! Look at me, Dulcie. Want me to be your pet? Fine. Your servant? Done. Anything."

"Anything?"

He tipped his chin down in a solitary nod. "I *need* this."

"What *I* need," she said, leaning forward until her face hovered just over his, so close he felt her breath curling over his chin, "is for you to obey me."

"I'll polish your damn boots for the rest of my life if you want. Just give me this," he pleaded through clenched teeth.

"You're not listening, Jake. I'm not asking for shiny boots. I'm asking for your obedience. If I tell you to follow me, you do so without question. If I need you to duck out of sight, you've got to move fast," she said, and Jake kept nodding along. He was right there with her, agreeing to everything she threw at him. With her help, her trust, he might actually have a shot at catching Tulio, and that was better than the hollow nothing he was living with right now. She continued her list of demands, but slower, "And if I need you to keep that smart mouth of yours shut, you will do so. I can't have you saying the wrong thing at the wrong time to the wrong person and getting us both killed."

His eyes widened. "That can happen?"

"With certain vampires." She shrugged lazily. "Yes."

All he had to do was stop looking at her as jailer, and start thinking of her like she was his captain. Jake was an officer, a SWAT member. Following directives was second nature. On top of it all, she wasn't wrong. He was walking onto a battleground he didn't know how to navigate. She did.

"Yeah, we're good," he said, nodding his compliance. "I'll follow orders."

"No matter what, Jake. If you're going to walk at my side out there on the streets, you're going to encounter a way of life you don't understand. That means if a man is attacking me, you don't move unless I say."

"Listen, if someone is—"

"Nothing. You do *nothing*. If the situation is bad enough I think I'm in danger, then I will tell you to run. And you will." At his questioning look, she shook her head to quiet him and continued, "If something happens to me, and demons don't get you first, there will be a kill order out on you. You will need to know where it is safe to seek sanctuary."

"I'm in. You lead," he said, though he was a little unsettled by the devious smile that suddenly curled this beautiful woman's lips. He was in for a hell of a ride.

• • • •

Dulcina had reaffirmed the rules of their new relationship and now stood in the middle of an eerily quiet street, Jake at her side. Always one to keep her word and follow through, she'd intended to head straight for the best source of information.

Dulcina was putting herself out there, for a man, for a human. She, more than most, understood Jake's soul-deep need for revenge, as well as the devastation and helplessness felt when it could not be found. She could show him that, over time, the pain faded, and an enemy's death rarely provided satisfaction.

And just like that, she was fully invested. She was keeping him. No, the situation wasn't ideal, but Dulcina was a big believer in dealing with what fate tossed your way. If she'd been handed this broken, vengeful human, there was a reason.

Dulcina was rational, changeable, and Jake seemed to be cut from a similar cloth. Jake living above ground with her could work, if they both gave up a little. Jake would have to give up a few major freedoms, and Dulcina? Well, her freedoms would also suffer. No more solitary existence, no all-night hunts. She should be highly irritated at the thought of living so restrictively. Somehow though, she couldn't bring herself to care. Jake was genuine, selfless, fun, and for the first time, her initial instinct was not to run.

"We good?" Jake rubbed his eyebrow, clearly a little unsettled by her silence.

She didn't answer. Instead, she looked him over, head-to-toe. Standing there, ready to follow her every direction, he wore faded and ripped jeans with a tight white T-shirt. Jake looked every inch the muscled temptation he was, and that had been her goal when she'd pulled out the clothes she'd wanted him to wear.

"Do not interfere with anything I do, and don't speak. If you must, call me D." She looked over to the nearby building and squared her shoulders. "Let's go see if Ruskin is in a mood to play."

Together they moved down the sidewalk. The buildings here were nondescript, one blending into the next with little significant differences. She turned down a narrow alley, then down an equally narrow set of stairs leading below the building. Ducking inside, she and Jake paused in the tight vestibule, their entry blocked by a big, strapping bouncer.

"Humans aren't allowed, D." The bouncer's deep voice matched his size.

"My pet goes where I go. You know how I get after a fight, Miloslav." She smiled up at the bouncer and the burly man blushed as he grumbled something under his breath, and allowed them entry.

Jake raised an eyebrow, clearly wanting answers, but he might find out firsthand. At the suggestion, her mind happily went there. A good adrenaline-pumped tussle, whether with demon or vampire, left her aroused and in search of a worthy bed partner. Every time. As Jake was within arm's reach, she was having a hard time considering anyone else for that position.

People stared as they stepped deeper inside, but not in the way she was accustomed. Sure, a few lustful gazes followed her, as well as a healthy amount of apprehension, but most sized up Jake. They probably couldn't figure him out. With his brownish hair, he certainly didn't appear vampire. He would either be pegged as demon or human, and both could have some nasty repercussions. Walking in with her was a deterrent, but his supremely confident attitude was likely what kept anyone from approaching as they headed for the bar.

"Hey, Gage!" Dulcina yelled to the bartender as she leaned over the counter. Looking dapper and dangerous, Gage reached out, and she grasped his forearm in a traditional vampire greeting.

"D, I didn't know you were around," Gage said, his words slow and deliberate. She loved his oddly thick accent, similar to Ruskin's.

"Always, my friend," she said, still grinning as Gage handed her a tumbler of dark amber liquid. Whiskey. Probably top shelf. Gage had a soft spot for her because she always put Ruskin in a good mood.

Dulcina knocked back the drink and handed him back the glass. "You sure know how to make a girl happy."

"So I've been told." Gage snagged a new glass, cleaning off the rim and nodding toward Jake. "Why's *that* here?"

Dulcina shook her head, hoping this was the worst of the attention Jake received. "The poor man can't help what he is."

"Yeah," Gage said, eyeing him with a new interest. "And exactly what is he?"

"Mine." That single word came out more possessive than she'd intended, but Dulcina didn't regret it in the least.

The single word statement was so clear that Gage's eyebrows shot up in surprise. "Really?"

Leaning over the bar again, this time nearly nose to nose with the bartender, Dulcina changed the topic, and whispered, "I need to speak with Ruskin. Keep the human in one piece for me, will you?"

"Fine," Gage grumbled. "Damn, I need a better job."

One problem settled, she turned her full attention to Jake. Hand in the center of his chest, she pushed him back until his legs hit the bar stool. She was putting on a show, and that meant selling it to anyone who might be watching. Skimming her hand over his chest and past his abs, she stopped at his waist. Taking hold of his belt, she pushed him down onto the bar stool where he plunked down awkwardly.

Dulcina leaned in, her lips against his ear. "Do not move. And don't forget you belong to me."

Her voice had come out a little more throaty than she'd anticipated, so she ran with it, taking his earlobe between her teeth and gently pulling away. She turned and left, not having the guts to glance back and see the look on Jake's face after she'd publicly claimed him.

Chapter 15

PARIS

This hard to find, no name bar was more than his livelihood. It was his home. A home he never left. A prison he'd created. Ruskin slowly pushed away from the chain link wall with a deliberate show of rippling muscle, turning only to lean lazily against the links and face the next man who'd entered his cage within a cage.

Average man, average build, average intelligence. It was always the same. Someone drank too much alcohol and suddenly found himself ballsy enough to take a shot at Ruskin. Either that or a man's so-called friends pumped up his ego to the point the poor sap actually believed he could beat the house champ.

Mr. Average stepped in, glancing back at a group of young men. Ah, the second classification. Ruskin had begun to suspect that over the years, climbing into the cage with him had somehow become a rite of passage to young adult vampire males of the surrounding cities, provided they knew where to find him.

There was no buzzer to start the brawl, no signal to begin this contest of brute strength. The fight began at the first act of aggression. Rarely did Ruskin begin these cage fights, but he always finished them. One way or another.

His opponent shuffled his feet slightly and took the first swing. Ruskin pulled back, easily avoiding the flailing fist. Taking a slow step away, he allowed the man to regroup before trying again, curious to see how he would change his strategy. Quick thinking and creativity could get a man far, but youth rarely posed a challenge.

His opponent suddenly charged, but Ruskin hit him across the jaw hard enough the man stumbled. His line of sight suddenly clear, he watched in absolute awe as Dulcina Casteel strutted across the room toward the bar.

She greeted Gage and he immediately noticed a new face followed her. Something about this man was off. Ruskin couldn't put his finger on it, but bottom line...he wasn't vampire, and therefore not a threat.

The man inside the cage with him regained his footing and attacked, trying valiantly to pummel him. Again. Dodging to the left, Ruskin twisted and thrust his flattened palm down on the oncoming man's shoulder blade, sending him to the floor where he belonged.

Ruskin stepped over the man's sprawled limbs, his rapt attention on Dulcina. She leaned over his bar, that firm ass of hers in the air as she had a private word with Gage. His bartender nodded toward the metal linked cage, and the instant their eyes met, his desire flared. She was here for him. There was nothing in this world he enjoyed more than tussling with this hot-blooded female.

She faced the man she'd arrived with, and pressing a firm hand to his chest, backed him up to a bar stool. Then she slid her hand down his chest to his jeans, took hold of his belt, and pushed him down into the seat. She leaned in close, and whatever she said into his ear had him fighting to control the desire that had flashed across his face. Ruskin raised an eyebrow in disbelief.

She headed his way and his blood ran hot once again. Ah, the way she moved... It had been too damn long since he'd seen her, since he'd had her. That lovely sharp gaze met his, and he smiled wickedly. Tonight was going to be fun.

The impulsive man inside the cage with him finally pulled himself off his knees and barreled toward him once again, but Ruskin was done. He had a better prospect approaching. Fingers splayed wide, he cupped the back of the man's head. Ruskin spun him just enough to throw his balance and add momentum, then sent his opponent face first into the floor. This time he didn't get up, didn't even twitch. The drunken crowd cheered wildly.

Ruskin leaned back against the metal link fence and lit a cigarette, his every gesture exuding boredom. Others opened the door and pulled the unconscious man from the cage while Ruskin watched Dulcina approach, allowing her to make the first move.

Dulcina wove through the mingling crowd, her destination clear. The measured grace in her every movement as she climbed onto the raised platform was hypnotic. When the only thing that separated them was the metal mesh, Ruskin approached her slowly. Meeting her toe-to-toe, he linked his fingers though the fencing above her head. He leaned down until his face was a breath away from hers.

On the rare occasion he spoke, Ruskin tried to hide his accent, though it never went well. He only managed to sound Russian. Over the years, speaking had become an extreme rarity, until Dulcina. There had been no mistaking the heavy cadence of his words when they'd first tumbled into his bed, and he'd never hidden that sliver of himself from her since.

"What can I do for you, *my darling*, and for how many hours?" Ruskin said just for her, giving over to his natural born accent, his voice thick and rich.

"Behave, Ruskin," she scolded firmly. "Only information tonight."

A flit of movement behind her drew his attention. The human stood, but Ruskin wouldn't dignify his presence with a glance. Something else was going on here and he might just require some answers of his own.

"All information comes at a price," he whispered. "What shall I ask of you?"

"What do you want?" she asked, her tone more curt than usual.

"If I told you, you might blush," Ruskin said with an idle, lustful perusal of her from head-to-toe and back again.

"You know I don't blush," she said, seemingly unaffected by his interest. "What else do you want?"

Ruskin cocked his head slightly to the left. It was not like Dulcina to pass up a tumble in bed with him. He didn't know what game she was playing, but if he couldn't have her in his bed, he'd settle for the next best thing.

This green-eyed beauty was a creature of habit, a woman of action, and he knew her well. Slowly, emphasizing each word with a seductive purr, Ruskin said, "I want you in my cage."

She lifted an eyebrow, feigning annoyance, but there was no way she hadn't seen his demand coming. It had been years since she'd stepped into his cage.

The first time she'd dipped her toe into his world, he hadn't expected a slender female to provide him with an ounce of challenge. Moments after they'd called it a draw and both leaned against the fence, panting for breath, Ruskin had discovered just how much a good brawl stoked her wild and lustful side.

In the years following, she'd come to him at least once a week, releasing what was left of her pent-up aggression...inside his cage, or in his bed. Ruskin wasn't stupid. He saw clearly what she needed. What they'd both needed. This wasn't love. Hell, he'd soon learned it wasn't even lust. What they had together was a sliver of time when neither was ending lives or being hunted. They were solitary creatures who secretly craved companionship and physical contact, but on their own terms. She was the only woman he'd been with since leaving his home, and one of three vampires he trusted to stand anywhere near him. He had a sneaking suspicion she felt the same way about him.

Ruskin curled his fingers around the metal, desperate to have her under his touch once again. "Make up your mind, darling."

Dulcina's steady gaze broke away from his to glance back at the human. The male shook his head, a silent plea for her to stop. What was this? His wild Night Stalker hesitated. And for what? To ponder the wishes of a human male?

"I'll have you under my hands tonight," Ruskin said low and firm, deliberately drawing her attention. "You choose. In the cage or in my bed."

"Done," she said before turning fully back to face him.

Embracing her Spirit, she vanished, slipping through the metal barrier to reappear at his side. Ruskin turned to her, an appreciative smile curving his lips. Show off. She could easily escape this cage, but her pride would never allow retreat.

Dulcina's keen gaze tracked every movement he made. She'd never been intimidated by his looks, an image that made others approach with caution. Ruskin's tousle-spiked black hair, black kohl eyeliner, and black t-shirt stretched tight over his thickly muscled upper body made him an imposing figure. But not to her.

The heavy rhythm of the drums in the music nearly drowned out the confused chattering of the crowd. After what Ruskin had just done to his previous opponent, they seemed to collectively worry for Dulcina's safety. There was no need. Dulcina had been known to kill full grown, battle-ready demons, but that was not what made her extraordinary. She was unique to anything he'd encountered, because nothing rattled her.

Ruskin lifted his closed fist, an intentional test of her reflexes, but she didn't flinch. She knew his habits and tells, too, and she wasn't about to give away any hints that might help him. They circled each other, for more than a mere few steps. No one, not even Dulcina, took this long to start a fight. She was stalling.

"Dulcie," the human male called, his voice low and beseeching. He had left his seat and cautiously made his way toward them. Even now he edged closer. Dulcina cocked her head toward the human, listening without looking.

"Dulcie?" Ruskin asked, shocked at the endearing way her name sounded on the human's pleading tongue. Without warning, Dulcina struck quick and hard, catching his chin in a vicious uppercut. His head cranked back, but when he faced her again, he was smiling. "Ah, there you are, *my darling.*"

She launched her fist again, but this time he dodged her swing and grabbed her shoulder, flinging her back against the cage. The metal rattled as it caught her, and like she'd done it a thousand times, Dulcina sprang off the links and ducked under his arm, meaning to attack him from behind.

He was ready for her. Ruskin twisted out of reach, hooked his arm around her neck and locked her back tightly to his chest. She didn't struggle. No, not Dulcina. She was too much of a seasoned warrior for such nonsense.

"You seem tense," he whispered into her ear. Her mind was elsewhere tonight, and he did not care for the slight. "I can help."

Her elbow caught him just below the ribs, a superficial blow meant to distract, and it did. Her head whipped back, connected with his chin. He released her, a grunt escaping his lips.

"I brought my own cure," she gritted out between clenched teeth.

Ruskin glanced over to the human. A fight was foreplay for him, and for her. Always had been. But slaking her desires with a human? Unheard of.

"Truly?" Ruskin asked, not bothering to hide the surprise plastered across his face.

She shrugged, not answering.

"*My darling,*" Ruskin all but purred, sending her a gentle, knowing grin. "He's human. You'll break him."

"I haven't yet," Dulcina said.

Her voice was smooth, but something about his mention of the human had put her on guard. That, and she was not at all trying to win this fight. He was missing something, a vital piece of this puzzle before him.

Ruskin leaned on the one pressure point he had and, as he pushed harder, he allowed his words to curl with his accent. "You *will* break him, sooner or later. Humans are weak. He can't give you what you need."

"There's not one damn person in this world, above or below, who knows what I need," she snarled, then belted him across the jaw.

He was ready for her strike, had provoked it, and though the hit hurt like hell, he used the moment to hook her foot with his and catch her off balance. Tripping her, Ruskin shoved her back into the cage and was on her in a heartbeat, the metal bowing under their joined weight.

Again she struck that spot just below his ribs, catching an opening. The jab hit a nerve in more than one way. Instead of letting this play out, Ruskin twisted his body hard, sending them both rolling across the cage floor. He landed on top, using his natural weight to his advantage. She could barely move, though she thrashed beneath him, trying to buck him off and break free.

Ruskin caught her wrists, pinned them above her head, and bent to her ear. "I'd prefer to do this without clothing. Yield."

Her response was visceral. Dulcina bolted up and cracked her head into his nose at the same time she rolled her body, the combination enough to throw him off her. She was free, as was he. Ruskin took her by the arms, lifted her to her feet, then slammed her against the cage wall. His temper, always leashed, flickered to the surface. Wrapping his hand around her throat, he lifted her off the ground. He leaned heavily against her, using his body to pin her against the metal cage, but did not release his grip on her throat.

Bowing his head, he took a breath, reigned in his aggression, and allowed the calm to wash over him again. Controlling his temper was a learned skill, and the fact that he could, didn't guarantee it happened swiftly.

Ruskin took a mental step back and replayed every movement she made, every moment with her this night. The similarities of their past encounters, the differences. He looked at Dulcina through a different lens. She was hurting. Desperate. Something within her screamed of...hope?

"What is this, *my darling*?" This time the word 'darling' was sweet and intimate. He liked this woman, very much, and was concerned. She was not acting herself. In any other fight they'd both be panting from overexertion and bleeding by now, gleefully impressed by each other's brutality. "You're not even trying. Why allow me to take the upper hand for a scrap of information?"

Her jaw clamped tight, eyes cold and hard. She was refusing to answer him?

Ruskin's eyes narrowed, then his gaze slid to the human who had eased closer. The man's eyes were wide, fearful, and his hands gripped the metal links tight enough to turn his knuckles white. This inferior species looked as if he wanted to rip open the cage, kill him, take Dulcina out of here...and at the same time, was furious he wasn't capable of doing any of the above.

Fascinating. The human was emotionally attached to her, and she ignored him. Completely tuned him out, like she did everything else when in the middle of a fight. The difference? They'd stopped fighting, and still she refused to draw attention to him. She was protecting him.

He voiced his theory as fact. "This is for *him*."

He didn't need Dulcina to confirm anything. Releasing her to the arena floor, he took a step back. Her denial would do no good at this point, not when the human she'd arrived with appeared thoroughly concerned for her in a way that belied his true feelings. It was mutual. She belonged to this human, whether she knew it yet or not.

"Go. Go to your pet. He is...distraught. Comfort him," Ruskin said quietly, his words rough and choppy as he pushed through emotion he hadn't realized affected his heart so deeply. For so long, Dulcina had been his hope, and once again this cold, harsh world left him with nothing. "Stay the day here and rest. My home is yours. Come nightfall, I'll give you what you want. Anything you want."

"Ruskin, I—"

"Anything."

Dulcina nodded, embracing her Spirit only long enough to leave the cage without a word, or even a backward glance. The human was at her side in a heartbeat. His hands went straight to her face, tilting her head to inspect her neck. When he saw the reddened skin marking the exact spot Ruskin's hand recently occupied, the man whipped his head around and glared hatefully at him through the metal.

Well, well. Human or not, it seemed the man had a fire in his belly Ruskin could respect. Dulcina would naturally be drawn in by that fierceness. It hadn't appeared as if she'd told him of her plan to take on a male vampire in a fight, which was likely why she allowed him to fuss over her.

Dulcina was wrong. There was in fact one person in this world who knew exactly what she needed. Good. At least one lost and tormented soul in this world had found their other half, and he would never begrudge her happiness, even if it meant his would be forever denied.

Chapter 16

PARIS

The hand print turning red across the right side of Dulcie's neck was more than enough to make Jake want to throw fists. It was a damn good thing that brute was locked inside a cage. Tilting Dulcie's chin up, he stroked his thumb over her neck, checking her delicate flesh for any tissue damage.

"Not here." Dulcina batted away his searching hand.

"Then where?" he asked, not about to back down. When she said nothing, he pushed harder. "I got two things screaming in my head right now, woman, and if you don't let me check you out, I'm going after him."

Jake pointed at the man in the cage, though he didn't need the emphasis. She knew who he meant. A flare of fear crossed her features, and she quickly locked her hand around his wrist and pulled him with her. Near the back of the room, where the lights were dimmer, she led him down a short hallway. At the third room, she opened the door and shoved him inside.

The instant the door shut, Jake scanned the room for occupants. Empty. He turned back to her and resumed his inspection, checking the other side of her neck.

"Are you hurt?" Jake asked, point blank. He skimmed his hands over her arms next, and when satisfied she wasn't truly damaged, he returned his focus to the red marks on her neck. "What the hell were you thinking? What was that all about?"

"You wanted information," she said, surprisingly still allowing his hand to guide the tilt of her head.

"That was...you did that for me? To find..." Jake clenched his jaw tight, absolutely livid at the idea of her willingly putting herself under the hands of a brute. "Figure something else out. You are *not* doing that again."

She wasn't listening to him. Jake hadn't noticed at first, but now that he awaited her vow, he could see all her attention was on his hands, leaning into his touch. Savoring. He recognized her sudden ardor had a whole lot more to do with the adrenaline response after a fight rather than the man in front of her. Not uncommon after a brawl, but not something he'd expected from her.

"Dulcie? You listenin' to me?"

Her fingers curled into his shirt, clenched into fists, and she jerked him up against her. Jake threw a hand out to the door behind her, only just catching himself from fully crashing into her, but it seemed that had been her goal. Dulcie's lips landed on his with the surety of a woman who knew what she wanted, which meant she wasn't stopping with just a kiss. After seeing her walk into that cage for him, Jake had a need of his own to feel her safe and warm in his arms, but he wouldn't take what she offered now, not when he was dead certain it wasn't an act of true affection. This was the adrenaline junkie in her, riding the high.

Jake groaned and pushed away from her, breaking the kiss. She tried to pull him close again, but he managed to keep them mostly separated. "Hey, now. Not like this."

Dulcina hooked her palm around the back of his neck and spun him hard enough they switched positions. His back landed heavily against the door, and it rattled under his weight.

"Hey!" he yelped, taken off guard by their sudden shift, feet tangled. He'd barely barked out the word when she braced her forearm across his upper chest, pinning him in place with her otherworldly strength.

Dulcina paused long enough to draw in a breath, then cranked his head to the side and sunk her teeth deep into his neck.

Jake's cry of surprise soon shifted to a low moan as a shudder of overwhelming pleasure coursed through his body in tidal waves, crashing through him again and again. He didn't know how long she drank from him. Seconds? Minutes? The pleasure eased into a soothing sense of contentment even as his vision hazed, giving everything around him a soft dreamy edge.

Muscles weak from the toe-curling pleasure thrumming through his body, Jake leaned back fully against the door. Senses dulled, he felt nothing more than the hard door at his back and Dulcie's warm body against his chest. Those last two anchor points to reality were being threatened by a dizzying euphoria, and Jake fought hard to remain conscious.

Her warm breath tickled against his neck where she fed. The lingering sweep of her tongue across the bite hurt. Not physically, but because it was a harsh reminder he'd only been a fixture in this exchange and now she was done with him.

As she stepped back, Jake shook his head hard, fighting to stay awake. It was obvious by the way she looked, cheeks pink and quickened breathing, that the pleasure involved with biting him had been quite mutual. Seeing this hot-blooded woman flushed with passion had been on the top of his list, but he did not like the way she'd gone about initiating their first kiss, his first bite.

Jake closed the gap between them again. He was angry as hell and trying to put up a good front, but his muscles were quickly turning to jelly. His weight shifted forward, invading her personal space, and it might not have been entirely on purpose.

He met her stubborn gaze and practically growled his words. "Next time you wanna have a go at this, there won't be any biting. I'll want it and you'll want it. Until then, don't touch me."

"You're mine," Dulcie said, chin tipped defiantly. "I'll do what I want with you, sweetheart."

"Maybe I am yours, bad luck of the draw and all, but I'm *not* your sweetheart. Step off," he said, holding out his arm to keep her at bay as she was coming toward him. Or was he moving toward her? "What'd you do to me?"

Lord above, this must be what the town drunk felt like on a bender. His vision wavered, awareness faded, and the last thing he felt before his eyelids slammed shut and the blackness took him, was his body hitting something damn solid. Probably the floor.

• • • •

Dulcina had maneuvered Jake to the bed and settled him under the blanket, and had slept at his side through the daylight hours. He barely stirred, which was expected. She'd drank deeply enough from him to knock him out and alter his ability to clearly remember what had happened.

He shifted beside her, lifting his hand to his chest, guarding his injured rib in this twilight of consciousness. She closed her eyes as the memory of those searching, caring hands on her neck spiked her desire for him again. The way he'd looked at her, so concerned and ready to battle on her behalf...she needed him after that very public display of care and affection. His emotional response had broken loose the barrier she'd put up.

He'd watched in silent rage as she'd scuffled with Ruskin, never distracting her, never telling her she couldn't do it, or demanding she get out and stay safe. It was after she'd stepped out of the cage that the gentle caress of his fingers over her neck told her exactly how concerned he was over her. It was his willingness to fight an unbeatable opponent to seek retribution for her that shouted to everyone in the room how much he truly cared for her. She'd never known how much she craved a man's genuine concern born from affection until that moment.

No, perhaps that wasn't entirely true. Affection was one of those subconscious needs she'd easily pushed aside or ignored. The thought of receiving such attention from lovers in her past was unsettling. To think of Dario checking her for injuries after a scuffle was nauseating. Nico? If he'd tried to protect her in any way, she would have knocked him on his ass for the insult. Bottom line, she didn't think she could take gentleness or doting attentions from any man other than Jake. Everything about him rubbed her the right way.

Dulcina didn't nurture relationships. She'd never trusted anyone enough to let them into her life. People who got close to her ended up dead. Solitude allowed her to survive.

She wasn't alone anymore, though. Dulcina rolled to her side and watched Jake sleep. His body was completely lax. This was the most peaceful she'd seen him, which hadn't occurred to her until now. He must have been in far more pain than he'd let on, or perhaps more tense about his new living situation with a vampire than he'd expressed.

The way he looked at her after she'd fed from him… There were no words to describe the sheer volume of betrayal she'd seen shining in his eyes. Her actions had hurt him, and for once, she cared.

Dulcina slipped her fingers through his short hair, taking this quiet moment to touch him without his knowledge. He'd been so angry with her, and now that she'd had time to rationally think things through, he had every right.

• • • •

Jake groaned, rubbing his hand over his face. Floating somewhere between sleep and consciousness for several minutes, he finally woke to the feel of fingers moving through his hair. That would be Dulcie. Had to be.

Drowsy, and off kilter, he gingerly pushed his body upright and out of her reach. He definitely still hurt, but it all felt different. Muted.

"God damn, woman," Jake slurred his words, his senses and coordination slowly returning. "My head is foggy as all get out. How the hell did I get a hangover? What did you do to me?"

"It's only the effect of my bite," she said, and that's when Jake realized how close she was to him, sitting right there at his side. He hadn't felt her move.

"That why no one remembers what you do to them?" Jake rubbed the back of his neck and stretched it out, working the lethargy from his muscles.

"We need to talk," Dulcina said, and although they sure did, the thought of it made him uneasy.

"What, like that coming to Jesus talk we had when I was trussed up like a pig with your knife in my chest? None doin'," Jake said firmly.

Jake stared her down, hoping the stern set of his jaw relayed how damn upset he was with her.

"Clearly there's been a misunderstanding," she said, but he wasn't following her train of thought. His silent, level stare must have been too much for her to take, because Dulcina snapped, "Whatever you're dying to get off your chest, just say it."

"Say what?" Jake snapped back, so irritated the muscles in his jaw twitched. He felt them. Like cords strung too tight.

Dulcina refused to back down. "Whatever it is that turns your stomach, let's hear it."

Jake didn't say a word as he eased off the bed. The pain in his ribs he'd expected, but the kinks in his body and wobbly way his legs struggled to get him from A to B and back was concerning. Still, he paced as best he could, sorting through his scrambled thoughts and memories.

"Sugar, I think I missed a step here. But okay, if that's what you want, I'll have a go. You walked into that cage knowing damn well you were gonna give that big ol' boy something. Something of you. And no, I didn't like it one damn bit, but that was your call. I have no say over you. But this?" Jake pointed to her, then to his neck where she'd bitten him, and again to her. He paused for a breath, then two, taking the time to calm himself. "I don't like what you did to me. You *took* my blood from me. Too many things have been ripped away from me. What little I got left is precious because it's *all* I got. This won't happen again. You hear me?"

"You forget, you have no say," she said, her words a flat, heartless reminder.

"You wanna bet? I can play nice, or I can walk out that door. You think I won't? Back me into a corner and see what happens. I got nothin' left, and I won't be used," Jake said, his dark words hanging between them.

"Everyone is used, for one purpose or another." Her words were fact; she'd meant them as such, but they came out hollow. She stared at nothing in particular, completely zoned out.

Jake slowly approached the bed, leaned down, and hooked a finger beneath her chin to bring her gaze up to his. She didn't pull away or fight his touch.

"Do you even know what it feels like *not* to be selfish?" Jake asked, for the first time seeing the world through her skewed perception. She took before someone could take from her, left before someone could leave her. It was how she survived, how she came out on the other side of a relationship unscathed. Dulcie's brows furrowed, and the moment they did, he shook his head. "Yeah, I didn't think so."

Silence hung heavy between them. This wasn't what he'd first assumed. She hadn't hurt him because she didn't care, but more like she didn't know *how* to care. This was all new to her, and she was probably struggling.

Jake cleared his throat and asked, "When you first stepped up to that cage, whatever he said, you shut down. What did he want from you?"

"Nothing I haven't willingly given him before." Dulcina shrugged. "I've never said no to Ruskin. Tonight I denied him."

"And that's what landed you in the cage? You had two options? Sleep with him, or fight the man?" Jake waved his hands, a stopping gesture. "Correction. A grown vampire man with, what, a good ten years of life and combat experience over you?"

"At least fifty."

"Fifty. Sure." Jake nodded, then exploded, "What the hell were you thinking!"

She stood then, meeting him toe-to-toe, her lip twitching in anger. "I thought about *everything*! Ruskin has connections I don't have, and you could never get. He *is* the answer. If I don't get that information from him, you'll go out on your own. You do that? You die. If that man you hunt doesn't kill you, the Stalkers will slaughter you."

"You're doing this to keep me from dyin'?"

She looked like she wanted to move, to pace, but there was nowhere to go. In a rush she barked out her frustration, "I don't know how to do this!"

"Do what?" he asked, his brows scrunching together at her outburst.

"You!" she yelled. Jake straightened, eyes wide. She kept rolling, spilling a lot of what she kept all pent up. "I need you, Jake, and I don't need anyone or anything."

Jake may have been stunned by her admission, but it was Dulcina who stood there with her jaw gaping. She hadn't wanted any of that to come out, and it had spilled like someone had shot a cannon through a dam. Standing there in the aftermath, she looked positively terrified.

He reached out to her, and she flinched. Jesus, that was a reaction he hadn't expected. He'd never hurt her, but he suspected she glitched out on him for an entirely different reason. Tenderness was foreign to this woman. Hell, she probably craved it so badly it frightened her.

"Don't move." This time Jake lifted his hand slowly. His palm slid against her cheek, cupping her face. "Just...don't move."

She didn't, and he took that as a good sign, like a skittish creature learning the world could offer kindness. She trusted him not to hurt her, not to take advantage of her, and to approach his every move thoughtfully. Deliberately.

Jake cupped her neck, just under her ear. Dulcina's short hair shifted as his fingers delved underneath, satisfying his need to maintain contact with the warmth of her skin. Jake moved at a leisurely pace, proving with every touch she had the freedom to escape. She didn't. Pulling her to him wasn't an option, not now, so little by little Jake closed the distance between them until his lips settled over hers with a firm pressure that wasn't assertive or even soft. This kiss was steadfast and sure, a promise of everything he could be for her. When she made no move to reciprocate, he pulled back, only to see she was stuck like a deer in the headlights. Stunned to the point she wasn't moving or speaking.

Undeterred, Jake came back for seconds, and this time he lingered. His lips sweetly teased hers with sweeping caresses and measured nips, until hers parted slightly. He pulled back just enough to break contact, hovering close without touching her, waiting. Dulcie hesitated only a moment before she replicated his actions, teasing until he joined in, creating a sensual give and take.

A heavy fist pounded on the door, and they both startled at the intrusion, but he wasn't willing to release his hold on her. She ignored the door as well, pressing in closer to him, her fingers curling around his biceps in a way that did all sorts of things to his ego. A second knock filled the room, louder and more impatient. She finally broke away from the kiss but made no other move to untangle herself from him.

"What?" Dulcina snapped toward the door, the hardened edge of her voice shifting to a gasp as Jake nuzzled her cheek.

"He wants to talk. Now," the familiar voice of the bartender demanded from the other side.

"Be right there," she called, just muffling a moan as Jake planted teasing kisses below her ear. Dulcina's fingers curled into his shirt and tugged him tight against her.

Jake didn't give in to her wordless insistence for more kisses and instead pulled back, a grin spread broad across his face.

"That, Darlin', was mutual. Which is why it was so damn good." Jake took a step back and hiked a thumb over his shoulder. "Best get going."

"Mutual," she said in an odd, deadpan tone as she eyed him warily. "So you can just shut it off?"

"Off?" Jake laughed. "Hell, no. Just barely under control. You've had me at a simmer since you let me rub your feet."

Her lip curled in revulsion, but then she seemed to truly ponder his words. "Seriously?"

He nodded, small smile turning up the corners of his lips. "That was big for you, giving me a pinch of control. I know you measured out all the scenarios in your head and made damn certain I couldn't somehow use the situation to hurt you, but you still let me put my hands on you. Sexy."

"I almost shoved you off the bed and made you sleep on the floor," she said, her eyebrow raised in challenge.

"Yeah, but you didn't." He grinned, feeling free enough for the first time in a long damn while to let the truth spill from his mouth. "You wanted me there, my hands on you."

She eyed him like he was a snake ready to strike, but she didn't back away. "Are you still angry?"

"Yeah. I am," he said, a serious statement, but his voice was laced with desire that refused to fully let go.

"When we come back we'll..." Her voice trailed off, clearly all jumbled up in the logistics of a relationship.

"Figure it out," he finished her sentence. No hesitation.

She tilted her chin up, a little show of courage.

Jake went straight for the door, but when he glanced back, Dulcie still stood in the middle of the room, her gaze a touch unfocused. He grabbed the handle, the twist of metal on metal drawing her full attention to him.

"After you, Sugar," he said, pulling the door open for her, making it abundantly clear he was following her lead.

Matter of fact, he'd follow this woman about anywhere. Fiery. Gorgeous. She may not have left the room as confidently as normal—he hoped because she'd been shaken by their kiss—but her steps were sure. The farther she moved down the hallway, the stronger her strides became, like she was walking into a confrontation and she would damn well prepare for a fight. That right there was the sexiest thing he'd ever seen.

Dulcina led him into the bar. It was all closed down, probably for the daylight hours. Everything was quiet, minimal lights, and no sounds other than some soft shuffling from behind the bar. In fact, he wasn't quite sure where they were headed until she led him to a corner booth where Ruskin sat, arms spread wide over the back padded cushion like he... Well, he did own the place.

"I've never seen you outside the cage," Dulcina said as she slid into the seat, leaving enough room for Jake to slide in beside her.

"Is that so?" Ruskin asked, a twitch of his eyebrow hinting that there was something more to this exchange. "We're lying now?"

Dulcina refused to acknowledge his statement. She pulled a slip of paper from her pocket and handed it to him. This was the information Jake had written down for her earlier. The fugitive's name, airport where he'd landed, and last known location.

Ruskin didn't glance down at the paper. Instead, he continued to stare at Dulcina, studying her face like he was searching for clues. He found them when his gaze shifted to Jake's neck. Ruskin's brow lifted. Good.

Smug as all get out, Jake let his grin curl the left corner of his lips. Well now, maybe he wasn't as mad at Dulcie as he'd thought. He'd known the mark on his neck was healing rapidly and he hadn't thought much about it, but that bite gave Ruskin clear evidence of what had happened between them behind the closed door.

Ruskin turned to her and shook his head, still not seeming to understand her choice. "We could have done this the easy way, love. The pleasurable way."

"No," she said, casting a quick sideways look at Jake. "We could not."

Well, hot damn. That sounded like a whole love letter to Jake's ears.

"You've chosen a mere human over your most devoted lover?" Ruskin sighed, hand over his heart. "My pride is thoroughly bruised."

"Devoted?" she questioned sharply.

"Most eager. Available?" When Dulcina's expression remained impassable, Ruskin laughed in defeat and waved his hand dismissively at her. "Fine then. Stay another day. My treat. Tomorrow I will provide your answers."

"Tomorrow?" she asked, all fired up at the change of plans. "Gage said you wanted to talk."

"Not really. We both know how aggressive you can be when fighting, tumbling in the sheets, and drinking your fill," Ruskin said with a sly grin, and before she could protest, he pushed on in that weird curling accent of his. "You didn't let it loose on me, so... I had to make sure the human still lived."

The glare she sent him would shatter windows. Piercing. "Walk that back."

"Apologies. Not for a second would I believe you would harm the human *intentionally*," Ruskin said, hands in the air in mock surrender. "You understand, I had to know for certain. Can't have a drained body decaying in my establishment. Give me time to gather information. We'll talk tomorrow."

"Agreed," she said smoothly.

Ruskin smiled, then stood and headed for the bar without a backward glance. Jake had no idea how a man could gather enough information in one day to be any help, but he seemed to think he could, which meant waiting it out was definitely worth a shot.

"Cocky son-of-a-bitch," Jake grumbled. "What's the accent? Is he Russian?"

"No..." Dulcina said, truly seeming to process his question. "Not Russian. Not Romanian...but something close."

"You trust him?"

She looked over to where Ruskin talked quietly with Gage, then tipped her chin up. "Not at all."

Chapter 17

PARIS

Jake left the underground, no name bar, just a step behind Dulcina, though once on the sidewalk they fell into sync. They'd spent the day hunkered down together, just talking and resting. Well, he rested. Dulcie would fidget and pace, then plunk down next to him, only to get up and fall prey to her restlessness again.

He hadn't expected her to stay, not when she seemed to know all three men who seemed to both work and live here, but she never left him. Maybe because she wanted to be with him, and maybe because she didn't trust any of them. Hard telling where her mind was most of the time.

This woman had done the impossible. Through her rather aggressive contact, she'd secured a last known location on Tulio. It was on them to verify the information, but if he was still hanging around, they could keep tabs on him long enough to pinpoint when he boarded a plane bound for the States. Then, all Jake had to do was report the destination to the proper authorities. Nothing different than his job. Former job. Shoot.

Jake scrubbed his hand over his scruffy face and jerked his brain down a different road. He tapped Dulcie on her shoulder, drawing her attention. "You trust that Ruskin fella's information?"

"I do. For a man who never leaves his bar, you'd be surprised at how far his reach extends. Information is his main source of income," she said, glancing over at him as she spoke, but never fully taking her eyes off the path before them.

"Clever diversion. He's masquerading as the damn entertainment. Everyone probably assumes Gage owns it all. Keeps the focus off him." Jake laughed, his short outburst drawing her irritated glare. "Heck, half the info they catch probably comes straight from Gage. Bartenders get all the local gossip, and good old Ruskin is just raking in the profits."

"I assume so," she said, but was no longer invested in this conversation.

Her hand smoothly dropped to the Bowie knife on her hip. Jake's gaze locked on her knife, still holstered, but now unstrapped. "Rough neighborhood?"

Dulcie paused, turned, and chucked him under the chin. "Not for me. Now go on ahead. You know the way home."

"Funny," he said, her dig at his attempted escape not going unnoticed. She was right, of course. He absolutely did know the way back, and Dulcie let him take the lead.

They walked for a stretch, crossing several intersecting streets. Jake didn't know where he was in relation to...well, anything else in town, but as he caught little landmarks he knew he was on the right path.

One eye on his surroundings and the other constantly catching Dulcie in his peripheral, he kept them on the move, setting a steady pace. He thought, after putting a healthy distance between them and the bar, Dulcie would stretch those beautiful legs and walk at his side, but she hadn't closed the gap. He would like to think she was mooning over their kiss, but when he turned and got a good look at her, he noticed she hadn't come any closer to him.

Jake stopped in the middle of the sidewalk, waiting for her to catch up. Side by side once again, he asked, "Why you hanging back?"

"Gives demons the impression I'm an easy target," she said simply.

"Oh," Jake said, not knowing how else to respond. She made herself bait? Expected an attack in the streets? Right out here in the open and at his back where he couldn't see the fight coming? "You're drawing them out?"

"Yes. If any are around." She sighed, as if speaking again was the greatest annoyance she'd had to suffer through. "And I suppose, if I'm being honest, I rather enjoy watching you walk."

"Yeah, well, just don't trip over something while you're staring at my ass. I'm gonna get movin' and you try to keep up. Our show's gonna be on soon, and I don't want to miss it." Jake turned, walking with a bit more swagger in his step.

Dulcie laughed. Outright laughed. "You have no worldly idea what is happening in that show. You couldn't form a sentence in French to save your life."

"No, but I get the gist of it, and I don't want to fall behind," he said over his shoulder, never slowing. "Hustle, woman."

Maybe it was dumb, but he kinda did want to watch the show with her. She was right. He didn't have a blessed clue about the plot, and sure, he could guess some of what was intended by context, but what made it enjoyable was that Dulcie would be sitting right there with him. She might ignore him like usual, but sometimes she let out a little huff of a laugh, and he relished witnessing her armor crack open just a fraction. Hell, maybe she'd let him sit right up next to her instead of against the headboard. Didn't hurt to try.

"Hey, Dulcie. How 'bout when we get back—" A short, muffled yelp sounded from behind him. It was not Dulcie's voice, but when he whipped around, she was gone. Jake saw nothing, heard nothing. The dimly lit street behind him was empty. Someone had taken her.

Adrenaline catapulting him into high alert, Jake scanned the street for possible exit routes. He hadn't heard any doors, or vehicles, so that left alleyways. Unless someone could do that vampire-vanishing thing and grab her. Jake shook his head hard. Nope, he had to focus on what he could work with, and not the wild possibilities he didn't understand. Reality-based. That's all he had right now, and Jake backtracked, retracing their path. The first alley was clear. Well lit and quiet. The next alley split the facade of the decorative building fronts.

Dulcie had been prepared, had known there might be an attack, and still she let them take her? She fought these things all the damn time, right? At least that's what she said. So how had they caught her unaware? And how the hell was he supposed to handle a demon if she couldn't?

Jake slipped into the alley, moving as quickly and quietly as his busted, out-of-shape body would allow. If Dulcie was down here, then she'd been pulled deeper into the darkness. His trained eye caught no sign of movement, heard no scuffles, and found nothing to indicate she'd been taken into that gaping maw of blackness ahead. He was going in anyway.

A muffled slide of shoes on pavement echoed off the buildings surrounding him. He was on the right path. Jake surged forward, only to stop two steps into the darkness. It was damn near impossible to get his bearings. If he wanted to do more than walk face first into a wall, he'd have to wait until his eyes adjusted.

Mere moments passed, but it felt like an eternity. Nothing moved, making it impossible to separate the vague outlines of shadows in the alleyway.

An overly feminine whimper sounded from just ahead. For a flash of a second, he panicked, but something was off. He couldn't bring himself to believe it was Dulcie. The voice was too wispy, too helpless. Was she pretending? Maybe. Maybe not.

Jake moved forward slow enough to secure each step in the dimly lit terrain ranging from a sepia glow in the center, to barely visible objects around the edges of the alley.

A blast of chilled air hit him in the face and he pulled up short. Suddenly, a solid wall of a man stood before him, and Jake took a couple of steps back. Toothpick hanging from between his thin lips, this guy was intimidating on a whole different level.

Big guy flashed a set of misshapen, pointed teeth in a crooked grin. Was he vampire? Funny thing was, he kind of hoped so.

"Best let 'em be," the man's bass voice matched his size. "You hear?"

The hell he would. He wasn't leaving Dulcie to fend for herself. Jake stepped around him only to be blocked again.

"They'll be just a tick. Why don't you come with me?" The man's eyes flashed red when he spoke this time. Nope, not vampire. The other kind. Demon.

"Nah, I'm good," Jake asserted more confidently than he felt. The demon advanced, closing the already short distance between them. "Hey, big fella. No means no."

With his side still tender, and his whole core stability questionable, his options were limited. Surprise and disorientation were key. Arm tucked at his side to guard his ribs, Jake fought dirty. The heel of his palm shot up without warning, catching the demon in the nose. Jake felt the crack of bone against his hand, confirmation of a broken nose. Grabbing the guy's shaggy blond hair, Jake held him steady and brought his knee up to the man's groin. As any man of any species would, the red-eyed demon toppled to the ground. Jake stepped over him, on the move and desperate to find Dulcie before she was hurt.

"Jake," Dulcie snapped, and the sound of his name on her lips jerked his body to a cold, hard stop. He couldn't see her. "Remember your promise."

Stunned at the harsh directive in her tone, he remained rooted in place. Though he was pleased to realize whatever was happening in the dark, she was not harmed, he also recognized she was right. He promised not to interfere no matter what happened. The only thing he was allowed to do was run, but only if she said so. These were the terms. He wanted so badly to jump in, to help, to prove to her he was worth keeping around, as a man and partner. Still...something deep inside his skull screamed: *trust her*.

He remained motionless, listening intently to the sounds around him. The man on the ground behind him groaned in pain. Up ahead in the darkness, that soft murmur of distress had changed drastically. Now sensual, feminine gasps and sighs played off a very masculine groan of pure indulgent pleasure. The combination explicit enough to heat Jake's cheeks.

Being here for such an intimate moment made him want to avert his gaze, even though he couldn't actually see anything. The girl vocalizing her enjoyment of whatever the heck was happening, was not his Dulcie, that was for sure. Too innocent and sweet. What he didn't quite understand, was why Dulcie was hanging around to listen to this. Or was something else going on?

The stillness of the night was frequently punctuated with pleased sighs and savoring moans, telling the tale of their mutual and full enjoyment of one another. Eventually, the night quieted once again.

At last, he recognized the silhouetted outline of Dulcie walking toward him. He reached out to her, asking softly, "You okay?"

"Damn it, Jake. You were supposed to stay put," Dulcina snarled at him, smacking his hand away. "Why did you follow me?"

"What do ya mean? You disappeared. I'm sick of everyone dying on me!" Jake snapped back, adrenaline still coursing through his veins. "You're all I got, and I'm not losing you too!"

She looked at him with a wide-eyed shock he hadn't expected. That was fair. He'd just unloaded a hell of a lot on her. She didn't seem to know what to say, how to respond. For half a second, he thought she was going to say something, admit she hadn't fully prepared him for what was going to happen up here, or even acknowledge there was mutual care and concern happening here between them.

Instead, Dulcie shouldered her way past him to...check on the fallen demon? She crouched down, turning his head to inspect the damage, but once he groaned in protest, she stood and ignored him.

Dulcie smoothly wiped her hand on her pants. "No one took me. Demons like that alleyway. I only checked it. One was feeding. They weren't going to harm me, and unless they showed signs of harming the human, I had no intention of engaging."

"Monitoring their habits?" His head was spinning with all this new information.

"This is what I do, and you could have gotten us both killed. The demon lives, and for that, we should be thankful."

"If that demon attacked her, he could have attacked you!"

"He didn't attack anyone, and he certainly wouldn't have tried with me. Demons know better than to pin a vampire down for sustenance. That sweet little human was his meal choice for the night. End of story. We have one human dazed, practically sedated, and full of lustful dreams. One demon, blood-sated and riding out the remnants of his euphoric feeding." She pointed to the demon rolling on the ground, and sighed in disappointment at the scene before her. "And their protector all busted up and rolling on the ground."

"Protector?"

She nodded. "We used to think demons hunted in packs, but they're usually in pairs. One feeds, the other ensures the female's safety and protects his friend who remains vulnerable for a period of time after the feeding."

"You're okay with them drinking from a random human on the streets?"

"Everyone feeds, Jake. You. Me. These demons. Our sustenance may vary, but the need is universal." When he continued to give her a look of sheer disbelief, Dulcie merely planted her hands on her hips and shrugged. "I've taken an unsuspecting man or two into an alley to feed from him. It's how I survive."

Jake remembered vividly the bite she'd taken from him, the roiling desire shaking his body to life, and then nothing. Blissful blackness and wild erotic dreams. But Dulcie? The thought of her alone and vulnerable in an alley somewhere didn't sit right with him.

"When you feed," he said, the words coming out slow, and a little more hurt than he'd intended. Jake cleared his throat, trying to block the image of her sinking those pretty teeth into another man's neck. "Do you have protection?"

Dulcie smiled, tight-lipped, but gave him nothing more. Instead of answering, she pointed to the ground. "Now that you've incapacitated his protector, I'll have to stay and take over. Do his job."

"His job?"

Jake ruffled his fingers through his hair, frustrated and confused. "I need a drink."

She snorted. "Well, I'm not giving you one. If this is how you act sober, I can't imagine— Move!"

Dulcie shoved him hard, pushing him toward the wall. The demon he'd temporarily grounded had made it to his feet and lunged for him, but Dulcie got in the way, shoved him backward and took the hit full on. They scuffled for a bit, twisting and struggling for the upper hand. Jake stayed out of the way this time, harshly reminding himself that he didn't know the rules to the game.

The big man had a knife clenched in his fist and was pushing past Dulcie as he tried to get to Jake, his red eyes flaring like he was in a craze.

"Back off, Cooper!" Dulcie gritted through clenched teeth. "It's me!"

The big man slowed his momentum to a full stop, and stepped back, blinking hard and shaking his head like he was clearing some kind of fog from his mind.

"D? What are you..." He scratched the back of his head, looking between her and Jake. Cooper looked down at the knife in his hand and offered it to her, palm open, knife balanced. "D, I didn't know. Didn't know he was with you. I didn't mean to hurt you, wasn't trying to..."

"I know. Just like I know it would never cross your mind," she said with a definitive nod. She took his hand, folded his fingers back around his knife. "You good, or do I need to stay?"

Cooper adjusted his stance and tipped his head down, looking at the pavement. "Nah, I'm good."

"You go on. Take care of your friend."

This woman was confusing. She'd been ready to jab a knife into the throat of a vampire in her own city, but here with demons, her supposed enemy, she was understanding and patient.

Cooper may have looked thoroughly confused, but he didn't hesitate to take her up on the free pass. He nodded, wiped the blood from his nose, and slipped off into the darkness of the alley toward his friend.

"We're leaving," she said, leading Jake from the alley.

They walked in silence. She was probably furious at him. For most of the walk home, Jake made an effort to see things from her perspective. He'd messed up her mission. Whatever it was, and however her world worked, he'd gotten in the way. She had every right to be pissed.

He'd seen all sorts of reactions and emotions from her in their short time together, but he'd never seen her pissed. There was no way to guess how upset his interference had made her, and how long she'd stay mad. Which was not unlike any other woman he encountered in his life. The difference was, this woman had the burden of an entire species resting on her shoulders. And a really big knife.

Jake was...well, he was processing. This was a lot to take in, and because of his limited knowledge about the species and their society in general, he was trying to reserve his judgment, but it was hard. Damn hard.

When they stepped into her apartment, Dulcie locked the door, switched on the lights, and headed straight for him. She checked him over, head-to-toe, front and back side.

"Your ribs?" she asked, blunt and to the point.

"Sore, but fine."

"You're bleeding." Dulcina shoved him backward until he sat on the edge of her bed. She left him there, headed into the bathroom to rummage around.

Jake was feeling off, not really lightheaded, but displaced. A little out of body. Probably because of the adrenaline. It did things to a person. Made you keep fighting when normally you'd be crying for your mama. Hell, he hadn't realized he'd been injured until she'd pointed it out. The demon must have come close enough to snag the back of his arm with his knife.

She emerged with a tincture in a small brown bottle, and a large bandage. Jake reached out, snagged her hand and turned it palm down. An angry red stripe marred the top of her forearm. "You're bleeding, too."

She glanced down where blood welled. Instead of washing the cut, patching herself, or even ignoring the injury, she licked it. Twice. The skin...stopped bleeding and knit together, a thin and nearly transparent layer of skin forming. She'd sealed the wound. No gap in the flesh and only a somewhat angry welt left behind. Then, she carried on as if the entire event of being injured held no meaning to her. No anger, no irritation, no pain. The cut was there, then it wasn't.

"So you magically heal and I get a Band-Aid?" Jake pointed at her hand, disgruntled, and honestly dismayed by her bizarre healing abilities. She had to have done the same thing to his neck, he just hadn't seen it happen.

She said nothing, concentrating instead on dabbing his wound with warm water. Twisting off the bottle cap, she squeezed several drops onto the bandage, soaking the white pad with the liquid.

She secured the bandage over his cut, and two seconds later pain zinged through the wound. "Stings like hell."

"I could have healed you, but I didn't think you'd appreciate being licked," Dulcina said, fighting a smile.

His jaw dropped slightly, half struggling to believe her, but mostly turned on at the thought. So that was the trick. She didn't just heal naturally. Something in her saliva had healing properties.

Jake cracked a grin. "You're wrong there, Sugar. I would be most appreciative of your tongue on me."

She wrinkled her nose at him. "I think I'll pass until after you've showered."

"Ouch. Point taken, though." He watched in silence as she finished gathering the Band-Aid wrapper, her nimble fingers tucking the pieces together. Who patched her when she was really busted up from a fight? "You know, I'm slowly coming to terms with what you are, what you do, but, Sugar... I don't like that you're alone out there. Why don't you have a partner, or a friend with you?"

She shrugged. "If I get into a bad situation alone, then I die alone."

"But you're not alone anymore. I'm stuck, right? So, I'm here." The look she gave him was one of someone who had just been jarred from their own reality. Had she not admitted to herself that she now had a permanent roommate? "So what happens if you die? What if your life doesn't hinge on your strength and abilities for once and ends simply because you land in an unbalanced fight...like twenty to one?"

Her back straightened, jaw clenched, but she answered, "Then I die."

"And when you don't come back here?"

She flinched, ever so slightly, but he'd seen it. "Then you die."

"Exactly." Jake paused for a moment, then said softly, "Dulcie, I get it. I do. Your drive to stop the evil in this world lives in me, too. Deep. But fact is, you're not alone. I'm here."

"What are you going to do? Fight with me?"

"Why the hell not?"

Everything about her became stone cold and tense. "No."

Jake leaned back, testing out his bandaged arm. "Listen, give me the layout, the rules, and a weapon. Once I'm fully healed, I'm good to go. I'll do this with you."

"For how long? A month? A year?" She shook her head slowly. "This is my life, Jake. It's not what I do, it's who I am."

"Ditto." Jake stood, having no interest in backing down.

Dulcie just looked at him with the most resolute, hurt stare he'd ever seen on a woman. Why did it feel like he'd just kicked her in the gut for wanting to stand at her side? Or was this something else? Not him, but something beyond his control. Something spurred her fear to have someone standing at her side, in her life, having her back.

"What did he do to you?" Jake asked.

"He?" Dulcina asked, brows drawn in confusion.

"Yeah, *he*. The man you think of when you shut down and shut me out. Who put that fear in you? What did *he* do to you?"

Her eyebrow twitched, then softly, she answered, "He shattered my ability to trust."

Jake opened his mouth to ask who, but she spun on her heel and left, walked right out of her home and into the hall. The slam of that door following her departure reverberated through him.

Scrubbing a hand over his hair, Jake stayed put, determined to give an emotionally vulnerable woman her space. She hadn't produced details, but he'd caught the vital bits. Someone close to her had hurt her pretty bad. Whatever had happened probably set her goals and fears for life.

For a woman who guarded herself so closely, and still allowed this ol' country boy to wiggle his way into her life, well, it gave him hope. Hope of change, maybe for both of them.

Chapter 18

PARIS

Stubborn. Driven. He was just like her. Dulcina knew exactly what it would do to Jake if he was forced to sit on the sidelines and watch the fight happen around him. She'd been in that same position. Dying inside to protect those who couldn't protect themselves, desperately craving that moment she was allowed to set things right in the world.

Jake wanted to fight alongside her. Of course he did. Wouldn't that just solve so many problems? She wouldn't have to worry he would escape while she was gone. Except he was a human, a risk to himself, and to her.

Ruffling her wild, short curls, Dulcina aimlessly wandered through her building. With a need to simply clear her cluttered mind, she walked a familiar loop through the hallways that would eventually bring her back home.

If she were being brutally honest with herself, she should have left Jake behind in Balinese. She hadn't because…well, the idea of being apart from him was even more grating than his presence.

She liked him, she did, which was exactly what made this difficult. As a human, he was vulnerable, his life more fragile than hers. Dulcina had seen vampires die under a demon's blade time and again. Not just any average vampire, but trained and conditioned Guardians. Their lives over in the blink of an eye. Her eye.

She'd witnessed so much death at an incredibly young age. Dulcina had watched her father fall under a demon's blade, had seen the moment the spark of life left his eyes, and all while she'd been draped over a demon's shoulder as it carted her from the city. Helpless.

The demon had never stopped, carrying her past the spot where Lord Navarre had been sprawled on the floor of the chateau, blood pooled beneath his shoulders as he lay still as death. In the great hall, as she was taken from everything she'd ever known, she'd seen a pair of feet peeking from the shadows, heard ragged breathing. The Gatekeeper, Steffen, lay dying. Three of the strongest protectors of her life and her city, taken down in one night.

She hadn't known at the time, but Lord Navarre had barely survived, and would linger in a healing sleep for years. Steffen had been brutally incapacitated, and though he lived, he was forever changed. Her father had not been so lucky.

If men such as the lord, decorated Guardians, and the Gatekeeper were taken down so easily, she'd lose Jake in one night. One fight. She'd become blessedly numb to the natural order of life and death in the years since the attack, but something about Jake's life being completely in her hands made her overly cautious.

Even if Jake were capable, his species more resilient, she couldn't bring herself to trust him with her life. As a rule, she didn't trust anyone.

Dulcina paused, hands on her head, and stared at the striped burgundy wallpaper. Trust was possible. She'd done it before. Once. Nico had been her only exception. Years ago she'd returned to Balinese, chasing a rumor of Captain Savard's return. Before she'd even opened the door to the training room, she'd known her fated mate was one of the men inside. Though her first instinct had been to bolt, curiosity won. Without a single doubt, she'd known her fated mate was none other than the barbarian recluse, Nicolai Moretti.

Until that night, the man had lived only in whispered tales of his outrageous and savage tenacity. His reputation hadn't swayed her in the slightest. She'd trusted in the driving need of a fated mate to protect his other half above all else, and so she'd boldly encouraged Nico's untamed and lustful side to life, and it surfaced with a vengeance.

Their meeting of pure chance, the joining of fated mates, had soothed both their turbulent souls. Since that night, Nico no longer possessed any lingering urges to walk into the sun's lethal glow. And Dulcina? Her driving anger had mellowed, she'd left behind her need to execute every demon she encountered, and decided to trust the man and the path fate had placed before her.

Nico must have recognized their connection as well, but to his credit, he never pushed her for more. Never begged her to stay, to marry. He'd given her freedom, and because of that, she'd returned to him often.

Dulcina laughed. Her fated mate had given her the ability to trust again, to live in the moment without a weapon in her hand, to allow another to watch her back. In turn, she'd coaxed Nico to recognize the man he was at his core, showed him there was no need to fear unleashing his true self. They'd given each other a form a freedom they'd never had before, lessons they wouldn't have been able to grasp with any other, and it was clear why the fates had matched them.

But fate was only half the equation. Dulcina had never felt the need to simply be in Nico's presence the way she did with Jake. Half the reason she antagonized Jake so much was to draw a reaction from him. It was a test, but for herself. No matter what he did or said, she remained perfectly at ease and in enjoyment of his company. Was that not the work of fate as well? She'd had many opportunities to collect a human, save a handsome man from a demon encounter, but never had. Why this one? Fate had thrown him in her path. Repeatedly.

Something about Jake just fit. She'd never been more comfortable around a person in her life. She talked to him. Listened to him. His voice settled her restlessness. She'd always imagined being tethered to a man would make for the most miserable existence. Men had always been leery of her quick temper, unsettled by her innate ability to vanish on a breath, and then there was the matter of her Bowie.

Jake wasn't intimidated. He'd been a little confused at first by her shift into Spirit, but had adapted swifter than some vampires to her effortless ability. He challenged her flares of irritation with teasing. And her knife? It was a tool she needed and used, and Jake had never asked her to leave it at home.

Home. Jake was alone, in her home, and...untied. She'd left him loose. Damn! This was becoming a problem. He'd become such a familiar presence she hadn't given a second thought to walking out without him. She hadn't been gone long, truly wasn't far from her home, but he was clever.

Dulcina headed home, looking for Jake as she moved. He wanted to leave, had tried it before, and now that he'd gained the information he needed, there was no reason for him to stay. Except he'd promised. Jake had promised not to leave, to see this out with her, to follow her directive. She believed him, but years of ingrained mistrust made her doubt.

Dulcina moved faster, hustling through her building. She wasn't thinking straight, afraid he'd already left, even hoped to pass him along the way back. Nothing. She burst through her apartment door. The door closed at her back, she took two steps in and scanned her small home. Empty.

"Jake?" she called, but he didn't answer. He wasn't here. She would have to search the building first, then the surrounding streets. Dulcina turned on her heel, headed back out.

A solid arm hooked around her waist, jerking her momentum to a halt before she could touch the doorknob. Relief instantly bloomed inside her, and she sagged back against him. He hadn't left her.

The cold, sharp edge of a blade pressed against her throat and Dulcina instantly went still. For the first time since she'd come to live above ground, terror slithered through her veins. His fingers bit into her side, inflicting more pain than the knife at her throat.

Everything inside her just...shut off. Like someone flipped a switch and she'd powered down. Her memories lashed at her mind with a vengeance. She'd had a knife at her throat once before, held by a man everyone trusted, and all she could do was wait for the moment he would slice her vein and leave her to bleed out. How had she not seen this coming? Of course Jake would try and turn the tables, to escape. This was why humans were not kept above. Jake had made her promises, they'd made plans together, and now he was going to kill her.

"Why?" Dulcina asked, her voice flat, no emotion bleeding through on account of her broken heart.

"I need answers," the man snarled in her ear. This was *not* Jake.

If it was not Jake holding a knife to her throat, then who? She felt it then, in a rush of recognition. The man behind her was taller than Jake, though not by much. The similarly hard planes of this man's body were unfamiliar, and the touch of his hands uncaring. Had she not been so frantic in fearing Jake had run, and in turn hurt by what she assumed was his betrayal, she would have recognized the difference instantly.

Her thoughts came in a rapid, disjointed stream, her instincts struggled to surface. With just enough of a distraction, and the right amount of leverage, she could extract herself from his grip. Probably not without injury, but she'd make it work. Dulcina forced herself to relax, not willing to give away her preparation with tension-coiled muscles, and the plan was simple. Kill the demon. Find Jake.

"What do you need to know?" she asked.

"Where is Jericho?"

"Jericho?" A demon was questioning her about a demon city? This made no sense, and was the last thing she'd expected to hear from a demon's mouth. She'd thought every demon knew the location of Jericho, leaving only vampires in the dark about the location. Her Bowie knife was across the room on her dresser and her best bet was to stall for time. "I've never found the city."

"You must know something." The demon squeezed her tighter, his frantic aggression becoming more concerning by the second. Frantic equaled unpredictable. She needed a new plan. Give false information, distract the demon, then kill him.

"Hey, sweetheart?" Jake called from the bathroom, that twangy voice echoing off the tile walls as he came through the door. "We're either gonna need more towels, or I gotta do some laundry."

He was still here? Jake stepped fully into view, a towel in his hand and a toothbrush hanging from his mouth. At the sight of her, he froze in place, careful not to make any sudden moves. The man behind Dulcina tightened his grip on the blade, twisting it against her skin.

This was bad. Jake had no escape route. He was backed up to the bathroom. No windows, no way out. So her plan altered again. Protect Jake. Kill the demon.

"Whatcha lookin' for, man?" Jake asked around the toothbrush in his mouth, leaning heavily against the door frame like this entire ordeal bored him. "Can't speak for the lady, but I don't have any money."

Lady? Jake wouldn't refer to her as a lady, and he'd certainly never called her sweetheart. Jake was up to something. Whatever he was about to do, he was doing from where he stood. Impassive. Leaning against the wall. Instantly she realized his plan. Resting against the door was not laziness, but a tool to steady his damaged body. The towel in his hand? Jake had his gun.

"I don't want your money. I want Jericho! Stalkers know all the cities, above and below ground. She will give up Jericho, or I'll take her blood," the man said against her ear, sending a revolting shudder down her spine.

"See now," Jake said, his solemn tone nearly lost by the toothbrush bobbing between his lips as he spoke. "You're not getting any part of her."

"I already have her," the demon said, the blade pressing deeper against the soft skin at her throat.

"No, man, you don't. She's mine."

Jake moved, and the second he did, Dulcina swiftly reacted. Turning her head away from the knife, and pressing her cheek against the demon's shoulder, she left her throat fully exposed, but it gave Jake a broader target. A split second later a gunshot sounded.

Dulcina flinched, fighting the urge to pull from the demon's weakening grasp. When he dropped to the floor at her feet, she opened her eyes to see Jake's gun raised and steady, the towel askew on his arm.

Jake spit his toothbrush from his mouth and jogged over to the fallen demon, checking his shot. The demon had caught the bullet between the eyes, or at least close enough to make the claim.

"I took my gun back. Don't be mad. I heard someone come in, and I tell you what, he sure didn't walk like you, Sugar," Jake said while checking the demon for any other weapons.

She just blinked. Dulcina always controlled the situation, made the kill, saved her own ass. She'd never had anyone to count on, until now. Jake had been calm and collected, his frighteningly accurate shot a testament to his abilities.

"Probably gonna need to invest in a silencer," Jake said with a sheepish grin. He glanced up at her, and whatever he saw flipped his tone, and he softly said, "Dulcie? Honey, you good? You hurt?"

When she didn't answer immediately, he closed the distance between them, enfolding her in his arms.

The vibrations of the gunshot seemed to repeatedly rock through her, skewing the surety in her voice, but she answered, "I'm fine."

Jake kissed her temple, whispered into her hair. "Don't you ever scare me like that again."

Her jaw dropped. "Me? What about you? I thought you'd run off again! I thought I'd turned my back, and—"

"Nah. Wouldn't do that to you. I promised I wouldn't." Jake skimmed his thumb across the underside of her bottom lip, the motion gentle. "Just wanted a shower. And my gun."

"I didn't fight him at first, because..." She looked down at the dead demon, and her words slipped out in a whisper. "I thought it was you, at my back, knife to my throat."

Jake sucked in a breath, and before she could look up at him, he tugged her against his chest and locked both arms tightly around her in the most genuine and secure hug she'd had in her life. "Never. You hear me? *Never.*"

His voice was raw against her ear. Because she had assumed it was him? Or was he merely worried for her safety? He must have been at least a little worried, because she'd never been so completely engulfed by an embrace. With one of his arms around her shoulders, and the other tight around her waist, she was thoroughly clasped against him and it was...lovely.

Dulcina melted into him, and not just from shock, or because he felt damn good all firm and warm. Trapped in his arms, all movement hindered, she found herself in awe of how easily she gave up the urge to hold a weapon should there be a need to turn and fight. As Jake held her, he faced the door, and she willingly allowed him to watch her back. He'd just proved he would.

"Sugar, as much as I would love to stand here all night and hold you," Jake said, giving her one more squeeze before pulling away, "someone was bound to hear that gunshot, and we've got a body to take care of."

A smile twitched at the corners of her lips, amused by his practicality. He was right, of course, and she pulled her phone from her pocket and dialed.

"*Dulcie,*" Jake said, drawing out her name in a very cautionary way. "Who ya callin'?"

The line connected and from the other end Geoff answered, "Yeah?"

"One body," she said evenly.

"Location?"

She glanced at Jake and his brow furrowed with worry as he watched her intently. "My place."

"Holy mother of... Are you kidding me? Are you... Damn it, D, are you jetting?"

"I'll be gone. And Geoff, there is not much mess, but there was a considerable amount of noise."

"Christ. I'm on it. Just go. You get safe," Geoff ordered and hung up.

Jake crossed his arms. "The body guy?"

"He's more than that, but yes. Pack your bag."

"And this?" Jake asked, holding out his gun.

She wasn't sure if he was asking if she wanted to take it back or if they needed to ditch it but neither was going to happen. "Keep it within reach."

Jake's eyebrow popped up in surprise but then he nodded, seeming to catch the severity of their situation. The next few moments were a swift mission to gather their things. Jake had already been living out of a duffel bag, meaning he did little more than snag his discarded clothes from his recent shower.

Dulcina was always ready to leave at a moment's notice. She pulled out her packed bag, and strapped her Bowie onto her hip.

Together they wiped down anything either of them might have touched, and once again Dulcina was thankful her apartment was small. Doorknobs, faucet handles, and bathroom mirror cabinet topped the list for her, and Jake caught anything else he remembered touching.

Geoff appeared out of thin air inside her home near her front door, falling out of his Spirit form, his big army boots thumping her floorboards as he touched down. Jake reached for his gun, but she threw her hand out to stop him.

"Authorities are in your hall. You're not going out the front door," Geoff said, the tight curls of his long hair moving against his neck as he shook his head. "Northeast corner. You ready?"

Dulcina nodded sharply and, as Geoff squatted down and took hold of the dead man, she sucked in a deep breath and locked her arms tight around Jake.

"Hey, now," he yelped, and a second later they vanished.

Spirit was simple when she only had her own body to contend with, but hauling another, somewhat unwilling entity, was a trial. His Spirit weighed her down, and constantly threatened to pull them both from the protective shelter of invisibility.

Just inside the alley by the northeast corner of her building, she dropped them both from Spirit. Jake stumbled, his bag falling off his shoulder, and braced his back against the brick wall as he dry-heaved. Not surprising. Traveling in Spirit was rough, especially with no prior experience. Taking him with her while he was conscious had not been easy, and for the first time in many years, she was feeling the effects. Her vision wavered and her stomach roiled.

Head hung, Jake said, "I don't want to do that again."

"Next time I'll leave you behind," she said, still trying to catch her breath.

"Liar." He glanced up at her and grinned. Damn it, that smile of his was contagious, and she found herself smiling back. He was absolutely right.

A heavy, muffled thump drew their attention to the faded blue van parked in the alleyway. The vehicle rocked with no visible reason.

"What the hell was that?" Jake asked.

"This is Geoff's van. He collected the body, dropped it inside. He'll be heading straight back to clean up the blood. We can't go yet. I need to know he made it out."

"All right," Jake said with a slow nod, and took up a position opposite the way she faced so they could watch each other's backs. She appreciated his act of pure, instinctual protector.

Moments later the van rocked again, though not as forceful. Geoff was inside now, behind the wheel. He leaned across the passenger seat and hand cranked the window down.

"You need a ride?" he offered.

"We need a hideaway for the daylight hours." Dulcina jumped in first, making a barrier between Geoff and her human. Never one to miss taking note of an odd situation, Geoff got a good, long look at Jake before throwing the van into gear. Dulcina intentionally gave Geoff something else to think about. "Are we clear?"

"Yeah. Cleaned up the floor, tossed a spare rug from my van over the wet spot. Now it just looks like you have bad taste," Geoff said with a confident wink. Sure, the man looked like a reject from an 80's hair band, but he was efficient.

"I owe you."

"Not just me. It was a close one, and you won't believe who stalled them. Our lord and sovereign himself cracked his door and had a conversation with the authorities. Threw a bit of misdirection their way. I don't think it went how he planned. Big, scary bastard like that pointing them in the opposite direction after a gunshot? They searched his place top to bottom. Probably wasn't what he had in mind, but it bought me enough time."

Well, now. There was some information she never had before. Of course she'd known the Stalker Lord was in her building, on her floor, and exactly which door he lived behind, but she never saw him. Geoff's description of the lord being a big, scary bastard made her wonder why he never took care of problems himself. But then, he had a multitude of Stalkers and his assassin to take care of business. To her knowledge, only a rare few people had ever caught a glimpse of their Stalker Lord.

"He'll keep an eye on things. If they don't find the wet spot under the rug, you could probably go back in a week. With no room pinpointed for the gunshot and no body, they'll probably give up pretty fast."

"They won't monitor the location?" Jake asked.

"No, probably not, unless people call in another gunshot," Geoff said, rounding yet another corner.

The van eased to a stop in front of a complex and Geoff threw it in park. With a stretching reach, he leaned across her, his fingers fumbling with the handle on the glove box. After a little bit of fishing among what was, in her opinion, far too many keys, he dropped a set in her hands.

Dulcina inspected them and the number stamped into the metal plate attached to the ring. Her eyebrows raised. "Third floor?"

"Yeah, well, short notice. It's the closest location, most well stocked apartment, and not much happens around here."

"Thanks again."

She clutched the keys tight in her hand, and leaned over Jake's lap to pop the door handle. When he didn't move to get out, she looked up at him.

He just sat there, grinning ear to ear. "Aw, you opened the door for me. Thanks, Darlin'."

"Shut up," she grumbled, shoving him out the door.

The van door shut and they started for the building, but suddenly Jake left her side, dashing back toward the van. Leaning through the open window, he reached across the seats, hand extended, and said, "Thanks for the save, man. Appreciate you takin' care of Dulcie and me."

Geoff hesitated for a brief moment, but met him halfway, shaking his hand. "It's what I do."

"Amen to that," he said, hitting Geoff with another smooth grin. Geoff's van rumbled off into the night as Jake made his way back to her side.

"What was that all about?"

Jake shrugged. "I always make friends with the driver."

"Geoff doesn't have friends," she said, eyes narrowed, watching him suspiciously.

"Sure he does." Jake hiked a thumb toward his chest and grinned. "Me."

"You're impossible," she said, shaking her head as she led him into the apartment complex and the elevator.

The gentle whir of the elevator gears was the only sound in that intimate space. She expected them both to simmer in silence after the night they'd just had, but Jake cleared his throat, caught her gaze, and asked, "Hey, is this safe for you? You know, above ground? Daylight?"

"It's either this or the catacombs."

He shuddered slightly. "That's a hard pass on catacombs for me."

She smiled, shaking the key at him, and said, "Then it's third floor, number seventeen."

Jake took the key, but also snagged her hand and never let go. They remained silent as the elevator door slid open. He led the way, though he didn't actually know where they were going. His uncanny sense of direction got them headed the correct way to the room. It was that intuitive instinct that had brought him to Paris and got him this far.

Pausing in front of their room, Jake surprised her by disentangling himself from her hand and motioning for her to stay back.

"What do you think you're doing?"

"Get all bent out of shape if you want, but you're staying outside that door until I check it out," he said, that oh, so serious tone surfacing and throwing an unexpected shimmy of delight down her spine.

Dulcina liked this headstrong, take-charge man. He'd always been this way. The difference between how he took over a situation and how others had in the past was he did it out of genuine concern for her, and not because he thought her incapable. She was here in the hall alone, easily able to fend off any attack, and he damn well knew it. He just had the forethought to prevent her from being trapped within a room on the third floor of an unfamiliar building.

Just a handful of seconds later, Jake waved her inside. The modest little room had a few frills, like the lace trimmed pillows on the bed and the vintage writing desk tucked tight against the wall, but otherwise was rather simple. The gem of this place was the view overlooking the city. It didn't capture the larger landmarks, but still, it was stunning. She'd been in Geoff's hideaways before, and comparatively, this one was lovely.

Dulcina opened the balcony window, taking the few short steps that brought her to the railing. Jake walked out, stood at her side. His presence felt so natural.

"I'm sorry," he said, his sincerity infused into every word. "That was your home, and I know he said you could go back, but you shouldn't."

She shrugged. "I need nothing I left behind."

Jake hooked his arm around her shoulders and pulled her to him for a side hug.

"I don't need this, you know," Dulcina said, her voice as tense as her muscles.

"I know, but I do," he said, wrapping his other arm around her, fully locking her against him. "Thought I was going to lose you."

"You're not that lucky," she teased, but when he squeezed her a little tighter, she let go of the tension in her body and melted into him. Okay, so maybe she didn't need hugs, but she needed him.

Chapter 19

PARIS

Jake woke to the dim light sneaking in beneath the curtain and streaking across the floorboards. It wasn't anywhere near the bed, but still, his first and instant reaction was to curl onto his side and protect Dulcina. That didn't happen. He couldn't move. A heavy weight pressed down on his chest, pinning him to the bed. Groggy and disoriented from sleeping more heavily than he'd expected, he lifted his head, peering down at what had him trapped.

Dulcie lay across him, head on his chest and arm draped over his belly, avoiding his damaged ribs even in sleep. A smile tugged at his lips. She could be pretty sweet when she wasn't all worked up and primed to kill something.

Everything had changed last night, and Jake wasn't naive enough to ignore that fact. It could have gone south fast, and because the brain liked to do its own thing, different scenarios flashed through his mind's eye. If he'd confronted the demon when he'd first known it was in the house, Jake might have been killed and unable to protect Dulcie. Had he lingered in that steamy, satisfying shower a tick longer, he could have come out to find Dulcie dead on the floor of her home.

A sharp pang of grief hit him hard, had his heart wrenching for a hot second. It would be like Rita all over again. He loved Rita. They'd been close as partners and friends. Their relationship could have eventually grown into a deeper love, but Rita's time was stolen. They never had a chance to see where their easy-going relationship would take them.

This thing he had with Dulcie was drastically different. Instant and easy. Together they were magic. Firecrackers. Ice cold beer by a bonfire. Slow dance in the moonlight. All the good stuff in life.

Dulcie was...well, she was special. In a weird way, he felt closer to Dulcie than he had to anyone in a hell of a lot of years. They read each other well, anticipated reactions, and both seemed naturally drawn to the other by an unseen, indescribable force.

He knew for a fact that had he struck out on his own to take care of Tulio like he'd planned, he would have landed right back on Dulcie's doorstep when he was done. Somewhere along the way he'd given his heart to her, and that was just fine. Didn't hurt a thing.

Unable to lay here any longer without touching her, Jake swept a stray curl from her face. Wrong move.

Dulcina woke like she'd been jabbed with a firebrand, already in motion, instinctively reaching for his throat. Up on her knees and hovering above him with one hand curled around his neck, her weight pressed down on his windpipe.

Years of training kicked in and Jake reacted, taking advantage of her elbow's natural weakness. Striking the inner crook, the force caused her arm to buckle. Now somewhat free, Jake took hold of her shoulders and flipped her around, pinned her back against the wood paneled headboard. He wanted to shake her, to yell, to get it through her thick head that he would never hurt her, but he was so angry the words stuck in his throat.

They stared at each other, both breathing heavy, her eyes wild. Now she knew it was him. Didn't stop her from hating that he'd turned the tables. Anger burned in her eyes, and she was fighting it, slowly coming down. Something hit the mattress with a soft thud. Something heavy.

"What the..." Jake glanced down. Her knife lay beside her knee. "Jesus, you went for the knife?"

He whipped his head up and met her gaze full on. In sleep she'd taken his gentle touch as an intruding threat, and it broke his heart. She could have accidentally gutted him, and even though she dropped the knife, he could tell the need to retaliate still burned in her.

Suddenly her eyes narrowed. Jake had a split second to prepare for her counterattack. Dulcie twisted sharply, wrenching one shoulder from his grasp, and just like that, she was back in the fight.

Dulcie flipped him onto his back. Yeah, he landed on the mattress, but the fall and twist jarred his ribs. Gritting his teeth, he growled through the pain. Though she had him flat on his back, she did nothing more than search his gaze, the look in her eyes challenging.

Keenly aware the chances of hurting her were slim to none, Jake sent her over the side of the bed. He held on, going over with her. They rolled across the floor, a mess of tangled legs and flailing arms, until she gained leverage. Dulcie threw her weight into the heels of her palms, thumping his shoulders to the wood floor.

"What are ya still fighting me for, Dulcie?" he demanded, pissed off and a little confused. Well, maybe a lot confused.

"I think I need you," she said, but her voice sounded off. Airy.

"Damn it, woman, I'm right here," he said, wanting more than anything to reach up and shake some sense into her, but she had him pinned good.

"No, I *need* you," Dulcie said with a suggestive roll of her hips.

"Oh," he said, the response automatic. A full second later, his brain caught up with her meaning, along with his body's reaction. "*Oh*."

She sat upright, easing the pressure of her palms on his shoulders. Jake took advantage. He took hold of her wrists and yanked them off him, and she landed on his chest with a huff. The impact of her weight on his tender ribs made him flinch, but he rallied quick.

Chest-to-chest, nose-to-nose, Jake dropped his voice low. "Like I said, Darlin'. I'm right here."

"Jake," she moaned his name. "Now would be good."

Now? Just...now? If that was all she could say about this whole thing bubbling between them, then nothing was going to happen. "Damn it, Dulcie, this isn't sex. Would you just let me love you?"

She went still on top of him, her breath fanning over his cheek, but she gave no response. Did she not know how to let someone take care of her, to love her?

Jake rolled them over, keeping her hands clasped above her head as he settled on top of her. Yeah, she could absolutely break his hold, do whatever she wanted with that otherworldly strength of hers, but she didn't. "Let me show you."

She made no move to deny him, so he pressed a soft kiss to her lips, then another, ignoring her attempts to make this exchange more aggressively carnal. He could absolutely go there with her in a heartbeat, but now was not the right time. Jake kept every brush of his lips sensual, soft and gentle.

"What are you doing?" she asked, breathless. Her eyes squeezed shut, her brows crunched together, like she was all kinds of confused.

He grinned against her lips and admitted his tactical approach. "Taming you."

"Jake—"

He cut off her words, derailed her train of thought with a beautifully executed kiss, then pulled away long enough to murmur against her lips, "Not completely. Just a little."

He understood her. Dulcie was always in control, and a woman like that needed someone to give her a break, encourage her to let go and enjoy herself. Trust was key, and she was giving it over to him.

Jake plied her with fleeting kisses, darted his tongue across the seam of her lips. Enough to tease and tempt, but not to intrude. He was making her go slow, giving her time to think through what she wanted, to fully immerse herself in the sensations he was kindling in her. She could easily deny him, decide she needed instant gratification rather than a dose of slow loving, but he hoped she learned to crave the slow burn.

Dulcie whimpered, waging some internal war over what she wanted versus what he was giving. A couple more drawn-out kisses and he pulled away, pressing his forehead to hers, his breathing ragged. He was addicted to her lips, her reaction to his touch. This is what his soul had been searching for all his life. This woman. This moment. Nothing had ever felt so right.

"No one's ever let me love on them before, not like I wanted to." Jake placed little nipping kisses along her jaw until he was once again hovering over her lips. "And, Sugar, I'm dead certain no one has *ever* loved you the way I do."

Dulcie gasped, her lips parting, and he took that chink in her armor to give her the slowest, most deliciously deliberate kiss. He may have shocked her with a dose of truth, but he meant every word.

He'd fallen for her, and could absolutely tumble forward full speed, dig deep and never leave her side. Didn't do anyone any good to pussyfoot around the situation or pretend, so Jake was laying all his cards on the table. Whatever happened between them after tonight was her call, but he'd voiced his stance on the matter.

A knock sounded at their door, even and insistent. Jake tensed. "You expectin' someone?"

In a daze, she scrunched her brows together and fought to come back to the here and now. "I...I ordered food."

"You takin' care of me? That's sweet," he said, a smile curving the left side of his mouth, but then his amusement fizzled away. His voice low, as if just for her ears, he said, "This isn't over."

"Promise?" she asked, all soft and vulnerable.

Jake swooped down, taking her lips in a quick, intense kiss, and then rolled off her and popped up to his feet. He gave himself a moment to take a breath and settle back into his own skin, then went for the door. Looking back was not an option. He'd either find her sprawled on the floor, forget about the door and get right back to her, or she'd be on her feet with her knife in her hand again. He grinned. Yep, those were the two options with this woman, and he kind of savored the fact that he knew there would be nothing in between.

Jake opened the door a crack, not really expecting any danger, but prepared nonetheless. The man on the other side was benign, a typical delivery kid. Nothing about him waving any red flags.

Jake took the package, then called out to Dulcie, "Hey, Darlin', you got any—"

Dulcie reached around him, handing the man some money. The man murmured a thank you and bustled back down the hall. By the time Jake had closed the door and turned around, she was already seated at the little table in front of the window. Legs crossed, leaning back on the chair and looking out the window, she waited in silence. Dulcie was different right now, lost in whatever puzzle she was working over in her head. He'd thrown her off, and she was still dealing.

She wasn't there yet. Jake could sense it in the way she distanced herself now. Afraid to take the leap. Her holding back could have stung his pride a bit, tanked his excitement, but it was only a delay. This woman was worth the wait, and he wasn't giving up.

"Do we need to ditch this room?" he asked, reverting to the practical.

"We can keep it for now." Dulcina leaned back, propped her foot onto her chair, but didn't look at him. "We're not terribly far from the building we'd planned to watch."

"You're serious?"

"Calm down, we're not going in guns blazing," she said, shifting her gaze to the general area where he'd stashed his gun.

"But we're going?" he asked, not bothering to hide his eagerness.

"Yes. We'll go tonight."

"Well, hot dang," Jake said, settling his hand over the bag of food. "We sharin'?"

"No, this is mine." She took the cup from him and set it before her, then pointed at the bag. "I got you the tourist breakfast."

Jake fished the container from the bag and popped it open, sighing as he took in the sight of eggs, bacon, and fried potatoes. "Woman, you're an angel."

"Don't read into it, Jake. You get contrary when you're hungry. Really, feeding you is for my benefit," she said, but he caught a hint of her smile behind the cup she held to her lips.

Yeah, she didn't have to admit it, but Jake could see she'd been more thoughtful than what she let on, that she enjoyed his appreciation. Pride might be holding her back, but this was a step. She was falling for him bit by little bit. Initially there had been a goal, an end game. Now he just craved her attention. That twitchy little smile of hers was like basking in the sun's rays.

Chapter 20

PARIS

From the shadows, Dulcina studied the layout. The location Ruskin had provided was easy to find and the setup surprisingly similar to the where she'd found Jake beaten and unconscious. Corner building, two entrances, and a service door in the back alley.

Jake remained silent, close enough his arm brushed hers. He seemed to have the same approach for observation, which she appreciated. Actually, there was a lot about Jake she admired. His entire demeanor projected a steady calm and she knew without a doubt he would approach any situation in the same manner. He thought things through, weighed options, and maybe that's what she liked most about him. He never felt like a liability, a wildcard, or a hindrance.

Even when he'd rushed in to save her from demons in the alley, the missteps of that situation had been her fault. Without preparing him for what might happen, how was he to know she didn't need saving? He was, in essence, like the Guardians of her city. When someone needed help, Jake assessed the situation and charged in to fix the problem. And truly, he'd functioned as the human version of a Guardian for so long, half of what he did was likely ingrained behavior.

Before leaving their temporary home tonight, she'd gone over the major details of her life as a Stalker, what rules must be followed, and which could be bent. She'd prepared him to stand at her side tonight.

He'd asked all the appropriate questions, provided his own tactical insight, and tossed out at least a dozen ways he could help her, even in his fragile human state of existence. It was hands down the best conversation she'd ever had with a man. She didn't believe he was capable of everything he'd claimed, but even half would be a boon.

A sharply dressed man stepped from around the corner and walked right up to the door of the club. He was allowed entrance by the brute of a doorman stuffed into a suit lingering inside the entrance. This was the fourth man in an expensive suite to enter the club tonight.

"It's a gentleman's club," Dulcina said, a hint of amusement in her tone.

"So, what, like boring conversation, brandy, and cigar type stuff?" he asked quietly, inching closer to her. "Gambling? Or dancing women?"

"Likely all of the above. But take it down a notch. You're not going in there," she said, surprised by the flare of jealousy at his mention of women. It dissipated quickly the instant his brows scrunched in confusion. Dulcina shrugged. "I assumed."

"I'm not above appreciating a dancing girl, just not while I'm on a job. Or attached. I asked because his normal game includes drugs. Makes everyone a bit more edgy. I'm not going in because they'd recognize me. This is recon only, and my ugly mug would blow it. You can't go. I doubt they'd.... No, they'd let you in, but it's not happening," Jake slid his arm around her waist and it felt protective, possessive.

"Why not?" she challenged him.

"Well," he started, clearly a little ruffled about producing an answer. "It's just not..."

"Safe?" she asked, loving that frozen look that came over his face, but in the end, she helped him out and prompted, "Because demons may be inside, just like his last establishment you tried to enter?"

"Yep, that's it. Good reason to lay low," he agreed, that quirky smile curling his lips like he knew she'd just saved his ass.

"So, we need an in," Dulcina said, watching his profile as he fixed his stare at the building. She could have been burdened with any type of man, with any number of personality flaws when she'd scraped Jake off the pavement. He was perfection, from his go-with-the-flow personality, to his earthy speech, to his scruffy whiskered face. Turning her gaze back to the building, she stated the obvious. "Easy. We need a gentleman."

Jake's left eyebrow popped up. "You driving back to Balinese to steal a whole person?"

"No stealing," she promised. "I might be able to talk a fellow Stalker into helping."

"So you know a guy?"

"I've heard rumors. Supposedly he's close, which makes him our best option."

"All right, then. Let's go get him."

"I can't guarantee he'll be there. Or help." Truthfully, she'd never met the man, but the rumors were consistent.

"But it's worth a shot?" he asked, leaning forward, his eagerness bleeding through his normally relaxed demeanor.

"Absolutely." Dulcina motioned for Jake to follow her, and he did.

They walked side by side in silence for a long while, contemplating what was to come, and that didn't seem to bother either of them. Gradually the world around them changed into something darker, dirtier, and the abandoned streets screamed of hidden dangers.

"This seems...unsafe," Jake said, taking an uneasy look around.

"It is. Don't worry. I'll protect you," she said, smooth and confident.

Jake immediately laughed, though it was tamed down so as not to draw too much attention.

"It gets eerie before entering the homeless district," she said quietly.

Sad to say, but the homeless were easy pickings for demons, not to mention the regular band of cutthroats and thieves. She'd always heard a certain Stalker had a constant presence here, keeping the area well protected from demons. He must be supremely sure of himself to telegraph his location.

"You lost, sweet one?" an incredibly deep voice called from a darkened alley.

She turned, facing the gaping maw of the alley on the other side of the street, Jake calmly standing at her back. She couldn't see the man in the shadows and, without the tell of red eyes, this man could truly be any species.

"Not lost. Not sweet." Her confident tone never wavered.

"No," he said, a dark chuckle rolling off the building. "I've heard you're not as sweet as your name suggests."

He knew her name? Then he knew her reputation. "So you know my name. Does that make you a friend?"

"No," he said as nothing more than a fact. Jake shifted at her side, probably not caring for the man's answer.

"Then a foe?"

"Not unless you cross me," he said, his words followed by a deep, hushed laugh.

The Stalker name circled around in her head, trying to form fully. She had a wisp of a memory... "Kael. Yes?"

"Ah, you've heard of me." Kael's voice was unsettling in its lack of origin. "Perhaps I am doing well then."

"Well enough," Dulcina hedged, never one to diminish her own talents in comparison to another.

"Well enough," he said, seemingly agreeing. "What brings you to my territory?"

Dulcina watched the dark entrance of the alley for any hint of movement, but all was still. "You."

"This should be interesting," Kael said, his voice a slow drawl as he stepped from the shadows of the alley. Dressed head to toe in black, Kael looked like only a face floating in the midst of darkness. He stood on the other side of the narrow street. Motionless.

When he said nothing more, Dulcina continued, "We have a request of you. We're looking for a man named Tulio Suarez, and we need someone he won't recognize to enter a gentleman's club and gather information."

"This is for our lord?" Kael asked.

"No. This is personal," Jake clarified.

Kael ignored him completely, as if he hadn't spoken, didn't exist. The Stalker's full attention remained on her.

"And you can't do this because you are female," Kael said evenly and without question. Then he pointed to Jake without looking his way. "And this one... I take it this human is not capable."

"He is capable," Dulcina said with a fair amount of pride she didn't feel the need to hide. "But he is compromised. They know him, or at the very least, know he is coming for Tulio."

Kael studied them both for a long moment, then finally said, "What will you give me in return for this favor?"

"I have nothing to give. No possessions, no home. Only my sword," she said, doubting for the first time that this might actually work.

"I have no need of help." Kael waved his hand dismissively. "I'll do this for you, if you patrol my zone while I'm away."

"That's it?" The simplicity of his request surprised her. "You don't want to barter?"

"It's enough." Kael looked up the road. Nothing but a gaping emptiness in the still night. "I'm bored. A change would be most welcome."

Jake elbowed her and she pulled out of her stuttered shock in time to seal the deal. "Done."

"Give me the address, and I'll make myself presentable," Kael said with a grin.

She held out her hand, offering the man across the street the same slip of paper Ruskin had given her. She'd committed the address to memory, as had Jake. There was no loss in giving up the paper.

Kael vanished, then appeared three feet closer, only to vanish again. He repeated this haunting process several times until finally plucking the paper from Dulcina's hand. If he expected her to flinch, she hadn't.

"Showoff," Jake muttered behind her.

"We all are. A lingering trait of every Stalker," she said. A smile curled Dulcina's lips. She appreciated a good show.

Kael walked away without a word, slowly vanishing fully into Spirit with each step.

"Damn unsettling," Jake said, shaking his head.

Dulcina ignored Jake's flabbergasted reaction and hooked her arm through his. "Shall we patrol?"

"You're serious?" Jake scratched his head, looking down the quiet street. "He was serious?"

"That was the deal," she said, tugging him down the dark street.

"You think he'll come back with anything we can use?"

She shrugged. "If not, we'll find some other way in. This just seemed the easiest."

Arm in arm, they walked at a leisurely pace and she split her attention between the road ahead and Jake. He had a similar pattern. Glancing at her, scanning the road, checking behind them on occasion. The man had good instincts.

"Do you have a zone, same as this guy? Like someone sectioned off the city and gave each of you a piece?" The curiosity filtered into his voice and she understood what he meant, read the statement for what it was because it came from Jake. He wasn't implying she wasn't capable. He just had a very real understanding of how much ground she must cover alone.

"I do."

"Was your home inside that zone?"

"It was," she said, followed by a sigh. No upset, no regret, just a fact of the past. "We'll find another place. It's best to stay close, to pick up on any local whispers, rumors."

Jake nodded. "I like the part in there where you said *we*."

Dulcie didn't respond, mostly because she'd caught the slip too. She'd never purposefully included anyone in her life.

Jake stopped, pulled her to a stop with him. "You okay with this?"

"There's no choice. We cannot live apart," she said, hoping he would drop the subject and not look too deeply into her hesitation to answer him directly.

"That's not what I mean. I'm asking if you're okay? If this is too much for you? Do you need me to back off?"

"I'm okay," she answered, once again recognizing that Jake wasn't asking about things on the surface level.

"Good." He took her arm and kept them moving along the path she'd originally set for them. "Hot damn, Sugar, we're going to have a good life, you and me."

"Is that so?"

"Now, don't sound so surprised. One day soon I won't be so busted up, then watch out," he said, all proud of himself.

"Watch out for what?"

"For fun. Sugar, we'll be a couple of peas in a pod," he said, that genuine grin spreading across his face, betraying the amount of joy her little use of the word 'we' had given him.

"Are you going to be like this every time your ego gets a little boost?" she teased.

Jake ducked down and caught her earlobe in a quick pinch between his lips, then whispered, "You bet I will and you'll like it."

Dulcina shivered, allowing herself to enjoy his playfulness, his touch. He pulled back, unhooked his arm from hers and brought her hand to his lips for a quick kiss.

Her hand in his, he tugged her along with him. Jake was leading her, deliberately urging her to pick up her pace. Something had changed in him from one kiss to the next. Gone was his jovial banter, the gleam in his eyes that followed her with interest. Jake wasn't exactly distant, but his every move had become...deliberate. Watchful.

A dozen or so steps down the road and Jake tugged her into a cubby of a building along the sidewalk. His back to the wall, he tugged her tight against him, his arm encircling her waist.

Jake took her lips in one heated kiss after another, and they parted long enough for Jake to whisper, "We're being followed. They're not close yet, but gaining ground."

"Obviously," she said with a soft laugh, leaning fully against him. "When did you notice?"

"A couple blocks back," he said, nipping her jaw line.

Dulcina practically hummed with desire. He'd noticed they had company at nearly the moment she had, and she found his awareness supremely sexy. She dare not tell him, though. Not yet. "So we're hiding?"

"No," he said, touching his nose to hers. "My plan was to put the immortal vampire between me and the demon."

She smiled. "Not immortal."

Jake stole a quick kiss. "Invincible?"

"Nice thought, but no." Dulcie stole a kiss of her own.

Jake thought for a moment, and then with a nod, said, "Death resistant."

Dulcina laughed, head thrown back, joy lifting her cheeks. She wrapped her arms around his shoulders and squeezed him close. Ah, this man.

"Don't look now," he said, nibbling at her ear. "But company is coming."

"Shall I save you?" she asked, her hand taking a lovely detour down his chest as she went for her Bowie knife.

"If you don't mind."

"Do a girl a favor?" she whispered. The flickering change in his gaze told her he expected them to round the corner at any moment. "When you're ready, push me up against that wall behind you and drop to your knees."

"Oh, honey." His eyes lit with excitement as he leaned forward, pressed his forehead to hers.

Jake didn't rush to take position, which helped her gauge the distance of the man coming for them. He stayed close, giving a convincing illusion of an intimate moment, but his attention was definitely focused toward the street. If Jake wasn't in a hurry, then the threat hadn't even entered the alley yet.

She heard the light tread of boots on pavement approaching, and that's when Jake moved. He spun them around and crouched down in front of her.

With no room to move, Dulcina pitched herself forward, throwing her knife toward the red-eyed man approaching. Jake caught her around her legs before she toppled forward over him, and set her back on her feet.

Her knife had sunk into the demon's shoulder. Not her best work, but it would slow him. Initially, she couldn't tell if he was armed, and couldn't justify a kill strike, but now she clearly saw the drawn sword in his fist the shadows nearly hid.

Blood surged through her veins, adrenaline fueling her actions. It wasn't just her life at stake tonight. Jake was vulnerable. Dulcie charged the demon as he struggled to pull her blade from his body. She crashed into him, knocked him off kilter enough to jerk her Bowie free and roll away. He hadn't expected her to fight back and was still dealing with the shock of being injured.

A second demon emerged from the street and came for her. She sidestepped, caught him in the leg with her knife, causing enough damage to leave him floundering, gritting his teeth to silence his pained cry.

She didn't hear more men coming, didn't sense anything else moving in the night, but she looked back at Jake for confirmation. He held up his hand, showing three fingers. He'd seen three.

Dulcina forced her breathing to slow and she focused, trying to get a sense of where the third man might have gone. The air beside her moved toward Jake, not like the wind, but heavier.

Her eyes locked on Jake, and his brows furrowed, head cocked to the side. She lifted her finger to her lips, asking for silence, and then she took her Spirit. This was a trick Captain Savard had taught her when she was young. Slip into Spirit, let your essence gravitate to the heaviness in the atmosphere, and you've found your impostor, the other person hiding in his Spirit.

She followed that heaviness, and within seconds, the demon appeared before Jake. Dropping from her Spirit, she was already in motion, driving her knife into the demon's back. The instant she did, both demon and knife were ripped from her grasp. Jake had grabbed the demon's head and twisted hard, breaking his neck and dropping him to the ground. All while dodging the demon's blade. Impressive.

"Sorry," Jake said in a rush, his hands going straight to his ribs, probably hurting from that abrupt burst of strength he'd needed to twist his body that hard. "Jumped the gun."

Dulcina crouched down and yanked her blade from the demon's back. She wiped the black blood onto the demon's shirt and stood, surveying the downed men on the ground.

"This happen to you a lot?" Jake asked, his unwavering gaze on her.

"No. It doesn't. Nothing about this is normal." Dulcina kept her hand on her blade, not trusting that this was over. "I can see why Kael jumped at the chance to walk away from this for a night."

Chapter 21

PARIS

Dulcina woke to the smell of...breakfast? Since Jake had healed enough to be mobile, he'd done little things she never expected to notice, let alone like. He folded the blanket at the end of the bed when he woke. Not necessary, but it was nice. And the food? She hadn't asked him to cook breakfast, and that's what made it special. Jake didn't waste time asking for permission, he just did things. For himself and for her.

He slid the pan over the burner like he'd done it a thousand times, which she had to admit, was a little sexy. Sure, part of the appeal was the actual cooking, but those jeans slung low on his hips helped, too. As he turned, Jake tossed the towel over his bare shoulder, the muscles of his back and torso shifting deliciously beneath his skin as he moved through the normal everyday activity.

In the past she'd fed off of a man's excitement, his lusts and desires, using it to fuel her own. Though, she sensed her true connection with them was decidedly less. With Jake? Nothing had dampened or changed her desire for him. It burned on its own, bright and sure.

Surprisingly, it hadn't bothered her that he'd held her wrists together the night before last, or that he'd pinned her down, because it wasn't about him being controlling. The illusion of being bound had been overpowered by the loving caress of his other hand, the sultry slow way his lips moved over hers. Dulcina had realized in that moment she trusted Jake.

Dulcina rolled onto her belly, devouring the sight of him. Oh, my, the way that man's body moved... Watching him was addictive. She could only imagine how intoxicating he would be once fully healed. For a human, he was strong, capable, but these lingering, discolored bruises scattered over his flesh were a brutal reminder of the fractured bones still healing deep within.

Last night she'd been well aware of Jake's vulnerability. When the three demons had come after them, she'd been genuinely worried. Her zone was well controlled, and her altercations had become more supervisory in nature over the years. Kael's was something else entirely. Raw and unruly, his zone seemed charged with something sinister.

Kael hadn't seemed surprised by the onslaught they'd encountered, brushing off the aggressive attack like it was a normal occurrence and instead going straight into details of his experience in the club. Kael had mingled, gambled, and enjoyed his time not worrying about the safety of what he referred to as '*his* humans'.

In the club, he'd noted there had been an odd mix of humans and demons, and the co-mingling had given Kael a sense of unease. According to him, it had been difficult to tell if one knew the other was a different species.

Kael had yet to find any specific information about Tulio. He planned to return tonight and become familiar with the people, their habits. And again, she and Jake would patrol his area. After what they'd witnessed, there was no doubt his zone required a watchful eye.

"Come and get it." Jake walked by her with a single plate. Omelet in the middle, surrounded by sausage and some version of fried potatoes.

"How hungry *are* you?" she asked, falling into an easy, teasing mood.

"Darlin', I know damn well you're not a breakfast person, but just in case you get the munchies, the big plate goes in the middle," he said, showing off its location on the table with both hands. "Just pick off what you want."

"How sweet." She sat, stretching in the middle of the bed.

"'Bout time you realized I'm sweet," he said, going back to the little kitchen and bringing a cup to the table and placing it at her seat. "Tea?"

"Yeah, that one I didn't know. Coffee or tea. I guessed," he said, sitting down and throwing the kitchen towel over his lap. "Hope it's okay."

Suddenly she was struck by two things. First, she slept so soundly in his presence that she hadn't realized he was up and about, let alone working on cooking breakfast. And the second? He hadn't left.

Dulcie got up and kissed his cheek before sitting across from him. He looked at her, his eyes wide and stunned. "You okay, Sugar?"

"I think I might be," she said softly, and it was the truth.

She loved him. No other emotion came close to describing what she felt for the man sitting across the table. He understood her, accepted her as vampire, re-calibrated his blurred lines of justice to keep her safe, and oddly enough, that was all she needed from him.

Dulcie had let the emotions take her over, emotions she had worked for years to block. She never felt girly or delicate, protected and cossetted, but Jake made her feel that way. He spoke to both the warrior side and the feminine side of her, and all with that Kentucky accent. She bit her lip, holding back a smile.

Too soon. This was all too much and too soon. She didn't trust a feeling she didn't recognize, and sorting out where her heart and mind truly stood on the matter of Jake would take time. Luckily they had plenty.

Breakfast was silent for the most part. What struck her was how easily they got on together. They were comfortable. She'd thought at first that the easy flow between them had been on account of Jake being mostly unconscious, and fairly amusing when awake, but it had been a constant in the nights and weeks following.

Even after she'd obligingly tried a few bites of everything he made, and Jake scarfed down the rest, they'd fallen into sync. On the same page. They cleared the table, strapped on weapons, and walked out the door. He looked left, she looked right.

This strange unison she experienced had been an unexpected result of...well, him. Jake was sharp. Acutely aware of his surroundings, he was careful to steer her away from passing pedestrians, even if it meant playing up his accent and showing her random architecture like a tourist for an excuse to get out of a growing crowd.

It was cute. He knew she was capable, had witnessed that fact on a couple occasions, but he was strategically dodging potential dangers for both of them.

Upon arriving again in the homeless district, they briefly touched base with Kael and went separate ways. Truthfully, the Stalker looked excited for another night free of responsibility, and she couldn't blame him, but being in this area left her on edge. Her territory was well in hand, likely due to the hard work of those who had patrolled prior to her arrival, but Kael's zone had an entirely different dynamic.

Walking at a slower pace now that they were in Kael's district, Dulcina noticed most had ducked into their homes and stayed. It seemed even the humans knew to have a concern for their own safety. Last night they'd skirted the edges of the homeless encampment, made sure nothing had come up, but tonight they would avoid the area entirely at Kael's request.

Though she was certain he had no direct contact with the homeless, Kael had made it sound as if there was some unspoken agreement between them. Maybe there was, and that was his business.

Dulcina strolled down the street, shoulder to shoulder with Jake, her hand tucked into his, and for once in her life she felt content. She was happy right here in this moment, with Jake.

"Never thought a city could feel peaceful," Jake said, tipping his chin up and scanning the sky. He liked to catch a glimpse of the stars as he walked down the street. "Not the same as looking at a Kentucky sky past the trees on a hilltop, but the company makes it better."

Jake nudged her with his hip, his playfulness coming through again. She smiled. Jake didn't let her shut him out, and he never gave up on her. That was priceless.

She looked up at him, that easy, half smile on his face as he watched the world around him. Dulcina decided to make an effort. She couldn't include him in hunting demons, but maybe just letting him know what was happening instead of walking out every night without a single word would keep them connected. It was worth a shot.

"Jake," she said, but then stalled out.

"I'm listenin', Darlin'," he said, as if prompting her to continue because she'd taken too long to finish her thought.

Truly, she didn't know how to say it, couldn't find the right words to tell him she wanted him with her, at her side, even after they found the man Jake hunted. How could she convince him her feelings were genuine? He wouldn't believe her, not since he had no choice in his future.

"Hey," he nudged her gently. "You all right?"

"Just thinking," she said, her answer automatic to buy her time.

"I see that," he said with an understanding nod. "Just don't take too long to say it. I know you. The second a demon walks around that corner I'll lose you again."

She huffed out a little laugh. He wasn't wrong. A particular few held her attentions more raptly than others, and demons made the cut. As did Jake. Jake was blunt, honest, rough around the edges. Her roughness was all on the inside, and that Jake spoke to it, acknowledged who she was underneath it all, left her feeling exposed. Defenseless.

Releasing her hand and swiftly disentangling himself, Jake hooked his arm around her back, and yanked her up against his chest. The heel of her palm reflexively went to his shoulder, prepared to push him away, jerk herself out of his hold, but it was only a reflex. Jake, as only he would, took her pause as a win. With a slight cock of his head and a victorious grin, his lips were on hers, the kiss deep and sensual.

Dulcina whimpered a split second before he released her, and if he hadn't been holding her tight against him, she swore her knees would have buckled. Her senses were disoriented, still lost in the sensations he provoked.

"Why..." Her voice faltered and she cleared her throat. "Why did you do that?"

Jake leaned in, bumped his nose to hers, then pulled back just as she thought he might kiss her again. "To stop you from thinking too hard. Whatever you want to say, say it or don't. That rollin' it over in your head a dozen times only mixes things up."

Her jaw dropped, stunned at his perceptiveness. She would have just stood there staring at him had he not planted a kiss on her forehead, put his hand at the small of her back, and led her forward. He was right. That kiss had stopped all swirling inner monologue, and now she just walked with Jake at her side, thoroughly aware of his every movement. Completely tuned in to him.

This was easy. Everything between them flowed smoothly. The trust she had in this man was frightening. The faith he had in her was equally astounding. It all felt so right, confirmed by the constant spark snapping back and forth between them, connecting them on a level she'd never expected to experience.

She looked up at him, memorizing his profile. It was the most familiar view she had of him. From him laying to the left of her in bed, riding with her in the car, walking next to her, it was the same. He was at her side. Always.

Jake suddenly jerked back and he cried out, staggering and cursing as he fought to stay upright. Curling his right shoulder forward, he turned and leaned against her with nearly his full weight.

Her instincts kicked in, assessing the situation. Jake was not moving, in pain, and blood seeped through his shirt where he grabbed at something protruding from his chest. He'd been shot. With...an arrow? How had neither one of them seen or sensed the attacker?

Dulcina scanned the streets around her, searching for an enemy even as Jake weakened rapidly against her. Everything was quiet. No whisper of movement gave her a hint as to where the attack had come from. With nothing and no one to fight, she turned her full focus to him.

"Jake?" Initially she hadn't been concerned, but his continued silence and the stain of blood blooming across his chest sent a rush of sheer terror running through her veins. "Talk to me."

"Sugar, I ain't doin' so good," he said, completely dismayed, his words slurring together.

He was losing strength, sagging, unable to hold himself upright. She eased him to the ground and knelt behind him, supporting his back with her body.

Dulcina didn't know what to say, what to do. She'd seen a hundred men die, in a dozen different ways, but she'd never cared. No remorse, no emotion. This was different. This was watching a part of herself die and being helpless to stop fate.

"Jake, I can't fix this. I can't," she whispered against his ear.

Everything in her demanded she get up, hunt down whoever had fired the arrow, and break his damn neck. The only thing that prevented her from exacting a swift revenge was Jake's constantly trembling body and oddly gasping breaths. His body was failing.

Jake reached up, the motion uncoordinated, lacking any specific direction.

"I'm right here." She grabbed his hand, and he passed out.

Once again, everything good in her life was shattered in an instant. Someone she cared for was being ripped away. Again. She wanted to scream at the injustice, but she was numb. All that mattered was holding Jake.

From the shadows to her left, something moved. The use of a silent weapon meant demon or vampire, and she tracked the shifting shadows, expecting another attack. Whoever this was, he lingered, observing. Then slowly, the man came toward them with a frightening and silent grace.

The shadow moved without walking, was here without her sensing his presence on the street. The closer he came, she realized why. He was a Fade, a state of existing somewhere between a man and a Spirit form. She'd thought the ability to be rumor, but he was transparent. There and not. She could see him, he was real, but in this state of sustained transition, she would never be able to touch him. Kill him.

She kept her gaze fixed on his every movement, hatefully staring him down. With each approaching step, she recognized his translucent face. Rafe, the Stalker Lord's assassin, stood over them. Crossbow in hand, nearly blending with his long black coat, he passively glanced over them as if neither were of any true interest to him.

"I'm doing you a favor, *querida*." Rafe's deep, thickly Spanish accented voice filtered through the rage buzzing in her ears. "A human cannot run free in Paris with a vampire. This, I will not allow."

"*You* won't allow?"

His lip twitched, and at last he looked at her directly. "Would you prefer I use the royal 'We'? His voice is mine, and mine is his. One and the same. Decide this night how much this man means to you."

His words barely registered through her shock, but when they did, she answered, "What does it matter now?"

"I've caused enough damage for him to die. Eventually. But whether he passes from this world or not, is up to you." Rafe looked away, bored already. "Decide. *Pero...rapido.*"

The assassin vanished into nothing. It was possible he lingered in the distance, hiding and watching, but she pushed him from her mind.

This was her fault. All of it. As much as she wanted to rant and rave, and scream to the heavens at the injustice, she'd been willfully ignoring one blatant fact. Keeping a human above had never been done, at least, not in France.

She could change Jake right now, convert his body to vampire, make him the same as her in nearly every way. The only thing giving her pause was Jake's inability to speak with her, to give permission. He could hate her, leave her, but it didn't matter. In the end, he would be alive.

As a young girl, she could only watch helplessly when demons ripped away her entire universe. Her father, mother, the familiar and grounding presence of the lord of Balinese, her security, sanity, personality. It was happening again. The one person she felt bound to, cared for, was being torn away. No more. She wouldn't allow anyone to take from her again.

"I'm sorry Jake, but I can't lose you. I won't," Dulcina said softly at his ear. Jake's body twitched slightly, but gave no other response. At this point, most of his muscle reactions were likely involuntary.

Calm and determined, she never wavered from what must be done. Dulcina shifted back, allowed his weight to slide down so he lay across her lap. With both hands she gripped the arrow near his chest, not shying away from the strength it might take to remove the arrowhead. This was not something she wanted to attempt twice.

She took one steadying breath and jerked the arrow straight out of his chest. Jake cried out, limbs flailing, but only for a moment. His muscles went lax, the pain nearly driving him into unconsciousness. She had to work fast.

Pushing up her sleeve, she prepared to give him what he needed to seal and heal the wound. Biting the delicate inside of her wrist, she fit the wound to Jake's parted lips, pumping her fist to speed the flow of blood into his mouth. He drank, and though it was more of a reflexive response, it got the job done. The wrist was not known for ease of extracting large amounts of blood, but Jake was making an effort, even if bordering on involuntary. Dulcina kept her wrist at his lips, coaxing him to drink more, and for several minutes, he did. A rough gasp rocked his body and his skin flushed with fever. It was working. He'd taken enough.

Jake reached up and locked both hands over her forearm, clamped her wrist to his mouth and drank like a man lost in the desert for days. Dulcina leaned back, uncertain of this swift change in him. His short beard was rough around her broken skin as he pulled nourishment from her. This seemed like too much, too fast, but then again, she'd never turned a man before.

Dulcina pulled her wrist from his mouth, and although he fought her, she was still stronger. At least, for now. The connection broken, he fell back against her, floating in and out of consciousness.

She licked her wounded wrist, sealing the two punctures, and preventing her body from losing more blood. She'd worry about her decision later, regret that he'd had no choice. Now, she held on tight to the man she'd come to love. He'd taken in more than enough blood to make the change, to heal, and that was evident by the way his ragged breathing had shifted into something deeper.

Suddenly his muscles convulsed, and his back arched. Jake cried out again, and that's when she saw his incisors. His body was still sorting out the details, but he was vampire. He had a fighting chance to live now. She locked both of her arms under his shoulders, lifting and securing him against her with what little strength she had left, determined not to lose him.

Changing the core script of DNA didn't always go well. She'd heard tales of humans breaking free and running, never understanding what they'd become, or how to survive. They were always put down. Once fully turned, Jake would be so much stronger than her, especially since he'd just sapped her of her own healing blood. What if she wasn't strong enough hold him?

"Don't you dare run. Do you hear me?" she whispered harshly against his ear. Dulcina's senses were lit up, heightened by adrenaline, focused solely on the man in her arms. She tracked his breath, the sounds he made, the beat of his pulse.

Running wasn't the only possibility. Waking as vampire was said to be disorienting, almost like a hallucination. Lost in the haze of craving blood to mend his damaged body, Jake could turn on her, drain her completely. He didn't have the experience to know how to strike a neck, when to stop drinking. How to seal a wound she couldn't reach. Similar result. Dulcina would be dying or dead, and Jake would be put down.

She squeezed her eyes shut and held him tighter. Minutes passed. She felt the pattern of Jake's breathing slow and settle into an even ebb and flow against her body. His muscles relaxed in her arms, the weight of his body pressed down on her.

Jake twitched in her arms, and suddenly there was a stillness in him she didn't recognize. He held his breath, like the sound was too much, and getting in the way of assessing his situation. He was awake, aware, and now fully vampire.

A feral growl emanated from Jake's chest, and he twisted in her arms, instantly breaking her hold. Not running, not attacking, but his focus was unmistakable. His intense gaze fixed on her neck, Jake licked his lips a half second before he lunged for her.

Dulcina braced for the strike, expected pain and clumsiness from his first attempt, but all she felt was his breath on her skin, heavy and hot.

He pulled back sharply, concern etched on his features even as he stared at her neck. "Dulcie? I don't want to hurt you. I..."

"You won't, Jake. I trust you." She took his head between her hands. "Feel that pull? That nagging instinct beating at the back of your head? Follow it. Do as it demands and bite me. You need this. I need this."

His gaze collided with hers, then immediately fixed on the other side of her neck. His lips twitched as she pulled him closer. The second his lips touched her skin, his needful groan sent a deep shiver through her.

Jake bit down, sunk his teeth into the vein at her neck and pushed her back onto the ground. She could do nothing but hold on, arms locked around his middle, her one free leg looped over his in an effort to pin him against her. Her body couldn't figure out what was happening. His inexperience certainly caused the pain she'd expected, but tendrils of pleasure kept spiraling through her, more and more as he continued. Like he was slowly figuring out how this worked.

The instant Jake had gained the strength to lift the weight of his body onto his elbows, the pressure eased from her neck, then everything changed. His fangs no longer pulled uncomfortably in her vein, and his aggressive feeding had morphed into something...reverent.

By the time Jake withdrew his teeth, she was gasping from the sheer pleasure, clutching his back as he kissed his way across her jaw to her lips. He kissed her only twice, then settled his face in the crook of her shoulder, seeming to simply breathe in her scent.

Only seconds later, his weight went limp on top of her. She let out a shaky breath of relief. He was unconscious. He wouldn't go crazed, wouldn't run from her. Still, Dulcina refused to let go of him, though her strength was severely depleted. She'd made a life-altering decision on his behalf. The damage was already done, and irreversible. He might hate her, but she'd cross that bridge later. Right now, she had to finish saving his life.

Dulcina pried the flip phone from her pocket as she lay on the ground, Jake sprawled across her.

Geoff answered with a sharp, "What?"

"I need a favor," she said, trying to pull the weariness from her voice.

"I don't do favors, D. Never have," Geoff growled into the phone. "I move bodies."

"I'm asking you to move a body," she said, then added, "As a favor to me."

"Woman, you don't ask, you demand. So whatever you got must still be kicking. I can't transport a living body while Stalkers have dead bodies for me to dispose of. I'm sorry."

"I understand." There was nothing more to say. She hung up.

Truly, she did understand. Geoff was an easy solution, but a long shot. No one else was within range to even bother calling. Weak from being drained, she barely had the strength to roll Jake off her. She scooted toward the shelter of the nearest building, dragging Jake with her inch by inch.

She kept moving, determined to get them both to shelter, but after at long last reaching the nearest building, her strength gave out. The best she could do was drag Jake up against a set of stairs where it met the building.

Tucking them both tightly into the nook, Dulcina waited. Initially, she'd hoped her strength would return, at least in part, but as the minutes stretched on into hours with no change, she abandoned that possibility. She couldn't get them inside without replenishing her strength by taking blood from Jake. This would interrupt and stunt his healing and conversion process. Too dangerous. If he didn't have the chance to fully change and heal before she took from him, he might not recover. Drinking from him was not an option.

She lifted his shirt near his healing wound, checking the progress. His skin was repairing, faster than she'd thought it would, but perhaps not fast enough.

The decision she'd made to save his life could very well be the catalyst that would end both their lives when the sun rose. They had half a night left together, probably less.

"Damn it, Jake," she whispered, stroking his cheek. "I was supposed to go out on the end of a demon's blade."

A single tear burned a hot track down her cheek. She'd do it again. All of it. Every moment, every choice she made regarding Jake. She would take him home and save him again, keep him, turn him. She was resolved, accepting their fate with grace, because she was always meant to end up here with him.

Boots hit the pavement, loud and heavy. The sound brought her head up, her movement sluggish. Whoever this was, he made no effort to hide his presence. Dulcina pressed her back harder against the brick wall, making certain she was hidden as much as possible, but she couldn't pull in their legs.

The figure came into sight, his height becoming more evident as he headed straight for them. A demon perhaps? Or it could be Rafe returning. She couldn't reach her knife. The man stopped, off to the side of them, the shadows hiding him well.

"Is he dead?" the man asked, and immediately Dulcina recognized his voice.

"Kael?" The hope in her voice was palpable. "How did you find us?"

"I found the assassin's arrow, but no body. Can you walk?"

"If I could get to my feet, maybe." She didn't know what she could or could not do. She hadn't tried, because honestly, she wasn't going anywhere without Jake.

Kael moved Jake effortlessly, pulling him from her arms and propping him up. He turned to her and held out his hand, offering her the help she needed. Reaching out, she gripped his wrist.

"Easy," Kael instructed, not allowing her to rise too quickly. Once she was on her own two feet, he slowly released her. "You good?"

"I think I can move, but I can't fight," she admitted.

"You will have no need," Kael said, then maneuvered Jake's transforming body over his shoulder like he'd done this a thousand times and gripped Dulcie's elbow. "Where to?"

"We're staying..." Dulcie turned to point toward the apartment they'd most recently occupied.

"No." Kael shook his head. "Where are you truly safe?"

Dulcina quickly sifted through the options. Jake had been changed, but he was in a healing sleep now, defenseless, and needed protection. As did she. There was only one place to go.

"How long can you be away, and..." Dulcina's gaze settled on Jake. He was fine, she knew this, and yet seeing him in this state was heart-wrenching. She wanted him back, and when he woke, she needed to focus on nothing but him. "Do you have a car?"

Chapter 22

BALINESE

Jake woke to his cheek smashed against Dulcie's shoulder and his right arm snug around her waist. This was the good stuff. The best part of life. Waking to the warmth of this woman in his arms started his night off right. He was growing on her, like moss on a tree.

Careful not to disturb her sleep, he rolled off her and crawled out of bed. He felt a little stiff from sleeping with his neck propped up on her, but as he stretched out his muscles, the ache subsided. He was good. Not even his damaged ribs aggravated him. About damn time. He was tired of holding her back. Jake was an asset as a partner, and he was ready to prove it to her.

Two steps toward the bathroom, he stopped, taking in his surroundings. This wasn't their temporary landing pad in Paris, and it certainly wasn't her apartment. He stepped into the next room and blindly reached for a light switch. He'd been here before, with her. She'd sat on that kitchen table and talked to him. They were in her home, deep underground, in her city of vampires.

How in the....? Jake rubbed the back of his neck as he tried to snag a memory of how they got here, but only came up with fragmented pieces. They'd been walking, happy together, and then...a big blank.

He turned, redirecting his path to the bathroom in this particular home. Whatever had happened, Jake let it go for now and chose to trust Dulcie. Explanations could wait. Right now he was all sweaty and gross, with more than a few streaks of dirt and grime across his forearms and hands. He couldn't believe she'd let him go to bed like this.

Shucking off his pants, he cranked the water up to piping hot, hopped in, and gave himself a good scrub. Halfway through tackling his clean-up routine with gusto, Jake realized he was better than good. He could reach over his head, and stretch without pain. Hell, he didn't even hurt when he rolled his shoulders, or twisted his torso.

For the first time since those red-eyed fellas took a crack at him, Jake felt like himself. Now that he thought about it, there hadn't been any hitches in his steps as he walked to the bathroom, no reflexive urge to guard his ribs. Everything felt smooth, easy. Pain free.

He stepped out of the steamy shower, dried quickly, and stepped into his jeans. One by one he opened the trio of drawers at the sink to see what he could use. Scrubbing his hand across the stubble of his chin, he wondered if Dulcie had brought his bag. If not, that was fine. He'd just be a little scruffy for a while.

He never asked, but it would be nice to know if Dulcie preferred him with stubble or shaved. Maybe he'd make a change if one look tripped her trigger a little more than the other. Just thinking of that live wire woman had him grinning. Jake checked his reflection to see how well he was wearing the stubble.

His smile faltered, then faded. Cranking his neck to the side, he tried to get a better look at the black markings on his neck.

"Hey, Sugar?" Jake called toward the cracked open bathroom door. "Was I drunk last night? I got a tattoo."

His right side was good and normal, but the left had a design with twin black lines twisting over each other in a symmetrical design. Certainly not tribal, but balanced. She didn't answer, so he continued to inspect the line work as best he could—part of it was out of sight. "I mean I like it, I just... Did you pick this out?"

Hearing a subtle movement behind him, Jake turned. Dulcina appeared in the doorway, wearing her typical tank top and undies. Turning her head, she showed him a strikingly similar tattoo on her neck. So identical they might actually be the same tattoo, except hers was slimmer to fit her smaller neck.

"*We* got tattoos?" he gaped, rubbing his palm over his damp hair. "How the hell do I not remember a damn thing?"

"Not a tattoo," she said, then her voice and features sobered, like she was gearing up for something big. "A mating mark."

"Mating? Like a mate?" Jake said slowly, pointing back and forth between them, from his tattoo to hers. "That's what this means?"

"Don't be angry," she said, her eyes tracking his every move.

"I'm a little thrown, but I'm not angry. You and me? This isn't exactly possible, is it? You're a—"

"As are you."

Jake spun back around to the mirror, popped his jaw open and checked out his grill. Yep, a couple pointy fellas sprung down from the top. Not horror movie slasher fangs, but something sturdy and practical. Kind of short and easily hidden. "Why? What happened?"

Her brows scrunched together. "You don't remember anything?"

"Nope." Jake shook his head, trying to draw deep. "I remember walking with you, then...nothing. This is your underground city, right? How'd we get here?"

"It is. Kael brought us here."

Jake turned back to face her, and for the first time since he met her, Dulcie looked vulnerable. Something bigger than catching a lift had happened and he wasn't understanding.

"Why can't I remember any of this?"

"You were shot."

"Shot?" His mind was racing. None of this made sense. "Honey, this body is running top notch. No way I was shot."

She reached out, touched his chest. "This is the scar."

Jake turned to the mirror once again. The silvery scarred skin puckered in the shape of what looked like a compass star hidden beneath his chest hair. "Is this a—"

"Arrow."

"Jesus, that was close."

"You were dying," she said, and though her stance was strong, her voice steady, her fingers twisted together. Something about this made her hesitant, nervous.

"So that's why my ribs feel good? You made me vampire to save my life?"

She nodded. "You've been in a healing sleep for a few days."

"I was really dying..." A hazy set of scrambled memories jumped into his head. His shoulder being kicked back, then a faint impression of frustrated anger, and then nothing but euphoric visions of Dulcie beneath him that walked the fine line between "PG-13" and a good old fashioned "R". He didn't have a damn clue if the memories had happened, were a hallucination, or maybe a dream. "So how did I get the teeth?"

"You drank from me," she said quietly.

Jake rested his ass on the sink and crossed his arms. He nodded like he understood completely, but truly, he was still thinking it through as he stared at his toes. "All right, so we're all clear... I'm vampire and we're mated. The tattoo makes it like we're married."

"Yes," she said all calm and collected, but of course this didn't shake her up. This was her world, her rules.

"Legit married?"

She cleared her throat and when he brought his gaze back up to meet hers, she pointed to the mark on his neck. "Yours matches mine. You bit me, took what you needed to change and heal, but were not conscious after and could not properly seal your bite. The mark is the result. It's known as a claiming mark, a mating mark, or a mark of possession."

Again, he was going with the slow nod. "I'm yours and you're mine."

"Yes," she confirmed.

"Because I didn't know how to seal a bite," he said, drawing the most logical conclusion.

Dulcina was being more closed off than usual and for a hot minute he thought she wasn't going to say anything, but then she said, "You wouldn't have any way of knowing that it should be done, or how. Even then, it makes no difference. You were not awake after."

"You should have let me die. That would have been best for everyone."

"How?"

"I wouldn't be out there tracking a man. You get your freedom back." Jake took a second, trying to pull the raw hurt from his voice. "Yeah. Should have let me go."

"Look at me, Jake," she said, her tone steady. He lifted his gaze to face whatever she needed to say head on. Her bottom lip quivered, but she pushed herself to speak. "I relish solitude. I left my family without warning or remorse. I left what had been my home since birth without a second thought. I work alone. I walk alone. I can, and have, turned away from everything and everyone in my life, but I couldn't let you go. Do not, for one second, forget that I marked you as well. Intentionally marked you."

Jake let every word she spoke roll through his head, seep into his soul. She was saying she'd chosen him. On purpose. "You really want this? You want me?"

"More than I ever realized," she said softly, looking all vulnerable, like his next words would make or break her.

Jake stepped right up to her, grinning. "Aw, Sugar, you do care."

Dulcie didn't say anything and he didn't need words from her. He wrapped his arms around her and squeezed, and when she squeezed back even tighter, that said it all. She'd given her whole life to him and he'd do exactly the same for her. Jake slid his tongue over his newly formed fangs. They were the same creature now. Anything was possible.

"You're gonna have to teach me a whole lot," he whispered, planting a kiss at her temple. "Like how to use these chompers."

"You'll only be using them on me," she said, her voice going sultry, as her hand slid down his back.

"Yeah? I might need a whole lot of practice." Jake touched his nose to hers, teasing her with his nearness just a bit, then swooped in, pressing his lips to hers. "You up for this? Sharin' your life with someone?"

"Only with you," she admitted.

"Aw, see now, that's what I needed to hear." Jake bear-hugged her, lifting her so her feet dangled off the floor, and carried her into the next room. "This is a two-way street now, Darlin'. I keep you happy, you keep me happy."

She laughed at his antics, but managed to ask, "And what would make you happy?"

A knock sounded at the door, heavy and loud. Jake groaned, leaned forward, and pressed his forehead to hers. "Not that."

"I'll get rid of our visitor." She kissed him twice, then snagged her pants and swiftly stepped into them.

Jake couldn't wipe the grin off his face as he followed her just to the edge of the little living room. He hung back, shoulder on the doorway, watching her tug her jeans on and button them just before reaching for the door.

She swung it open to reveal a weathered, bearded man on the other side. Jake didn't recognize this guy, but Dulcie gave no negative reaction to him showing up on her doorstep, so he let it be and hung back to listen without intruding.

"Rollin told me you'd come back for the rehearsal," the man said, his voice sounding even more worn out than he looked. "I didn't know."

"Few did. It was a quick visit." Dulcie's sentences were short, her words carefully chosen to neatly tie off the conversation. She didn't seem uncomfortable, but something was off.

"I used to be one of your few," he said with a small, sad smile barely visible through the beard covering his face. "You know you're always welcome in my home."

"I know I am," she said, but gave nothing more.

Jake could easily see their visitor only had eyes for his Dulcie, but what he was struggling to understand was why the man looked gut-hurt over a solitary and highly unsocial woman dodging a visit. The man nodded, seeming to accept her answer, and beneath the slight shift in his beard might have been a smile, like he understood her completely.

"You're here now." The visitor's voice dropped a little lower. "Will you stay with me?"

That question jerked through Jake like a banjo string snapping inside him. Nope. Not happening. He knew with everything in him that Dulcie could handle this situation, had complete faith that she would shut it down, but the surge of fierce protectiveness that whipped through him could not be denied. Jake was in motion, crossing the room in measured strides. He got to her side just as the man reached out to touch her cheek.

"Hey, now. Hands off," Jake said in the most casual tone he could muster as he stepped up to Dulcie's side.

Jake didn't feel the need to put his arm around her and stake his claim, or step between them, but a verbal warning had felt appropriate.

"Who are you?" the gruff visitor demanded, acknowledging him for the first time.

"Someone you're going to have to worry about if you don't step away from my Dulcie," Jake said evenly, matter of fact. Tilting his head slightly toward Dulcie, he asked in a sweeter tone, "Where do you punch a vampire, Darlin'? Don't want to catch a fang. Never mind. Don't answer. I'll figure it out."

"Dulcie?" the man asked, looking to Dulcina in surprise. He seemed stunned. Flabbergasted. A little more hurt. Jake was starting to feel sorry for him. "You've always said Dulcie was an endearment, not a name."

"I did say that," she said, not expanding on her stance. Well, that put a feather in his cap. She'd stopped correcting him a long while ago.

Dulcie stepped fully from behind the door, revealing the black tattoo lines on her neck. His eyes widened, shocked by the marks. "But we are fated to become mates, you and I. Could you not sense that connection? The strength of the pull toward each other?"

"I felt that tether when I first came to you in the training room years ago, Nico. We had a clear understanding of what each other needed and we healed through that fated tie," she said gently. "But connection, understanding, and fate are not love."

"And this man?" The gruffness returned as his gaze shifted to Jake. He didn't appear angry, and wasn't accusatory. Nico just seemed to have been blindsided.

"This is Jake," she said, reaching out to touch his forearm. Jake seized on that little gesture and snagged her hand, holding it to his chest. Sure, it was a bold little show of possession, and really unnecessary, but it felt damn good.

"Jake," Nico repeated numbly, and after a moment, shifted his gaze and really looked at him for the first time. "A human?"

"He was," she said proudly, the simple statement seeming to reveal so much.

"Oh," Nico said, his whole body strung tight as he looked over Dulcie with a concerned crease in his brow. "Were you harmed? Are you...happy?"

"I'm good, Nico." Dulcie reached out and gripped Nico's hand, at the same time giving Jake's hand a little squeeze. The squeeze helped. Kept him from getting worked up over her cutting a tie she clearly once had with this man. She smiled, friendly like, and said, "We're heading to Rollin's wedding in an hour. Will we see you there?"

"I...no." Whatever he was about to say, he shut it down sharply, looking her straight in the eye, hand over his heart. "I wish you both well. Sincerely."

She nodded her acknowledgment, a silent thank you, and when he turned to leave, she shut the door behind him.

Jake remembered her saying that fated mate business was heavy stuff, life altering, a higher power picking your person. He couldn't imagine someone just letting it go. "We gonna have a problem with him?"

"No, I can't imagine we will. We have a belief among our species, that the world has chosen one fated mate for you." Jake was still hanging on to her hand when she turned to face him, and said, "This faith is deeply ingrained into our culture, but I never believed it until I felt that invisible pull toward Nico. The fates were right. I needed Nico, and he needed me. We're both better people for having known each other, but I never stayed with him, never loved him. Even after I'd met the man the fates had chosen for me, I never wanted a mate, or anyone in my life. Then I found you. I chose you, Jake. I want to walk through this life with you by my side."

"Aw, Darlin'," Jake said, tugging her fully into his arms. "That's music to my ears."

"This ear?" she asked, and Jake was not prepared to feel her teeth nibbling on his earlobe.

He shuddered, then swiftly came to his senses. "Yeah, that and the other one."

She dutifully switched sides, taking his other earlobe between her teeth.

Jake groaned, lifting Dulcie off the ground and hugging her close. "Damn, you know just what buttons to push. How much time do we have?"

"Not much. How fast can you be?"

Jake threw back his head and laughed. "Yeah, honey, that's not going to be a problem."

• • • •

Jake walked through Balinese, not paying attention to a damn thing other than his sweet Dulcie on his arm. The rich, royal blue gown she wore covered her from collarbone to toe, but left her arms bare. The kicker was, the sides of the gown had tall oval cutouts trimmed in gold starting just under her arms, leaving her sides bare to the top of her hips. Gorgeous.

They walked into the church together, and Jake wasn't blind to the multiple levels of shock thrown their way. Some likely noticed their mating marks, a fair amount of his peeking above the collar of his button-up shirt and hers sweeping up past the neckline of her dress. Though if he had to guess, he was certain most were just plain stunned by Dulcie complying with the bride's wishes in wearing the dress.

They sat in the second pew. Jake looked around the church, soaking in this new world he was now fully a part of in so many ways. He noticed a few more of those fancy neck tattoos and now he understood. They were so unique and they only matched their mate, and okay, that was pretty amazing.

The permanency of their relationship didn't stop the urge to throw his arm around her, sort of give off the signal that she was his, so he acted on that instinct.

"Feeling a touch insecure?" Dulcie asked, one of those perfect eyebrows lifting.

"You bet I am. Don't know these people," he whispered at her ear. "Just have the need to mark my territory, if you know what I mean."

"Jake," she said in that patient, scolding tone that was growing on him. "You marked me. Very clearly."

Grumbling, he squeezed her shoulder a little tighter. "Marked don't mean happy."

"Ah. Then it's a good thing you've decided to give them extra visual proof," she said, a slight smirk to her lips.

"I know it's silly, but—" His throat squeezed off any words trying to form the second Dulcie leaned in and kissed his neck, darting her tongue across his highly sensitive skin right there in front of God and everyone. Jake cleared his throat, and just loud enough for her to hear him over the chattering people, said, "Sugar, this newly altered body of mine is gonna have a bit of a hair-trigger for a spell. Best go easy, at least in public."

"That should settle any doubts of my happiness," she whispered, giving him one last nibble before pulling away, sitting straight, and looking on ahead like nothing had just happened. He was one lucky man.

Organ music started up, and though stuff was starting to happen around them, Jake couldn't take his eyes off his woman. She was a knock out. Strong, determined, fiery. If she was pissed off at him, he was sure as hell going to hear about it in grand detail, and she was just as quick to show him how much she loved him when she was pleased as punch.

Dulcie elbowed him and he followed her gaze to the center aisle. Drastically different than what he was used to seeing, the couple walked toward the altar together. A massive, boring, brick wall of a man was marrying a very curvy, classic beauty. They didn't look like a match on the outside, but that wasn't the part that counted.

The ceremony seemed oddly similar to a normal human wedding, and wow was that weird to classify something as 'human'.

A bride, groom, priest, and a fancy dress all inside a church. The difference? No bridesmaids or groomsmen. Just the priest, the couple, and immediate family.

"Hey," Jake whispered as he leaned in closer to Dulcie, noticing something different about the couple. "They don't have marks like ours. Why's that?"

Dulcie whispered back, "Rollin and Bette lived together, figuring each other out before they committed. They waited to do the mark and marriage all in one day."

The bride was all smiles in a fluffy cream-colored gown with a heavy gold lace bodice and trim. Pretty, but nothing he ever envisioned for his own wife. His wife. Again, Jake's gaze drifted back to Dulcie. His wife was a warrior, backed him like a partner, and loved him like a woman in love. Dream come true.

The priest's solid voice rolled over the pews, drawing Jake's attention back to the front. Familiar verses were read, a little speech given about history and the future, and then he announced the exchange of vows.

Loud and clear, the priest asked, "Do you, Babette Dautry, promise to love and honor Rollin Casteel?"

"All my life," Bette said, her eyes shimmering in the light, probably about to cry.

"Do you, Rollin Casteel, promise to love, honor and protect Babette Dautry?" the priest asked.

"With my life," Rollin said, the words solemn.

Well, that was different, but he liked the concept. The couple shared a sweet kiss, probably a little more innocent for the sake of the gathered family. Bette popped up on her toes, Rollin's arm around her back to help guide her, and she deliberately placed her bite.

The only outward hint Rollin gave of her bite affecting him was his fingers curling on her arms. There was no actual drinking from each other here, so he guessed the sensations wouldn't be nearly as earth-shattering, but it clearly still made an impact. Bette drew back to study the two open puncture wounds, then smiled up at her mate.

Rollin leaned down, said something that had Bette gripping the sleeves of his new suit, then bit her in return. She got a little weak-kneed, but he steadied her. When they pulled back and looked each other in the eye, those beaming smiles on their faces, Jake could feel their joy from where he sat.

"Aw, now that's sweet," Jake said, and Dulcie elbowed him. Apparently he hadn't been given the all clear to speak yet. Oops.

The priest spoke a few more words of wisdom, and now that Jake understood how devastating a bite could be, he was sure the speech was more for the benefit of giving the couple time to recover. By the end of the life advice and recited verses, the subtle hints at the importance of their union and the future of the city, Jake could see the black marks forming on their necks. Holy smokes, it was a wildly impossible sight. That same thing had happened to him. To Dulcie. He hadn't even been aware in the moment, but the significance hit him full force now.

The music began again, and the newlyweds slowly made their way toward the back of the church where they waited to receive their family. They were Jake's family now too. Heirs to the city his Dulcie loved. After having not much and no one to call his for so long, a whole lot of family had just been dropped into his lap.

Jake liked this, the whole thing. No best man or bridesmaids. No obligation to anyone but each other. The sincerity of it all.

Dulcie's family stood and began filtering from the pews and making their way toward the couple near the back of the church. The priest remained, watching the entire gathering, a small smile on his face.

"We did that," Jake said, nodded slowly.

A smile tugged at the corner of her lips. "You can certainly bite me again."

She was perfect, and Jake had more than he could ever hope for, but still it wasn't enough.

"We can do that later. I want something else first." He grabbed Dulcie's hand, pulled her to her feet, and led her up to the priest.

"What are you doing?" she asked under her breath, lips tight.

People had noticed them going against the flow of the crowd to get up front, and now her entire family watched them, curious, softly whispering to each other.

Right there in front of everyone Jake held tight to her hand. "Will you marry me?"

Dulcie looked absolutely flabbergasted. A rarity for this sure female. Everyone else had gone silent, too. Jake hung on edge, waiting for her response.

"I already bit you, turned you. It's done, Jake." She reached out, touched his mark. "We *are* married."

"No, we didn't do this part. The promises."

Her hesitancy slowly eased over into, well, guarded amusement. So maybe it wasn't the promises and ceremony that was throwing her off, but being hauled up here in front of everyone on the spur of the moment.

Dulcie fought a grin, but it reached her eyes, lit up her face with joy. "All right. Say your pretty words."

The priest smiled, stepping forward to be useful. "A happy night indeed."

"Now, hang on a second," Jake said, then stepped up to whisper into the priest's ear, giving him the particulars of his intentions. When he backed away to get his response, the priest's bushy brows lift in surprise, glancing over at Dulcie, but then he nodded in agreement.

Jake was extremely aware that everyone, including her family, watched intently. Spotlight was on, and he hoped he didn't screw this one up. Taking her hands in his, Jake pushed the distractions to the back of his head, giving Dulcie his entire focus.

Clearing his throat, Jake took a deep breath and let whatever was rolling around in his head come out his mouth. "I didn't get to choose certain things about...us. Okay, I didn't get a choice on damn near everything, but somehow it never mattered, because it was you. That's the kind of fit people don't find in this world. I've been changed, Dulcie, in more ways than one. I don't have to stay now. I have the power to leave whenever I want. You and I both know I won't, though. Because right here, right now, I choose you."

"Aw," a young girl sighed in the back of the church, followed by multiple adults shushing her.

The priest ignored the commotion, and began, "Do you, Jake Martin, promise to love, honor and protect Dulcina Casteel?"

Jake couldn't help but puff up his chest a little. "With my life."

"Do you, Dulcina Casteel, promise to love, honor...*and* protect Jake Martin?" the priest said, a hint of a smile pushing through his serious demeanor.

Dulcina quirked a brow at Jake's alteration to the standard vows, but all he could do was grin. Chin up, she answered as regally as any queen, "With my life."

"Come here, Mrs. Martin," Jake said, hooking his arm around her neck and bringing her in close. Nose-to-nose, he whispered softly, just for her, "You mad?"

"I'll be mad if you don't kiss me," she said, all serious and prickly, but she was grinning.

Chapter 23

PARIS

A knock at the door snapped Jake out of sleep, spiked his pulse. He lifted his gun from the nightstand without a sound. Reaching over, he intended to tap Dulcie, but she was awake, Bowie knife in hand.

She pointed to the left of the door as she slipped off the bed, her bare feet deftly carrying her across the floor and approaching the right side. Jake had assumed the random visits would stop once they left Balinese, but the surprises just kept coming.

Gun low by his side, Jake crossed the main room and went straight for the door. He gave Dulcie a countdown of three, then reached for the doorknob. Opening the door only a fraction, he was met by a massive man on the other side. No expression moved the man's face, and he remained statue still. Jake didn't sense a threat, so he pushed for a little conversation, testing the waters.

"What can I do for you, big fella?" Jake asked, but the man said nothing. He simply blocked the whole damn doorway, arms crossed. Expectant. Okay, so maybe he was looking for Dulcie. He called out behind him, "Sugar, we got company."

The giant's gaze flicked through the room, and as Dulcie stepped around him to face their visitor, she froze.

"My lord," she said, a touch of awe in her voice.

The Stalker Lord remained silent, his keen gaze taking in every detail, while giving nothing of himself. He didn't smile, didn't flinch. No acknowledgment. No annoyance. Not a hint of emotion showed on his dark, stoic face.

"We in trouble?" Jake asked the giant.

"No' anymore," the Stalker Lord spoke at last, his deep voice thick with a distinctly Scottish twist. His steady gaze landed directly on Jake's neck, accompanied by a slight nod. Then, with absolutely no precursor, ceremony, or words, he handed Jake a thick piece of paper. It was tri-folded and sealed with blue wax.

Jake took the letter, checked out the blank back and wax-sealed front, then passed it to Dulcie. "What is this?"

Wide eyed, she stared at the letter. "A kill order."

"A what?"

"Only Rafe gets these," Dulcina said softly. She refused to take it, shaking her head when Jake tried to pass it to her a second time. "He gave it to you."

Jake popped the seal and unfolded the paper. One name, in black calligraphy, was scrolled across the center.

Tulio Suarez.

"Am I missing something?" He showed Dulcie, then addressed the lord. "Hey, not sure if you know, but this guy..."

The lord's dark voice filled the space between them, bent hard by his heavy Scottish accent. "This man ordered demons to execute you on sight. You are vampire now, a Stalker, and I doona take threats to one of my own lightly. End this."

Jake nodded, rubbing the tight scar on his chest, and though they both knew the answer, he asked anyway. "Did you have me shot?"

"Details are...irrelevant. You are where, and what, you need to be." The Stalker Lord vanished before their eyes. Jake literally blinked and he wasn't there anymore.

Dulcie shut the door, pulled the letter from his hand, opened it fully and pointed to the Stalker Lord's name signed across the bottom. The name was small and modest, and difficult to decipher, but was authentic. "This is a legal, authorized kill."

His thoughts raced, hope surged, and that anger he locked down at losing Rita resurfaced with a vengeance. This was going to happen. Jake took a long, slow breath, trying to find a calm center, but his hand was shaking.

"You with me on this?" he asked, his voice a little more raw than he'd expected.

Dulcie rested her hand on his wrist and gave him a gentle squeeze, and when he looked up at her, she answered, "Always."

• • • •

Jake tapped his thumb to the side of his leg. Repeatedly. He hadn't been this nervous since the day his SWAT commander said he was going in first. This was no different. New job, new rules, and going into a location practically blind kicked everything into high gear. His vampire senses turned all that up just one more notch.

He and Dulcie crouched across the street from the club Tulio owned and frequented, their intention to strike tonight, and the urgency to engage beat at him aggressively. Jake needed this take down, but had never questioned his end game, until this moment.

Dulcie's black curls lifted and floated on the night breeze as she turned to look at him. He was starting to doubt this plan, and she must have sensed the change in him. He was hesitating. Dulcie could absolutely handle herself, but his gut twisted with the simple fact that she would be outnumbered while Jake focused only on Tulio.

Jake had asked Ruskin to serve as back-up for Dulcie, to make certain she'd have someone to watch over her. The man had laughed at the idea of Dulcie needing help, but agreed to send his bouncer and bartender. Not what Jake had asked for, but good enough.

Ruskin's boys hadn't showed up yet, and he wouldn't give this plan a green light unless Dulcie had someone in her corner while he took care of business. He leaned close, and whispered, "Maybe we need to call this off."

"Have a little faith," she whispered back, then nodded toward the alley. "Kael is here."

"He is?" Jake looked, but had to admit he couldn't see or sense anything. "Why?"

She placed her hand over his, effectively stopping his nervous tick. "I'm certain Kael got you that kill order."

Jake nodded. Only two men had known the name of the man he hunted, which meant it had either been Ruskin or Kael.

They couldn't wait much longer, and he was willing to move forward with Kael as backup. Jake led the way across the street, edging closer to the building. Keeping low, they climbed the short set of stairs to the front door. He tried the knob. Locked. He steadied his stance, giving Dulcie a countdown to when he intended to bust through the door.

Her hand suddenly gripped his elbow, and he turned to her. Dulcie wasn't looking at him, but held her finger up, requesting he wait a moment.

He heard the bolt slide open on the other side and smiled. Thank you, Kael. A twist of the knob, and they were inside. Gun drawn, Jake entered the club. Without his helmet, bulletproof vest, or layers of gear packed around him, Jake felt exposed.

Lights were dimmed, tables cleaned for the night, and the muffled distortion of male voices came from a room in the back. The glow of the floor lamps tucked into the corners was more than enough to light their path through the gaming tables. He moved toward the lounge in the back. The voices came from beyond the lounge, filtering through a cracked open door.

He skirted around the edge of the room and eased closer to the door, pressing his back against the wall. Jake closed his eyes, took a moment to picture Rita in his mind's eye, recalling the way she'd always give him a small, sure nod when it was go time. The bittersweet memory was exactly what he needed in the moment.

Jake opened his eyes and Dulcie was on the opposite side of the door, tucked tight against the wall, looking right at him. A small smile curled her lips and she pointed to the floor between them twice. He got the message loud and clear. Right here. Right now. Together.

He sent his mate a small nod and entered the room alone, gun leveled at the man sitting behind the desk. Tulio glanced up from his books, a flash of confusion twitching across his eyebrows, but then he smiled.

Tulio motioned for the bodyguard beside him to remain in place. "How many lives do you have, Officer Martin?"

"Enough to finish this," Jake said, holding steady.

"You won't shoot me," Tulio said confidently as he stood, buttoning his pale grey double-breasted suit jacket. "You're an officer of the law."

"See now, you didn't get the memo. I left my badge in the States." Jake grinned, flashing his new set of fangs. "I'm a changed man."

The broad-shouldered bouncer huffed a little laugh, clearly unimpressed, and Tulio? He didn't even flinch.

"What I see, Mr. Martin, is that somehow you've found yourself a vampire willing to turn you. Perhaps you do not realize it yet, but you are now bound by more rules than ever before. Vampires are not permitted to kill humans, or possess firearms above ground."

The cool metal of what felt like a large blade pressed against the underside of Jake's chin, but he never lowered his gun. Glancing to his left, he caught the distinctive flash of red in the man's eyes. Definitely demon.

"I know the rules, Tulio."

"And yet you bring it anyway." Tulio tilted his head, eyes narrowed as he scrutinized Jake.

Jake grinned. "I brought my silencer."

The blade at his neck was suddenly absent, and the pained yelp of a full-grown man told him Dulcie had stepped in seamlessly. Free of the blade, Jake holstered the gun he'd never intended to use, and headed straight for Tulio. He reached the desk just as Tulio's demon bodyguard clamped his hand around Tulio's arm and sucked them both into Spirit.

"Dulcie!" Jake yelled, searching the room for the men he couldn't see, couldn't find.

She vanished, the seconds she was gone feeling like an eternity. He ran to the window, scanned the street outside. Nothing.

"Jake," Dulcie said softly behind him. He didn't turn. By her tone, he knew she hadn't found Tulio. "If they were still in the room, or very close by, I could find them, but…"

"He's gone. I lost him."

"We won't stop looking," she said, her hand settling over his shoulder.

Tulio had demons. Demons could take Spirit. This was the outcome they could neither plan for, nor prevent, but they had absolutely known he had a high probability of escape. Didn't make the loss easier.

The crackling of the fireplace in the still room was suddenly shattered by a strangled cry. He and Dulcie spun around in time to see Tulio hit the floor with a bone-rattling thud, looking for all the world like he'd just fallen from mid-air. The man had been dropped from Spirit, and he whined in pain, writhing on the floor.

Kael appeared, translucent at first, but in a matter of seconds his menacing form stood over Tulio. If something wasn't broken, it was definitely fractured.

Ignoring everyone in the room, Kael went straight for Tulio's desk. Opening and closing drawers, Kael shuffled around the contents, rifled through papers until each drawer was empty.

Jake glanced at his mate, but she shook her head slightly, seeming just as confused. Kael had presumably taken out the bodyguard, returned their target, and now searched for something he deemed more important than the murderer in the middle of the room.

Heavy footfalls approached from somewhere outside the room and...upstairs? At least two men, maybe more. If they were coming to get tangled up in the commotion, it stood to reason they'd be demon. Dulcie had a knife, and he had a gun he wasn't allowed to use. Not ideal.

Jake grabbed the fire poker on his way to the door, and he thought Dulcie would be on the same page, allowing him to go first and take a swing at one before she tore into them. She didn't budge.

"Darlin'? You gotta step aside," he said, tugging her arm.

She looked back at him over her shoulder, a pleased smile on her face. "Your backup just arrived."

Jake looked through the door and into the lounge. The men he'd heard running across the second floor, now hurried down a set of stairs somewhere out of sight. He didn't see Ruskin's boys at first, but as the red eyed demons emerged into the main room, he heard Miloslav say something dark and not English. This effectively drew the demons' attention toward the main entrance. Miloslav barreled into both demons before they could gather their wits and redirect their fight. The demons went flying back, hit the hardwood floor in a crash of grunts and flailing limbs.

Gage appeared, diving into the dog pile, fists flying. They were not to kill these men, only disable or deter, and clearly weapons were not necessary. The two men were back-alley brawlers. One of the demons let out a howl of pain before Gage silenced him with a fist to the face.

"Jake," Kael said, zero urgency in his bored tone.

Jake turned to see Tulio standing unsteadily, his weight fully on one leg as he reached into his suit jacket. No way he was digging for a cigarette. Before Tulio had the chance to pull a gun, Jake swung on him, cracked him across the chest with the fire poker, catching his arm in the path. This time bone cracked. Tulio went to his knees, cradling the damaged arm, his body awkwardly twisted.

Jake took advantage of Tulio's agony-stunned state, dug through the inner pockets of his suit jacket and removed the gun he'd known would be there.

Kael must have had complete faith Tulio would be handled, because he'd already turned his attention back to the desk. He sorted through several ledger books, tossing them aside just as haphazardly as he snatched them up. His disappointment lasted for only a brief moment before Kael turned his full focus to the heavy desk itself. Feeling his way along the edges and nooks, he eventually paused.

A soft snick released a hidden compartment on the side of the antique desk, and Kael pulled out a hidden, nondescript ledger. His hand skimmed over the cover like it was familiar, the single item he'd been hunting for in his grasp at last.

"What is that?" Jake asked.

Kael opened it, flipped through a few pages, then held it out. Closing the gap, Jake eagerly scanned the page offered. Bullet point notes, tons of them, orderly and short. Kael pointed to one particular line. The last entry: *Demon city. East of Rouen?*

Dulcina was at his side in an instant, reading over his shoulder. The words meant nothing to him, but they seemed important to Dulcina. She gripped Jake's arm and asked, "He's searching for a demon city? How did you know about this?"

"A couple demons mentioned heading East of Rouen, almost like the phrase was a code between them." Kael pulled the book back to him, continuing his search. "Tulio scribbled in this book anytime his men spoke of returning home, checking on a brother, finding a wife, searching for a child, or traveling in general. He was triangulating a location. This is why you had an official kill order."

"Not because Tulio put out a hit on me?" Jake asked.

"That too." Kael looked up from the journal, his hard gaze meeting Jake's. "But this journal, *this entry,* is what made his death a top priority."

"Tulio was right." Dulcina stepped closer to Kael, legs pressed against the desk as she leaned forward, her words and tone challenging. "You know he's right because you know exactly where that city is located."

A sardonic smile made an appearance beneath Kael's dark goatee. "This mission wouldn't be urgent if his entry had been incorrect."

Jake was not oblivious to the tension that had suddenly spiked between these two, but he had no idea what was going on here, so he let Dulcie drive. She reached across him, took the gun from his holster and leveled it at Kael's head.

"Who are you?" Dulcina demanded. "Why do you hold knowledge of a demon city's location?"

Kael dropped the book on the desk and leaned forward, no weapons in sight, and stared past the gun barrel at Dulcina. "There is more than the location of one city in this ledger. Another demon city is named, as is the nearly precise position of Balinese, though it is assumed by Tulio to be demon as well."

"I'll ask only one more time," Dulcina said, steady as a rock. "Who are you?"

"Kael Doran." For a moment Jake thought he wouldn't elaborate, but when a ripple of red passed through those chocolate browns and vanished just as quickly, Kael had certainly snagged their attention. "I'm a Stalker, functioning fully under the laws of your Stalker Lord. I *am* one of you. But I am also a Demon Enforcer. My primary job is to protect the city of Jericho, and all demons who have fled Calix in search of safety."

"You can be both?" Jake asked.

"As our goals are aligned, yes. I guard the secrets of vampires just as tenaciously as those of my kind. The security of every species benefits us all," Kael said, and though he backed away, no longer leaning toward her, Dulcina did not lower the gun.

"Jericho," she said the word slowly, deliberately. Like she'd rolled the word around in her mind a thousand times but had never spoken it out loud. "Is it truly a demon refuge?"

"It is, and I will guard the location with my life," Kael said with a deep sincerity that could be felt in his words.

"And Calix?" she pressed.

Kael shook his head. "Not currently up for discussion."

Dulcina glanced over at him, and Jake shrugged. He was okay with the situation if she was, but this was completely her call. Seemingly satisfied, she handed the gun back to Jake.

"He intended to sell the information. Profit off the conflict," Kael murmured, skimming pages and pausing to read what he must have thought were vital entries. "Tensions always run hot between demons and vampires. He could have triggered a war that would have spilled above ground. This knowledge must die with him."

Jake looked over to Tulio, where he nursed what was probably a broken arm or wrist. "I'm all for hitting back in a fight, but turning his lights out permanently while he's helpless ain't sittin' right with me."

Dulcie squeezed his shoulder, then released him just as quickly. He heard the ominous slide of her Bowie leaving its sheath, and turned to meet her steady gaze, but she didn't move to strike. He got the hint. She was backing him, no matter what he decided.

"No need. You had your orders. I have mine. They are of a similar vein." Kael shrugged, the epitome of indifference, then called into the other room, "Miloslav! Gage! Bring the demons."

They heard a small scuffle in the other room, and a moment later Ruskin's boys shoved the two demons into Tulio's office, keeping a tight hold on them. To say the office filled with eight bodies felt overcrowded was an understatement. Battered and bruised, the demons moved with unsteady gaits, silent and wary. Kael's eyes flared red for a brief moment as he waved the demons closer. Miloslav and

Gage hung back, uncertain of what was happening, but gave them space.

"You know what we are." Kael addressed the demons, speaking to them as if no others were in the room. "Do you know why we're here?"

The demons shared a look, confusion creasing their brow, but ultimately both men shook their heads. Kael turned the book around, pointed to the same entry. One demon covered his mouth, clearly horrified by the written information. The other only stared, eyes wide.

"You fled Calix, my brother?" Kael asked, his tone hushed. "I see it in your eyes."

Jake remained still and silent. A lot was happening here and hanging out in the background was the wise choice.

The big demon who seemed the most shaken by this revelation lowered his hand from his mouth, and spoke, his voice raw. "My family is in Jericho, safe and hidden. But, there is not enough room for all who seek sanctuary. If the location is known..."

Kael ripped the delicate inner page from the notebook and pulled a cigarillo from his shirt pocket. He lit the cigarillo, then put the match to the page containing the location and set it ablaze. With a minimal amount of bravado, he dropped the page into the metal trash can. Then he continued on ripping all the pages out, adding them to the small fire.

"They are protected." Kael pointed to the lone human in the room. "What would you like done with him?"

The big demon didn't hesitate. He wiped the black blood from his busted lip and pushed his sleeves up to his elbows. He took a menacing step toward Tulio, and a heartbeat later the second demon joined him.

Tulio suddenly realized the danger was real and how badly this could go for him. Panic and desperation had him twisting where he sat on the floor in his rumpled suit, searching for help. "Officer Martin, stop them!"

"Already told you I'm not an officer anymore. You're messin' with a world that's bigger than both of us. I can't help you." Jake shook his head and took a step back just as the two demons closed in on their former boss.

Eyes a brilliant red now, the big demon gripped Tulio's shoulders and jerked him upright, cutting his pleading short as they both vanished into nothing. The second demon nodded toward Kael, a clear show of respect, then disappeared.

• • • •

As the phone in the back of Ruskin's club rang against his ear, Jake was sweating. Sure, he was a bit nervous as he waited for his captain to pick up, but not because of what he'd done, or what he had to say. This exact moment just felt...life altering.

"Yeah," his captain's voice came through loud and clear.

"Hey, it's Jake Martin. Just wanted to update you. Tulio was killed. He got on the wrong side of the wrong kind of people. You know how he is," he lied, sort of.

"That mean you're coming home?" his captain asked.

"Nah. Figure I left a hell of a mess for you. Comin' home would just make it worse." Jake scratched the back of his head, then threw in the kicker. "Plus, I like it here."

His captain laughed. "Vineyards and rolling hills and what not? Doesn't sound like you, Jake. You're telling me you fell in love with that pretty scenery women are always going on about?"

"Yep." Jake looked over at Dulcie sitting at a booth in the back, pretending not to keep an eye on him. "Sure is pretty here."

Jake hung up the phone. There was nothing more to say. Weaving through the people, he made his way to Dulcie. He took her hand, helped her out of the booth, and together they walked through the dark vampire bar that had no name. As they passed the cage, Jake paused and looked up at the man penned inside. Cigarette trapped between two fingers, Ruskin's arms were stretched out like a big ol' vulture cooling down from the heat of the day.

This man had started him on the right path by handing him a scrap piece of paper, and when asked, he'd sent help. Time to give credit where it was due.

"Thanks for letting me borrow your phone. And your boys." Jake didn't reach out to shake his hand, didn't feel it would be welcome, so he just said, "I owe you."

"No." Ruskin took a long drag off his cigarette before looking him in the eye. "You don't want to owe someone like me."

"Maybe not. Doesn't change the fact that I do." Jake sent him a sharp nod, as if the whole thing was a done deal. Settled. Ruskin returned the gesture, and that was enough for him. They had an understanding.

Dulcie put her arm around his waist as they moved away from the cage, gave him a quick peck on the cheek, then whispered into his ear, "You've made your phone call, and indebted yourself to a man of questionable morals. What's next, my love?"

"We've got a fair chunk of the city to keep an eye on." Jake grinned at his mate, eating up the sight of his mark on her neck for all the world to see, and squeezed her close. "Let's take a walk, Darlin.'"

Epilogue

BALINESE

Nicolai Moretti might not be ancient, but he had a multitude of years under his belt, and with time and experience came wisdom. The truth of that was evident in so many aspects of his life, but for all the knowledge accumulated, he did not have the insight to understand what the hell had happened with Dulcina.

He shook his head, his shaggy hair shifting around his head with the spontaneous movement. Without a doubt, he'd expected she would one day return to the city and stay, become his mate, and make every moment of his life a wild adventure. After all, she was his other half. Not an assumption, a gut feeling, but a fact.

Even as she stood before him, a lovely mating mark from another man curling over the delicate column of her neck, he felt the undeniable pull toward her, verifying she was the other half of his soul.

As he walked above ground, a sad smile tugged one side of his lips. Perhaps, in this case, he did not have to mate his other half to be saved by her. He hadn't come to the chateau above ground to meet the sun, to give up on life without Dulcina, but to simply breathe. Oddly enough, he was doing well, and had been since that first moment she encouraged him to embrace the man he kept caged. She'd freed him.

Stranger yet was the fact he found no despair in knowing Dulcina was mated to another man. Completely inaccessible. None of his familiar aggression burned within him at the thought of losing her. She was happy, and that alone pleased him a great deal more than he would have thought possible. Love, so it seemed, could be found outside of a fated bond.

A shadow moved to his right, and Nico stilled, his keen gaze tracking the crouched figure ducking behind the half walls of the courtyard behind the chateau. This person wasn't short by any means, but the uncoordinated, rail thin body suggested a teenage boy. Sneaking back home, perhaps?

His Guardian instincts prevailed. Nico followed the boy into the chateau, watched as he edged along the wall, his every movement skittish and ungainly. Definitely a youth. He didn't recognize the lad, which was not unusual. Balinese was heavily populated. He had no reason to pay attention to anyone unless they crossed through the training room, and this weak boy most certainly had not.

Nico scratched his thickly bearded chin, watching the boy from the shadows. He expected to follow him below ground and into Balinese, but the kid didn't seem to know that was an option. Instead, he sought out the smallest room on the ground floor of the chateau. He was hiding.

Listening intently, Nico waited for the scuffling across the stone floor to cease. When all was silent and the boy's frantic breathing had calmed, he eased inside the room.

"Show yourself," Nico called. Though he doubted the boy would announce his presence, it certainly would make things easier.

Bathed in moonlight, the small, richly furnished library was eerily still. The room looked inhabited and well loved, but it was all for show. The books and chairs, and even the sturdy desk, had never been used. Cleaned? Yes. The illusion of a cozy castle home needed kept up should anyone come poking around, such as this young lad.

Slowly stepping farther inside the room, he kept a sharp eye out for any movement. There were several places to hide, especially given the slight form of the intruder, but as he'd chosen the smallest room deep in the back of the chateau, Nico surmised he'd likely do the same within the room. Smallest corner. Back of the room.

Nico peered over the arm of the couch, and there, hunkered down and flush against that barrier of leather and shrouded in shadow, was the boy. He looked frozen in the moment, remaining still as if his very life depended upon his silence. Did he even breathe?

"Mind if we have a chat?" Nico asked.

The boy scrambled away from the couch and lunged for the low, diamond shaped glass window. Nico blocked his path with a simple step to his left and caught the boy's forearms in a firm grip. They boy instantly went wild, like some feral child who'd been lost in the woods.

Nico struggled to keep hold of the flailing youth, but as he did, his keen mind sifted through the facts laid out before his eyes. There was barely any flesh on the thin arms he'd clamped his hands around, which meant he was weak, malnourished, and then Nico recognized something vital. The boy cringed away from his touch, terrified not of what was happening to him in the moment, but likely of an experience in the past.

Not about to let him go now, Nico adjusted his hold on the boy to encompass his wrists instead, and the boy winced, letting out a pained whimper. Nico was by nature one of the rougher Guardians, but he'd been so careful to check his strength.

He slightly loosened his hold, but that seemed to be just as painful to the boy. It was then he realized the skin beneath his palms had shifted slightly, wet and slippery. Turning the boy's arms out to inspecting his wrists in the dim light, he could see the flesh was abraded. Raw and damp with blood, the detached flesh had a pattern to the wounds. He'd been held captive.

Shocked to his core, Nico released him, and the boy backpedaled until he stuffed himself into the corner again and sank to the floor, holding his injured arms close to his thin body. Someone had damaged this poor child, and if Nico ever got hold of them, they would pay with their lives. He would rip them to absolute shreds!

The boy suddenly recoiled as if he'd been struck, cowering and shaking. Nico glanced down at his fists. Clenched. But they had been since the moment he released the boy. Something else had triggered his reaction. Something Nico could not see. Could the boy sense the anger roiling inside him? Misinterpret the source of his ire to be the victim and not the abuser? It was possible. Creatures who'd been battered were often quick studies of precursors to violence.

Nico slowly dropped into a crouch, eye level so as not to seem imposing, and without moving a muscle, he said softly, "I'm not going to hurt you, lad. That's a promise."

"Sh...shelter, please. Just fr...for—" The boy's gaze soared heavenward, as if searching the ceiling for the right word, but then his eyes widened and he snapped his mouth shut.

"The day?" Nicolai finished. The boy looked up at him, his eyes large and round with fear. He guessed right. "Have a set of fangs then, do you? Same as mine?"

Nicolai bared his own fangs, and the boy eagerly nodded, but said nothing more.

"Come on, then. Come with me." Nicolai stood and took two steps back, giving the boy room to rise without feeling trapped. "I'll scrape up some hot food to fill your belly."

They boy didn't move. Did he understand him? His speech had sounded forced, like the words had been a struggle.

"Have you got a favorite food? Meat and potatoes?" Nico asked, reaching his hand out to help him up. "I'll see you well fed."

The boy's eyes frantically scanned his surroundings, but why? Was he looking for an escape? Searching for an answer? Eventually the boy shook his head. Either he didn't understand what Nico was asking, or maybe he'd gone hungry for so long the word favorite had no meaning.

They boy tipped his head down, his tangled hair bobbing as he thumped his chin against his arm repeatedly. He was avoiding Nico, looking down, out the window, to the door. Anywhere but up at him.

Nico huffed a quiet, short laugh. Look at how much he'd changed, had suddenly become the epitome of patience. Not long ago he would have cornered the boy, threatened him, and hauled his lanky bones into Balinese to be interrogated. He'd have roared his anger, likely even taken it out on the boy for simply being where he shouldn't. It was clear the boy needed saved from the sun, and possibly something worse.

He hadn't acted like a beast since Dulcina crashed into his life. She'd gifted him with the ability to accept himself as he was rather than fight it, and if not for her, he wouldn't have been capable of calmly talking to this lad. God, he loved that woman, for who she was and how she'd changed him.

The boy's head jerked up abruptly, staring at him with wide, sorrowful eyes that all of a sudden held just an ounce of hope. Now, what brought about this change? Had his inner shift of thoughts and emotions transformed him so obviously on the outside? Must have, because the boy was now interested, watching Nicolai with intensity.

"What's it to be, lad?" He asked, softening his tone. "Plan on staying here alone all day, or...good food? Deep shelter?"

Nico held his breath as the boy studied him, then at long last, nodded slowly and stood. The kid was taller than he'd initially thought.

"Well, come on, then," Nico said, and with that simple offer, he turned and walked to the door.

After a short moment, the boy sent a concerned glare to the window near his hiding spot, then ventured out into the open. Nico pushed forward, pleased to note his shadow remained constant as he entered the main hall.

From the darkness at his right, a smooth, diplomatic voice of a Guardian posed a question, "Everything all right, sir?"

The boy scrambled back against the wall, terrified of the voice that had no body, and Nico pointedly ignored the voice, needing instead to first calm his young shadow. "Everything's fine, lad. He's a friend."

Nico was being watched intently by both parties, and he retained his unruffled demeanor in an attempt to both reassure Dyre and keep the boy from running. Holding a hand out in the Guardian's direction, he asked, "Can I borrow your radio, Dyre?"

"Certainly," Dyre said, slowly stepping halfway into the light to hand over his radio.

"See? Friends share things." Nicolai uncurled his fingers, showing the radio in his palm, then lifted the radio to his mouth and clicked the side button. "Oi, Briona?"

A click sounded, followed by a clatter, and then, "Yer no' my Dyre. Wha' the hey now are ye doin' with his radio?"

"Dyre is fine. Just letting me borrow his gear. This is Nico," he said, needing to pacify the edgy Irish coordinator before moving on to the matter at hand. "Ears on, now. I need a favor. Havelock and Elin, a bite to eat, Room Two. You've got exactly two minutes."

A short clipped cursed was followed by a sharp, "Aye."

He handed the radio back to Dyre, and the Guardian stared back at him in concern, though he was careful not to let his gaze wander directly to the boy. 'Ears on' was current code for an incoming, low-level alert. Was the kid dangerous? Not likely. His gut instinct told him the lad was only lost, afraid, and starving after having fled from some dreadful circumstance. Still, it was protocol, and when allowing someone into the city with only a guess at his species and intent, it was best to take caution.

Hopefully the two doctors he'd called in could give him some answers as to the boy's species, and his health. Nicolai took in the sad sight of the boy where he stood, pressed tight against the wall, his shoulders curved forward like he was using his own body to hide himself.

"I promised not to hurt you," Nico said to the boy. "You still believe me?"

The boy warily looked between the two men, then slowly nodded.

"Good," Nicolai said, doing his best to project a friendly smile. "Because I meant what I said, and I need you to remember that now."

The boy tilted his head to the side, either processing his words or their meaning. Nicolai seized the moment and reached out, grabbing his arm. A strangled cry of betrayal filled the chateau a split second before they both disappeared.

Nico snared the boy into Spirit with him, speeding them through the city. He hadn't taken another with him like this in a long time, but even so, he could tell it was different with this one. The boy fought him like the devil, so desperate to break free you'd never suspect his body had been severely weakened. Fear did this. Adrenaline.

Entering Room Two, he found both doctors waiting there. The quarantined room would be locked from the outside. Nico moved to the corner of the room, a somewhat vacant spot he figured might give the lad some comfort, and released his Spirit.

When his body returned to solid form and breath again filled his lungs, the boy let out another indignant yell, a jumbled mix of English and French laced with seething anger as he scrambled to wedge himself into the corner.

Nico motioned for the two doctors to remain where they were and he approached the boy. Crouching down so they were face to face again, he spoke very softly, "You're not hurt, as promised."

The boy hid his head in his hands, pressed closer to the wall, and in the light of the room Nico could clearly see the mangled skin around his wrists.

"Oi," Nico barked out of pure instinct, and the boy's head came up, eyes furious and glaring. "My promise stands true. You're safe.

Underground. These people want to help. You understand? I won't let them hurt you."

The boy's brows scrunched together in angry distrust, and slowly his gaze slipped beyond him to where the two doctors waited.

"Think I can take them?" Nico asked in a conspirator's whisper. "Because I will if I have to. They *will not* hurt you."

The boy stared at the doctors, and slowly held up two fingers.

"Yes, there are two of them," Nico confirmed.

His hard gaze landed on Nico, and in a fantastic show of defiance, he held up a single finger.

"You'll do as I ask if there's only one?" Nico was only somewhat surprised. Hell, the lad felt outnumbered one on one.

The boy nodded in agreement.

"All right. Which one do you want?" he asked, and the boy's finger pointed at Havelock. Interesting. Not how he thought that was going to go. "Don't go far, Elin."

She rolled her eyes at him, likely annoyed at having been called in the first place since she wasn't technically a doctor, but she obediently shifted into Spirit and left the room.

"Tell me what you need, Dr. Havelock." Nico only turned his head slightly, not willing to take his full focus from the boy. "You do nothing without my permission. And his. Understood?"

"I think that's a very good idea," Dr. Havelock said with a kind voice. "I'd like to check his vitals, teeth, and any injuries he may have sustained. I would also appreciate a sample of blood, if we can manage such a thing."

Havelock gasped, his shocked gaze landing on the boy. Nico turned fully back to find the boy had already bitten his own arm and offered it, the blood dripping onto the floor. He could hear Havelock behind him scrambling to find a container to catch it in, but Nico could only stare. What would possess him to do such a thing?

Studying the outstretched arm in front of his face, Nico's horror amplified. The boy's arm was marred with overlapping bites long since healed and silvered. Had he been biting his own arm? Needing sustenance but never understanding why or how to properly seal the wounds?

A wide mouthed jar was slipped between them and Nico automatically snagged it from Havelock and placed it beneath the boy's arm to catch the streaming drops. Judging from the stillness of the doctor, he'd seen the scars too. They were everywhere. Between the dim light of the chateau, his bleeding wrists, and unpredictable behavior, Nico had completely missed the multitude of silvery healed scars. He didn't know what happened, but every guess, each probability, was monstrously evil.

Dr. Havelock rose, and went to the door, giving a knock. Elin appeared in the window, scanned the room, and unlocked the door. When it opened just six inches or so, Havelock passed the jar outside the room to her. That blood had been dark red and thick, but neither were a guaranteed indicator of species. The tests Elin ran on blood were swift and fairly accurate. In moments, some questions would be answered.

While they waited for her return, Dr. Havelock washed and inspected the boy's raw wrists and open bite, then gingerly applied a gel-like salve. When Nico had grabbed his wrists above, the boy had been in pain as he panicked, flailed and twisted. Here? Nothing. Statue-still, even as the doctor manipulated the positioning of loose flesh to apply the salve beneath the flayed skin. Some wires in this boy's head were definitely crossed.

A gentle knock on the door had the boy recoiling once again, his eyes darting around the room.

"Well, I suppose now is as good a time as any to take a break," Dr. Havelock said, slowly rising and heading for the door. As he left, the boy leaned forward, his gaze locked on the one point of escape.

"Don't even think about it," Nico said, and to his surprise, the boy relaxed slightly, leaning back.

Not more than thirty seconds later, Dr. Havelock reentered, calling Nico closer with a single beckoning finger. Nico spoke directly to the boy. "Wait here. I'll be right back."

Nico approached the doctor on the other side of the room, but refused to step outside the door. He wasn't about to leave this boy alone. "Go on, what have you got?"

"For all Elin and I can tell, between the blood sample and giving him a look over, the boy is a vampire. He's severely malnourished, which makes it difficult to get an age on him. Anywhere from mid to late teens. He won't speak, so we're going with our best guesses on this." Dr. Havelock paused, his sorrowful gaze landing on the boy. "He's been held captive somewhere, abused, starved. He's likely been caged away from people. Unless you've seen something to the contrary, we don't specifically believe he's a danger to anyone other than himself. Our guess is that with nourishment and kindness, he should recover. He's not demon, so he'll be allowed within the city. Shall I call the authorities and have him taken into care?"

Nico glanced back at the boy who was straining to hear their words, worry and apprehension clearly stamped across his face. "No, I can't do that to him. I got nothing pressing. I'll keep him."

The doctor's brows shot up in surprise, but he quickly muted his reaction. "Then he's all yours. Good luck."

Nico wiped his palms on his jeans. "I'd best go tell him, I suppose. Would you mind giving us some space?"

"Not a problem. If you need me, I'll be just outside the door. Lord and Lady Casteel have arrived and are asking for details."

Dr. Havelock stepped out of the room, and the hushed mumbled conversation confirmed the Casteels had indeed arrived. This wasn't a surprise by any means. An injured youth not a part of the city was bound to draw attention for a multitude of reasons.

Nico walked over to the table set up beside the bed. Hospital stays for vampires were extremely rare and very short, and though the room was neat and clean, it gave a homey feel. On the little table was the plate of food he'd asked for, kept warm by a domed lid. He looked over at the boy and lifted the lid, pointing to food piled on the plate. The boy's eyes widened, and he started forward before thinking better of his rash decision to move from his protected corner.

"I'm not bringing it to you. You want to eat?" Nico pointed to the untouched bed. "Take a seat."

The boy stared at the plate, but his rapt gaze flitted to Nico once more. He was considering the offer. Taking a step away from the food, Nico sat in the visitor's chair between the door and the bed. His intention was to be the physical block to anyone who might enter the room. Slowly, the boy moved, hesitation in his every step, distrust in every glance at the door behind Nico.

"I'm not going anywhere. You eat all you want." Nico smiled, not that the boy could see much more than the edges of his eyes crinkle since his face was covered in a thick beard. "I won't let anyone stop you."

The boy dashed to the bed so fast a whoosh of air followed him. He ate with gusto, scooping up peas in his fist and funneling them into his mouth. For the first time since Nico had met the boy, his focus was fully on food and not marking everything surrounding him as potential danger.

Discreetly, and as swiftly as possible, Nico scored a vein in his wrist and dripped his blood into the cup he'd snagged from the little table. Once a sufficient amount had gathered, he stood, sealed his opened wrist, and took a step toward the boy, who remained food-focused.

"Slow it down, now," Nico said, sliding the cup onto the table beside the plate.

They boy didn't flinch at the object intruding on his personal space, but instead curled his hand around the cup, put his lips on the straw, and drank. The second Nico's blood hit the boy's tongue, he instantly stilled, his shocked gaze finding Nico.

"It's okay. Drink it all down." The boy made no move to obey, and so Nico added, "Heal yourself."

He did as he was told, looking every bit like a child, sitting there, sipping blood through a straw until the last slurp. The instant he finished, he turned to his food with renewed eagerness.

Nico had a sneaking suspicion this new ward of Balinese knew more English than he let on, though mistrust was understandable, considering the poor condition of his body. Time would tell if his mind remained intact.

Food devoured, the boy turned again to the cup of blood. He pulled the straw from the cup and sucked the other end to make sure he hadn't missed a drop, then reached his finger inside to catch any residue.

"Don't like being weak, do you?" Nico said. He'd considered keeping the thought quiet, but decided to test they boy's reaction.

The boy stared at him, and then after a long moment, shook his head.

"No one does." Nico tipped his head slightly, studying him as he spoke. "We can work on that if you like."

The boy nodded, shaggy, twisted black hair falling into his eyes. Quickly, he pushed his hair back, likely an instinctual reaction to keep his vision clear to watch for approaching danger. Unrestricted gaze jumping left to right in yet another sweep of his surroundings, the boy suddenly froze, staring intently at a single spot behind Nico's head.

Nico turned in his chair. Behind him, through the small window of the closed door, Cat and Elin were in the middle of an animated discussion, no doubt about the boy. Cat peered in, clearly concerned over the boy's health, now that his species had been determined safe by ruling out demon.

Turning back to the boy, Nico was surprised to find he still stared at the door, his gaze leery and defensive. Recalling how he'd sent Elin from the room, Nico had an unsettling suspicion he'd been abused by a female.

"Don't like women, do you?" Nico asked, needing all the information he could gather if he were to acclimate the boy to their city, integrate him into society.

Deep blue and hateful, the boy's eyes narrowed on Cat. Slow and deliberate, he shook his head. Not liking women was a serious hurdle to jump, but everyone had some kind of glitch.

"What's your name?" Nico asked.

Twice the boy tried to form a word and faltered, like speaking was foreign to him, but eventually, in stunted speech and a raw voice much deeper than Nico had expected, he finally said, "O...ber...on."

"Oberon. All right, then. I'm Nico," he said, and then leaned forward in his chair, taking care not to trigger whatever fear had made the boy run in the first place. "I'd like to offer you a home. I got plenty of space, a room of your own and protection. I'll keep you well fed. What do you say?"

The silence between them was thick as Oberon contemplated his options. His uneasy gaze slid over to the door again, and when his gaze settled on Nico once more, he held up two fingers as his eyebrow quirked upward.

"That's right. Just the two of us. Me and you," Nico said with a smile he hoped conveyed the promise he meant to keep. "Not gonna lie to you. My home is, well, it's pretty damn big. Plenty of places you can be alone."

A different kind of anxiousness lit Oberon's face as his brain likely tumbled through the possibilities and opportunities laid before him. The more he processed Nico's offer, the more excitedly his head bobbed in an affirming nod.

"If that's a yes, I think we ought to shake on it," Nico said, holding out his hand.

Oberon swiftly stood, reached out his hand, but at the last minute pulled it back. He was mentally stuck, comparing their hands. Nico's was large, the thick hands of a working man, set off nicely with his naturally tanned colored skin. Oberon's hands? Pale, bony, his long fingers thin and his wrists marred with abrasions and dried blood a stark contrast.

Nico never wavered, his hand remaining there in offering. In his opinion, that steadiness was what eventually won Oberon over. His hand met Nico's and they shook.

"Stick with me," Nico urged, knowing that the step he'd just taken had likely saved the boy's life. "I'll help you find your strength, Bear."

Suddenly he straightened at the new name, the promise of renewed strength, and for the first time Nico saw what the doctors hadn't been able to accurately decipher with their science. Bear was no boy.

Reading Order
<u>The Cities Below</u>
In the Dark
Bound
Beneath the Night
Sheltered
The Guardian
Night Stalker
<u>Coming Soon</u>
Jovan

Don't miss out!

Visit the website below and you can sign up to receive emails whenever Jen Colly publishes a new book. There's no charge and no obligation.

https://books2read.com/r/B-A-ICLR-ACQIF

BOOKS 2 READ

Connecting independent readers to independent writers.

Also by Jen Colly

The Cities Below
In the Dark
Bound
Beneath the Night
Sheltered
The Guardian
Night Stalker

Watch for more at htttps://www.jencolly.com.

About the Author

Jen Colly is the rare case of an author who rebelled against reading assignments throughout her school years. Now she prefers reading books in a series, which has led her to writing her first paranormal romance series: *The Cities Below*. She will write about anything that catches her fancy, though truth be told, her weaknesses are pirates and vampires. She lives in Ohio with her supportive husband, two kids, and four rescued cats.

Read more at https://www.jencolly.com/.